## Lora Leigh's novels are:

## ALSO BY LORA LEIGH

*Rugged Texas Cowboy*

# LORA LEIGH

## lethal nights

St. Martin's Paperbacks

This is a work of fiction. All of the characters, organizations, and events portrayed in this novel are either products of the author's imagination or are used fictitiously.

First published in the United States by St. Martin's Paperbacks, an imprint of St. Martin's Publishing Group.

LETHAL NIGHTS

Copyright © 2019 by Lora Leigh.

All rights reserved.

For information, address St. Martin's Publishing Group, 120 Broadway, New York, NY 10271.

www.stmartins.com

ISBN: 978-1-250-11036-7

Our books may be purchased in bulk for promotional, educational, or business use. Please contact your local bookseller or the Macmillan Corporate and Premium Sales Department at 1-800-221-7945, ext. 5442, or by email at MacmillanSpecialMarkets@macmillan.com.

Printed in the United States of America

St. Martin's Paperbacks edition / October 2019

10 9 8 7 6 5 4 3 2 1

In remembrance and deepest fondness.

Timothy Craig Justice

May 23, 1962–September 7, 2018

The world was a brighter place for your presence and has now dimmed at your loss. True friends are few and far between, and losing one leaves a wound upon my heart that I cannot describe.

You are missed, more than words can ever say.

I saw a butterfly today, strange but true, and immediately I thought of you. As I watched it flutter about the bush of blooms, I realized, we haven't completely lost you.

You left us memories of your smile, so free and filled with joy. Memories of strength, of gentleness, from the time you were a boy.

You left us memories to make us smile, those of butterflies and satellites and a gentle soul. And no matter the years away, no matter the scars your own heart held, your smile held hope and a friendship that would always remain.

I can't say goodbye, sadly that's true. I'm sorry, it's far too hard to let go. Till we meet again, dear friend, I'll always mourn the loss of you.

Love is just a word–
Until someone gives it meaning.

# prologue

Ilya Nicholas Dragonovich.

Son of the Dragon. She thought she'd heard somewhere that that was the literal translation of his surname. If so, it fit him from head to toe.

Emma Jane stared back at the tall, dark vision of pure danger and dark, carnal sex appeal and wondered why she wasn't shaking in her size 6 sneakers. A normal, everyday woman should never be forced to face such men. Just being in their presence drove home the fact that there might be pleasures, experiences, and hungers that would always be denied.

His sunbronzed face was covered on one side by a menacing tattoo of a dragon, red eyes glaring at her from just above his left brow. Rough-hewn features were arranged with a hint of aristocracy, but for the evidence of a once-broken nose and the shadow of scars beneath the dragon. The icy stoicism in his pale green eyes and expression called to her and made her heart ache as he stood before her, made her want to reach out and touch him.

She wanted to stroke him.

There was something about him that was just so primal, elemental. He was a force of nature. He made her heart race.

He expected her to be frightened. The man she'd always called Dragon when she saw him in the society pages stood on her front porch, all but glaring down at her. He seemed to be awaiting a less than welcoming response. She probably should be frightened. Would have been, but instead she was charmed.

"How can I help you, Mr. Dragonovich?" Was that surprise in his gaze? If so, she'd better hurry and relish the victory, because she had a feeling it wouldn't last long. "The society pages precede you," she assured him with a grin, pushing back her nerves. "I recognize you." She wagged her brows. "'Russian Lothario on the Loose'! I believe you had two young women of European royalty on your arm that night."

The slash of his dark brow arched slowly, causing the head of that tattoo to tilt its snout just enough to look curious.

She decided in that moment she was in love with this man's ink.

"If you recognize me, then perhaps you could invite me inside," he suggested, the subtle flavor of his Russian accent sending a tingle up her spine. "I have an offer I'd like to discuss with you."

An offer? For her?

She was ordinary. Men like him did not offer women like her anything.

"What kind of offer?" She couldn't exactly hold back her suspicion.

Was that a grin edging his lips? A hint of amusement in a man who the paparazzi swore never smiled?

"The kind that ensures you keep your home when your divorce is final, and one that aids an agency I represent. I refuse to stand on your doorstep while you consider it though."

An offer to save her home when she was certain her estranged husband was indeed going to be able to force her to sell it? Okay, she might want to hear this.

She stepped back. Not that she trusted him, but the call she'd put through to her cousin Mikayla Steele's husband ensured help was on its way. It wasn't every day a dragon stood on a girl's doorstep and she couldn't be too careful.

"I called my cousin's husband, Nikolei Steele, when you stepped from your car," she warned him. "He's a badass and he'll mess up your pretty face if I ask him to."

He stepped inside, and the once-spacious hallway suddenly seemed much smaller. He towered over her, surrounded her, the warmth of his body sinking into hers in a way that sent a shiver up her spine.

"Good choice." He nodded, his gaze direct, as curious as his ink now appeared to be. "Nik Steele's a good man. We'll just wait for him . . ." He tilted his head to the side, causing his dragon to watch her as though with interest. "I must admit though, I don't think I've ever had a beautiful woman call me pretty."

Was that amusement gleaming in his eyes? The faintest hint of a smile at his lips?

"It's the dragon." She shrugged, narrowing her eyes on the iridescent scaled face. "I think he's flirting with me."

Ilya, the Dragon son and heir, felt the oddest sensation in his chest when she wrinkled that cute little nose and told him his dragon was flirting with her.

Standing there in denim shorts cut just a breath below indecent and a white tank top, with beautiful creamy flesh that shimmered in the sunlight, she was laughing at a tattoo that grown men had been known to tremble at the sight of.

"Ink does not flirt," he informed her, trying to keep his tone cool with none of the amusement he could feel threatening his normally icy façade.

"I have sweet iced tea, water, or coffee," she stated, ignoring his objection as she turned to lead the way to the open, sun-filled kitchen, and all he could see was an ass he wanted to palm in the worst way.

"Coffee would be appreciated, if it's not too much trouble." He paused at the doorway, expecting her take the coffee and conversation to the formal living room they passed.

"Well, come in and have a seat." She gestured to the kitchen table where it sat in front of a wall of spotless windows looking out on the front yard and drive. "My family has a tradition of conducting business at the kitchen table." She threw a smile filled with warmth and dreams over her shoulder at him. "You know, where the food is."

The warmth of her laughter, her refusal to fear him despite the wariness shadowing her pretty gray eyes, was an enigma to him and he found himself craving more.

Never had a woman treated him so . . . normally. As though he were no better or worse than herself, simply different. He liked the feeling.

Moving to the table, he pulled a chair free, unbuttoned the silk jacket he wore, and took his seat as he set his briefcase on the floor beside him.

"My agency has actually worked with Nik's security firm in the past," he assured her, at a loss as to how to handle this spry little female. "It is one of the reasons I believe we could work well together."

"Hmm," she murmured, pouring a mug of coffee and moving toward the table. "Take your coffee black, don't you?"

He fought to find the normal badass he was told he projected so easily. Instead, he feared he was staring at her like a slobbering puppy desperate for a pat.

"Please," he agreed as she placed the cup before him. He waved his hand to the table. "Won't you sit? We can begin our discussion before Nikolei arrives."

"He made me swear I'd wait on him before I even let you past the door," she admitted, stepping back to the center island with a rueful tug of her lips. "You need to do something with that flirty dragon, Mr. Dragonovich, he's gonna get you in trouble."

Staring at her, he caught himself breathing out a sigh.

"It is just a tattoo, Ms. Preston," he told her as though the subject were of no interest to him. "Tattoos don't flirt, they are simply ink."

"Hmm," she murmured again, her gaze flicking back to the dragon at the side of his face, and nearly had him lifting his hand to cover the damned image. "If you say so."

"I say so," he decided, quickly, desperate to change the subject.

"But I think your dragon just winked at me . . ."

All Ilya could do was sigh. This was not an encouraging beginning at all.

Three days later the contract between Emma Jane Preston and the representative for Brute Force, Ilya Nicholas Dragonovich, was safely locked in his briefcase and, in an utter act of idiocy, Ilya decided, he was driving Emma Jane back to her home well after dark.

She was a shrewd negotiator, even without the suggestions her cousin's husband, Nik Steele, had thrown
in. *The bastard.* He'd refused to allow Emma Jane to
discuss the agreement with Ilya alone. And Emma Jane
had very shrewdly followed his suggestion, even during
the two days and nights Ilya, or Dragon, as she had
taken to calling him, had stayed under her roof to get a
better understanding of what her home would need to
ensure the security of any clients or agents sent to it.

And the agreement had come just in the nick of time
for her, as he knew it would. Within days she would
have lost the home she'd been fighting to hold on to
through her divorce.

He'd saved her home, just as he'd meant to. Because
to do otherwise was unthinkable. It would have haunted
him. He'd seen her briefly at the job fair when he'd been
meeting with the sheriff. He'd known then that he
needed to see her again.

It was her eyes, he decided. That soft dove gray, still
filled with hope despite the shadows and still bright with
dreams despite the difficult divorce she was involved in.
This woman was one a man kept.

If he was a man at all he didn't think to merely play
with such a treasure, no matter her claims that his tattoo
did just that.

Pulling into the driveway of her home, he watched as
the motion sensor lights came on, narrowing his eyes
against the glare until he glimpsed the tiny red dot that
indicated the security camera was activated.

The footage would stream wirelessly to Nik Steele's
server as well as to the Brute Force offices in New York.
Should the alarm activate then it would send out an alert
to several different locations, ensuring help would be
there quickly.

"Thank you for driving me home." Her voice was a gentle stroke on his senses, making him wish he were a different kind of man. The kind of man who could claim a woman such as her.

"I'll walk you to the door." He'd already placed his bag in the trunk of the car. There was nothing left of him in her home.

Moving from the vehicle to her side of the car, Ilya opened the door and reached out for her hand to help her out. Her hands were like silk, soft and warm within his palm as he held on to her.

He didn't want to let her go. Not yet. Not tonight. And yet he knew he couldn't hold her either.

"I want to thank you again," she said softly, glancing up at him as they moved onto the porch. "For saving my home."

The overhead light spilled down on them, and in her eyes he saw the same struggle, the same wants and needs.

Ilya took her keys, unlocked the door, and told himself he wouldn't touch her. He couldn't touch her.

She couldn't belong to him.

"You're leaving tonight?" she asked as he stepped back. "It's late."

Yes, it was late. Too late to believe a woman like Emma Jane Preston could belong to him. Too late to wipe away his past.

"If I stay, I'll fuck you, Emma Jane." The sound of his voice was harsher than he intended, but his hunger was almost out of his control.

Ilya watched her breath catch as a delicate flush swept from the modest cut of the neckline of her dress to the roots of her hair.

"I'm still married . . ."

"I wouldn't care if he still slept in your bed and had never thought to betray you as he did. I'd still do whatever I had to, just for one night with you." He'd never killed a man to have a woman, but Ilya was terribly afraid he'd kill one to have this woman. But in doing so, he'd be signing her execution orders.

Her heart was racing now, the pulse at the side of her neck throbbing with either excitement or trepidation. She'd do well to fear him rather than want him.

"Dragon," she whispered, surprising him when her hand lifted, her palm settling against the short cut of his beard. "Good night."

He let her turn away. He actually let her take a single step into the house before he was behind her. Pushing the door closed, he had her in his arms, her back against the wall, her surprised breath parting her lips even as he took them in a kiss he swore would mark his soul.

His tongue swept past her lips and the sweet taste of her went to his head as her instant response sent a bolt of pure lust to his already painfully engorged cock.

As short as she was, she fit him. As tender, as fragile, as she was, she met his kiss with a depth of need he hadn't seen in her. Her arms around his neck, her body arching against him, she held on to him with feminine hunger and a hint of desperation.

"No." As quickly as she gave to him, she jerked her lips from his, her cry a sound of regret, with a hint of tears.

Her hands slid to his chest, resting there, neither pushing him away nor pulling him to her as her forehead rested between them.

"Don't," she whispered again. "Please don't do this to me. I can't do this."

Because she was married and even if he wasn't an honorable man, she was an honorable woman.

"One day, I'll be back," he said softly, the words spoken against the softness of her hair. "Stay away from me when that day comes, Emma Jane. Stay far away from me if you don't want me to share your bed. Otherwise, I swear to you, you won't keep me out of it. And I'll hurt both of us then."

He released her while he still could. Letting her go, he jerked the door open and walked away.

"Goodbye, Dragon . . ." he heard her whisper as he left, and he knew it wasn't goodbye.

He had every intention of returning.

# chapter one

Emma Jane Preston wasn't certain what brought her awake, but between one second and the next she was fully aware, heart pounding, her mouth dry in fear.

She wasn't prone to night terrors, nor was she often plagued by nightmares. At twenty-seven, she'd known her fair share of heartbreaks and, since her divorce, faced enough nights so that the creaks of the house no longer sent her imagination spinning.

This wasn't a creaking house or her wayward imagination. This was something else. It was something more.

This was a full-on panic attack with no rhyme or reason.

It was asleep one second, fight or flight in the next.

Sitting up, she stared around her bedroom. The pretty white curtains and lace sheers, pale gray walls, and heavy chestnut chest and dresser her mother had given her loomed as dark shadows around her.

Everything seemed fine. But the stillness of the night was too damned still.

Damn, she knew she'd set the alarms on the new security system before going to bed. If someone had tried to enter the house, the shrieking blast of sound would be deafening.

But there were no alarms going off. There was nothing but complete silence.

Sliding from the bed, she hurriedly pulled on the pale peach robe that matched her gown and grabbed her cell phone from the bedside table and the handgun she kept beside it. Her father had made her promise she'd keep the weapon handy at night.

Standing by the bed, she fought to hear something, anything to explain her fear.

She'd never awakened like this, even during the worst years of her marriage. She'd never been this scared in her whole life. So scared that instinct kicked in.

Moving soundlessly into the bathroom, she hit her father's number on the phone and waited, listening careful. He answered on the second ring and just as quickly she disconnected the phone before sliding over the edge of her garden tub.

She listened, not that she could hear anything over the rapid thud of her heart, but she tried anyway. And all the while she was cursing herself for not taking her brother up on his offer to loan her that maniac Rottweiler of his.

And she still hadn't heard anything.

Not a creak of the floorboards, or the normal sounds of someone breaking in. Sounds like glass shattering, or whatever accompanied someone invading a home.

It wasn't like she had experience in this. No one had ever broken in on her before.

God help that demented ex-husband of hers if it was him. She'd shoot him just for being the dick he was in scaring the life out of her.

But Matt wasn't a quiet person. He wouldn't go to the trouble to sneak anywhere. He'd be banging on her door. And he wouldn't have a clue how to get past her security.

Maybe it was her imagination.

It had to be her imagination, because she couldn't hear anything.

Drawing in a deep breath and gripping the gun in both hands as she lay in the tub, she considered creeping out of it. Her father would be there any minute, along with her brother and probably the demon-from-hell canine as well. And of course, they'd laugh at her for being so paranoid. Her father would try to convince her to go home with him and her mother. Again.

As she tensed to pull herself out of the tub, the crash of her bedroom door being thrown open and the sudden explosion of gunfire all but stopped her heart in her chest. The chaotic violence of sound seemed never ending as her life flashed through her mind.

She was going to die.

Her father would find her in her bathtub dead. Her brother would go insane searching for who killed her.

Oh God, her father was on his way.

*No.*

He'd die trying to kill someone . . .

The sound stopped as abruptly as it started.

Her heart was pounding so loud she couldn't hear anything else. It was booming in her ears, stealing her breath.

She stared into the darkness of her bathroom, straight up, waiting. If they were going to kill her, she might get lucky and get at least one of them. One of them would be enough.

And she knew there was more than one. She could hear their voices though she couldn't process the words. They were angry though, furious.

They knew now that she wasn't in her bed.

There were so many sounds filling the night now. The flash of lights through her bathroom window, blue and white. Sirens were screaming. If the sirens were from her security system, it was a little late.

Nothing made sense.

The sudden shrieking, the lights, shouts—she could barely make sense of anything but the rapid crash of sound in her ears.

Her heart.

Terror.

She didn't want to die yet.

There were things she wanted to do. So, they weren't big things, but they were things to do.

"EJ!" At first, the nickname her family used for her didn't make sense.

"EJ!" Louder, filled with fear, and so familiar.

"Daddy. Oh God. Daddy." She was sobbing as she fought to get out of the tub.

The gun clattered from her hand to the bottom of the tub as she all but fell out, desperate to get away from certain death.

"EJ . . ." He caught her as she fell out of the tub, nearly going to her knees as she fought to find her legs, to make them hold her up. "EJ. What the hell . . ."

She latched on to her father's broad shoulders, shaking so hard her teeth were chattering, fighting just to breathe.

He was here. He was here with her.

"Oh God. Dad. Who was it? What happened?" Disjointed, broken by sobs, the words spilled from her as her father wrapped his arms around her and held her tight.

What had happened?

Why in God's name would someone shoot up her bedroom?

# chapter two

Ilya was restless.

Discontented.

What the hell was wrong with him?

He could feel the strange malady as it pulsed just beneath the skin the tattoo marked. It was like an itch he couldn't quite scratch, a prickling of his skin that was driving him insane. It was an ache that went deeper than he could describe, even to himself. Deeper even than the bullet that had struck his chest six months before.

He'd be more than happy to blame it on that damned bullet though, except he knew better. He'd known better for nearly a year and fought it. It was only in his deepest dreams that he acknowledged what he'd walked away from, what even now he refused to do more about than lie in wait to catch a glimpse of her.

There were nights, like tonight—this moment—that time seemed to wrap around itself, unending, looping endlessly until it deposited him back, exactly where he'd begun. What felt to be hours later was only moments later and he was still staring at the ceiling with the same intensity of a man who believed there were answers to be found.

He should be exhausted, sleeping the sleep of a man who had tried to fuck himself into exhaustion with the body of a very willing widow. The widow was damned sure exhausted, he reflected to himself as he glanced at the dark-haired woman sprawled in the bed beside him.

Unfortunately, the sight of the ceiling above him held more appeal than waking the woman next to him. Beautiful though she was, experienced as hell, still the thought of waking her was suddenly abhorrent.

The very fact that he'd used her to try to fuck the need for another woman out of his senses was sickening enough, but the feeling that he'd betrayed his heart made his stomach roil. He'd slipped into another town in the early hours of the previous morning, parked his car in the parking lot across from the office where she worked, and just watched her.

Through the glass window of the office he had an unobstructed view of her and he'd let his gaze stroke her as he couldn't, even as he called himself every sort of fool. He wasn't a besotted boy, he was a hardened bastard, a killer, his hands weren't just stained with blood, they were immersed in it.

Sliding from the bed now with a caution that testified to his unwillingness to wake the widow, he dressed with far more haste than was warranted before slipping from her apartment and striding quickly down the hall.

She'd wouldn't even curse him the next time she saw him, he thought in disgust. They all smiled sweetly, simpered, and promised they'd give him reason to sleep next to them through the night if he but gave them another chance. And perhaps he would have if just one time one of them had shown some anger that he'd left her in such a way. Or at least, before he'd seen *her* he would have.

Self-disgust pricked at him.

He was a man who had once sincerely appreciated all things female but was rarely treated to the proof that the women he'd slept with possessed enough fire to actually get angry.

His employer and best friend, Ivan Resnova, had such a woman. The redheaded wife of the suspected criminal kingpin had no problem whatsoever tossing her husband from their bed to a couch if he dared to overstep his bounds. Though admittedly, the redhead in question adored her new husband. Still, letting him know she was angry with him wasn't something she held back.

Women were either too frightened of Ilya's suspected power or too enamored of it to dare become angry with him.

All but one. With her cheeky smile and expressive face she'd teased him for his "flirty dragon" and warned him more than once that the tattoo would get him into trouble. And he was damned if anyone had ever known anything but fear when they let themselves think of the past that followed that ink.

The dragon was to be feared, he'd made certain of it, but his life necessitated it. Now he knew nothing else.

Stepping into the lobby of the apartment building, he nodded to the night manager where he sat in the glass-enclosed office, then to the doorman who swept open the door as he neared. He had only moments to wait before the sleek Jaguar he drove pulled along the curve in front of him.

The valet accepted his tip without glancing at the bills Ilya slid into his palm and within moments he was heading out of Manhattan on the return drive to the Resnova estate on Long Island.

There was no enthusiasm at the thought of returning to the house Ivan and his wife, Journey, were turning into their home.

*Home.*

That sense of belonging, of peace in one's surroundings, wasn't a feeling Ilya believed he'd ever known. The estate had always been a home of sorts for Ivan whenever his daughter, Amara, was there. Now, with the coming babe Ivan and Journey were expecting, it was becoming more so. For Ilya, the growing discontent was only becoming worse.

Why? Why was he doing this and not stealing at least one night with the woman haunting him?

The question was like a nagging mistress. It refused to be silenced or to abate.

It surely wasn't, as Ivan suggested, an inner hunger for his own home and hearth, a woman he could call his own, a child to restore his belief in something. He'd scoffed at his friend when he'd said those words. Such things had never been meant to be his, and he'd accepted it long ago.

But did the knowledge that one particular woman shouldn't be his keep a man from craving her?

Absently, he lifted his hand from the wheel and rubbed his fingers against the left side of his face. There the scars were hidden by an intricately curved tattoo of a dragon, complete with reddened eyes and subtle, iridescent scales. From his brow to his jaw, the sinuous lines of the dragon shadowed the scars left by the blade of Karloff Resnova, Ivan's father, with the help of Petrov Stefanovich, the uncle charged with Ilya's keeping.

Now the tattoo, just like the scars, marked him, ensured he could never escape what his uncle called Ilya's mother's shame.

Now, the tattoo marked him in other ways. The most significant was that of Ivan Resnova's lethal assistant. There was no evidence of the crimes he was suspected to have committed and there were definitely no witnesses, but the tattoo ensured he could never escape suspicion.

It marked him in another way as well. A mark that only a brother acknowledged and had sworn retribution should anyone strike against him, but more important, it marked a legacy of blood and death he could never escape.

Not that Ilya cared much for any particular distinction, just as he refused to admit that he cared little for that brother's life or practices. Blood bound them, whether he liked it or not. And sometimes, he actually liked the far too reckless, excessively intelligent man his brother had become.

The miles passed, rather like life lately, far too slowly and with far more too much time to think, to reflect on a life that felt more barren and far colder than ever as he drew nearer his destination.

Perhaps he should have never gone to the widow, but as he had, perhaps he should have stayed.

He would have preferred facing a rabid dog, he thought with an amused grunt. Not that the widow wasn't charming, she was and as experienced as any he'd fucked.

And he knew he'd never join her in her bed again.

Lowering his fingers from the scars that no amount of ink could fully erase, he watched the traffic as he drove instead. It wasn't excessive in the early hours of the morning, but there was enough to keep his mind on his driving rather than allowing it to wander too far.

Not that he was certain where it could wander that it hadn't already. He'd even entertained the idea of returning to Russia and overseeing the Resnova business concerns there. There was still a lot of work to be done there to legitimize those holdings. A lot of heads to knock together.

Blood that would have to be spilled . . .

At times, he swore he could smell the scent of blood surrounding him. His own, as well as the blood he'd spilled himself. No matter that he'd never taken a life that didn't deserve it. There had just been many that had deserved it. It didn't change the fact that he'd made himself judge, jury, and executioner.

Not that justice was plentiful in Russia. And, in many instances, in America either.

Spilling blood to ensure those under his protection weren't harmed was a small price to pay, even now. But it didn't change the fact that the blood stained him. That he'd taken lives with cold, hard purpose.

Perhaps he was having a midlife crisis? Not that he thought he was old enough for one, but he guessed anything was possible. If he began lusting after women far too young for him and looking for ways to be more appealing to such women, he was just going to shoot himself in the face and save his family the embarrassment.

Not to mention himself.

Not that he had younger women on his mind. The problem was, it was nearly impossible to keep one particular woman off his mind.

Whatever the malady attacking the contentment he'd once so prided himself on, he was going to have to find a cure for it. Something other than interfering in the life of the one woman he truly wanted.

*Then what?* the inner malcontent snarled in response.

He'd be damned if he could answer that question. Just as he had no clue how to fix it. A fix that didn't include pretty gray eyes filled with innocence and dreams.

Maybe Ivan was right about a vacation. Ilya hadn't taken one in years. Perhaps a few weeks doing nothing would help him figure this out. Working obviously wasn't helping. He'd buried himself in work for the past months and the discontent had only grown.

He frowned at the thought.

When had it begun though? He hadn't always felt this off balance, this dissatisfied. He couldn't pinpoint a date or a time when it had begun. At first, he hadn't realized why his temper had become so testy or why he'd found it more difficult than ever to sleep.

As he drove ever closer to the estate where he both lived and worked, that discontent echoed stronger inside him.

The thought of going back to work in the office didn't appeal to him. Witnessing the emotion and easy intimacy between Ivan and his new bride, Journey, held even less appeal. Those two could make a saint curse with all their lovey-dovey crap.

As that thought crossed his mind, the low ring of his cell phone through the car's speakers had him checking the caller ID in the dash display. Frowning, he answered on the first ring.

"Ivan? Is there a problem?" It was two in the morning.

"Are you still in Maryland?" Ivan asked, his tone uncharacteristically cold.

Ilya's brows lifted in surprise.

"Heading out of Manhattan actually and coming your way," he answered.

"Turn around." There was nothing resembling a request in his tone, it was pure demand. "Head for Hagerstown. The safe house there has been breached and the owner's bedroom destroyed with gunfire. The assailants ran when the sheriff arrived with her family, but from the report I was given, it was an interrupted professional hit."

*Hagerstown.*

There was only one safe house in Hagerstown, the one he'd helped set up the year before. His Emma Jane had been attacked.

"Did we have a client there?" Was the owner there? Was she safe? Questions he couldn't make himself ask. Hell, that safe house wasn't even logged into the system yet. No one should have been using it and no one should know of it.

He turned onto an exit to turn around and head back the way he'd come.

"No client." Ivan's voice was clipped, angry. "Ms. Preston followed protocol, but it was by chance she wasn't in her bed when they began firing. The security system failed."

Ilya felt pure, hard fury gather within him.

"Like hell. I installed that system, Ivan. It wouldn't have failed unless she didn't set it properly. And I don't believe that would have been the case." He hit the gas, shooting off the exit far faster than he would have normally.

"Well, it went off quick enough when her family went through the front door. Sheriff's deputy was caught unaware when four armed, black-clad assailants shot out the back door." Ivan's tone held a note of fury. "He's recovering, but that alarm didn't go off when they went in. I had the system's response analyzed by our electronic security database, and it shows the system was armed and active until the assailants went through it on their way out."

And that sure as hell didn't make sense.

Dammit, he'd done the work there himself. He'd picked the home's owner, worked up the agreement with her, and when he'd left, he'd been certain there would be no problems should trouble arise.

"Ms. Preston is unharmed then?" he asked, gripping the steering wheel and speeding past what little traffic joined him on the highway.

"Unharmed," Ivan confirmed. "I have Sawyer heading out with weapons, files, and clothes for you. He'll meet you at the safe house within hours of your arrival and stay as backup. This could be a strike against me or the work we're doing, rather than anything toward Ms. Preston."

"If so, then we have a leak!" Ilya snapped. "She's not even on the books, nor is the house listed among our locations. We've yet to even use the Preston location."

For whatever reason, he'd delayed listing it on their location database or recording their agreement with her. All he'd recorded were the payments to the Hagerstown account each month for keeping the home available.

Emma Jane Preston. Big haunted gray eyes, pretty pink lips that smiled even when she'd believed she would lose her home, and waves of lush thick brown hair falling just below her shoulders.

"While he's with you, I'll have Sawyer begin searching for any attempted hacks into the system . . ." Ivan began.

"She isn't in the system," Ilya gritted out. "I hadn't placed the location within it. Those files are in the office, period, in hard copy."

And they'd had an intrusion into the office several months before. The same intrusion that resulted in a gunshot wound to his chest.

*Son of a bitch.*

"Get to the safe house, figure out why she'd be targeted, and I'll work on this end to figure out who. I don't think it was a strike against her though," Ivan stated. "That doesn't make sense."

That didn't explain who it was a strike against then. Even had the men who shot Ilya the month before found her file, it would have no significance for them. No more than any other file would have had.

"Tell Sawyer to call when he's close," Ilya bit out, fighting to hold back his anger. "I'll contact you once I've met with Ms. Preston."

The call disconnected and as Ilya shot through the night, heading for the small town, he wondered just why in the hell anyone would strike against Emma Jane Prescott. There wasn't a chance in hell anyone could have figured out that even now, a year later, Ilya Dragonovich hadn't been able to forget her.

Her name hadn't passed his lips once those meetings with her were concluded, despite the countless times he'd spent thinking about her. Not once had he mentioned her, spoken of her, or so much as written her name as it passed through his thoughts. All he'd done was allow himself to be marked as hers alone.

At that thought, the phone sounded again, her name on the caller ID. He answered it before the first ring finished.

"Emma Jane? Are you well?" She was fine, he assured himself.

"Dragon?" Her voice shook, fear and shock still filling it. "I'm not hurt, but . . ." Her voice trailed off and silence filled the line for a moment. "I'm scared, Ilya."

And her fears hadn't been eased after she'd called Ivan. She had her family surrounding her and Ivan's promise to send help, but still he could hear the fear in her voice as well as in her words.

"I'm coming, honey," he promised, his voice gentling without thought. "I'll be there soon. I promise. I'll take of this, Emma Jane. I won't allow you to be harmed."

A hit of breath, a smothered sob. "Okay." He heard the shaky breath she took. "Thank you."

The line disconnected and it was all he could do not to throw the phone, to curse, to rage.

He'd done all he could to ensure no one knew the effect she had on him and still she was in danger. God help whoever had attempted to take her from him, because they were living on borrowed time.

# chapter three

It was nearly noon the next day before Emma found a chance to check her bedroom with any semblance of calm, and what she saw there had her heart racing with renewed fear. The walls were peppered with gaping holes, her mattress appeared shredded, while the rest of the room was littered with drywall and mattress filling as well as the shattered remnants of her bedside lamp and the table it had sat on.

The window was now boarded up. Evidently, the shooters found as much offense with the glass there as they did with her bed.

Dammit, fixing this wasn't going to be easy.

She propped her hands on her hips and began mentally listing everything that had to be done, who she could get to do it, and what they'd charge.

As she'd told Ivan Resnova, one of the owners of the security agency she'd signed with to provide a safe house if needed, she'd cover the costs. She had no choice; it hadn't happened while one of their clients was there. She had yet to actually provide a service to them, so it couldn't have been their fault.

He hadn't said anything. He'd just made a rather non-committal humming noise that had made her a bit nervous. She didn't know if he believed her when she told him there was no way the information could have leaked that her home was a safe house for the security agency, Brute Force. How could it have? No one had stayed there yet.

And she sure hadn't told anyone. She wasn't prone to discussing her life with those few who claimed to still be her friends, or her family, so she sure wouldn't have told anyone else. Besides, she'd promised not to. She didn't have much left that she could call her own but her word. She wasn't about to allow that to be stripped bare as well.

After hanging up with Ivan Resnova, she hadn't been able to help herself. She'd called her dragon. He wasn't hers, no woman could hope to hold a man like Ilya Dragonovich, but still, she couldn't help but think of him as her dragon.

Even if he wasn't hers.

There were days that she wondered what she could claim as hers though.

Even her home wasn't fully her own. To save it from foreclosure, she'd signed it over as a safe house whenever needed to the Brute Force Security Agency, owned in part by the Resnova Corporation. Who had suggested to the owner, Ivan Resnova, that she'd perhaps be interested in doing so she wasn't certain. She didn't even try to find out. She was simply thankful they had.

When the Resnova legal counsel, Ilya Dragonovich,

had shown up on her doorstep and made the offer, she'd been leery at first. It was her cousin's husband, one of the few people outside of family whom she trusted, who had assured her Ilya Dragonovich wouldn't betray her. Ever.

He could never be hers either.

Men like Dragonovich didn't tie themselves to the girl next door. The tabloids were filled with pictures of him with models, actresses, the rich and famous. He was so far out of her league as to be ridiculous.

He was an orgasm waiting to happen though.

He certainly wasn't like any man she'd ever dealt with, that was for damned sure.

"You should pack some things and go stay with Mom and Dad for a while," her brother, Ronan, spoke from behind her, his voice quarrelsome.

That whole big-brother syndrome was starting to get on her nerves.

"This is my house, I'm not going anywhere," she reminded him, shooting a frown at him as he leaned against the doorway beside her.

Ronan glared at her, his brown eyes narrowing as he tried to come up with an argument he thought would convince her. She was sure that worked with all the other women he knew, but he was her brother. She knew him for the softie he actually was.

"Give it up, Ronan," she suggested, giving a little roll of her eyes. "If Mom and Dad can't convince me, neither can you."

Besides, her dragon was on his way.

He'd promised her.

She looked around her room once again. Sleeping was going to be iffy for a while. The nights would be harrowing if by chance Ilya didn't show up. How she would actually survive another invasion to her home she wasn't certain. One thing she knew, she wouldn't hide in the bathtub again.

"EJ," her brother tried again. "This was serious business, sweetheart . . ."

"And I'm serious, Ronan, I'm not leaving my home and I won't further risk Mom and Dad's safety by staying with them." The very thought of it terrified her.

The sheriff's deputy was in the hospital with a knife wound. It could have been so much worse. The men rushing out the back door as he came up on it could have killed him. She knew his wife, he had kids, he and Ronan were friends. The knowledge that he could have died because of her filled her with guilt.

Ilya was coming, she promised herself again. He'd promised she would be safe. Not that it was his responsibility considering he had yet to even send anyone there who needed to hide, but he'd promised. And he'd called her honey.

"This is crazy, Sis," Ronan tried again, his tone angrier this time. "If we hadn't shown up when we did, some crazy bastard would have killed you. Is that what you want?"

She wasn't going to yell, she promised herself. If she got into a shouting match with him, she'd end up losing her temper. Losing her temper with her family never worked out. She ended up feeling guilty, then she'd give in to them. She couldn't do that this time.

No matter how much she wanted to run and hide, it simply wasn't going to work right now. Anyone that determined to kill her would only follow her.

"What I want is to keep my home safe and figure out

who it was and why," she told him, her voice highly reasonable, she thought. "I can't do that if I run and hide."

"You can't do it if you're dead either." Ronan's voice rose and Emma forced herself not to flinch.

If she flinched, then she had to admit that the past owned more of her than she admitted to. It would weaken her, and she couldn't let it weaken her ever again.

"She looks very much alive to me." Faintly accented, deep, like black velvet and midnight mysteries, the voice came from the staircase behind them and had her and Ronan both turning quickly to it.

Relief slammed into her with a force that nearly stole her breath.

Before Emma could blink, Ronan pushed her into the bedroom behind him, blocking her with his much larger body and ensuring she couldn't be seen. Instead, she peeked around him and gave her dragon an apologetic, if rueful, smile.

"Who the hell are you?" Ronan demanded, and she could just imagine her brother's expression.

"Ilya Dragonovich. As I explained to your parents when I drove in, I'm a friend of Emma Jane's. I came as soon as I heard that there had been a break-in," and didn't he sound so convincing?

Emma felt a shiver run up her spine as Ilya shot her a little wink and that almost smile he did so well.

"Ronan, move," she ordered her brother as she tried to push past him.

"You're no friend of Emma's." Ronan held her back despite her attempts to push past him. "I know all Emma's friends."

Ilya's brow arched. Black as pitch, terribly mocking,

and far too confident as his icy pale green gaze flicked back to her brother.

"Evidently, you do not," he stated as he stood at the top of the stairs, relaxed, almost lazily amused.

"Dammit, Ronan, move." Emma pinched his side hard enough that he flinched, but he didn't move. "I know him. Stop making a fool of me in front of him."

"Never fear, Emma Jane, I know you far too well for that," Ilya assured her, sounding too amused and far more familiar than she was certain they were.

She shot him a dubious look from beneath Ronan's arm.

"Ronan, I swear to God, if you don't move, I'm going to kick you." This was too embarrassing.

But her brother moved, albeit slowly, watching Ilya suspiciously.

"Who the hell is this, EJ?" he demanded as she moved into the hall. "And how exactly do you know him? You never mentioned him to me."

"There's a lot I don't tell you," she muttered, shooting him a silencing look.

"Emma Jane and I met last year at the job fair she attended," Ilya lied, and he did it oh so smoothly. Even his pale green eyes lied as he stared back at her as though they'd shared far more than a kiss.

Like he knew her more than he actually did know her.

It was all she could do to think. To breathe.

The tattoo at the side of his face seemed to flex dangerously, almost as though it were a separate entity, watching her as it glared a warning.

His thick black hair was cut almost military short, while his darkly tanned skin made the color of his eyes stand out even more. He was a shade taller than Ronan's six feet, two inches, and muscular. The white shirt and low-slung jeans he wore just emphasized his powerful build and made her mouth water.

She knew just how hard, how warm, he was when he was pressed against her, his lips on her, his tongue in her mouth . . .

"EJ . . ." her brother began, his tone low, warning.

"Stop making me look bad, I told you," she huffed, fighting to keep her own composure. "He's a friend."

She moved away from Ronan, intending to step past Ilya and, she hoped, to get them all downstairs where she didn't feel so hemmed in. But as she moved to pass him, his hand touched her arm in the gentlest caress, stopping her in her tracks.

Her head jerked up, and she felt her lips part as she tried to remember how to think.

"You're unharmed?" he asked, his tone low, seductive.

She felt the intimate promise that throbbed beneath his voice like a ghostly brush against her flesh and fought to hold back a shiver.

"I'm fine, Dragon." Geez, didn't she sound all bedroom voicy? She flushed at the knowledge and cleared her throat, hoping it would help. "I promise."

She wanted to tell him she was just scared, terrified, but as she stared up at him she couldn't find the words.

"Someone nearly splattered her blood all over her bedroom, that's not fine to me," Ronan protested, stalking toward them, glowering at her.

"Nor is it fine to me." Something hard and icy flashed in his eyes as he turned his gaze to her brother. "But reminding her of it simply to weaken her isn't exactly good form either, I'd say."

His hand slid back from her arm. She nearly shivered at the lack of the warmth.

"Let's take this downstairs, Ronan. I need some coffee and I'm certain Ilya really doesn't want to listen to us argue." She slid quickly past Ilya. For one insane moment she just wanted to press herself against him, feel his warmth all over.

She hadn't even realized she was cold until he touched her.

"Your manners are slipping," Ronan berated her as they reached the wide front hall. "You didn't even introduce us."

"For a reason," she assured her brother, leading the way to the kitchen. "Why don't you go find Dad? I'll fix some coffee."

"He's speaking to the sheriff in the front drive," Ilya spoke up. "I introduced myself when I arrived."

Emma Jane almost came to a stop as she entered the kitchen but forced herself to cross the wide, cheerfully sunny room to the counter where the coffeepot waited.

Her dad was worse than Ronan. How had Ilya managed to get into the house without him following and demanding answers she was certain Ilya wouldn't have?

"Emma . . ." Ronan's voice was a grumble of displeasure.

"Would you please stop." She turned, still gripping the counter desperately, needing just a minute to figure out what was going on, what Ilya had told her father, because God help both of them if their answers didn't match. "Just go . . . just for a minute, Ronan. Please."

She met his worried gaze and felt like the worst sister in the world. No brother should have to go through what hers was going through. Ronan had always tried to protect her and felt he'd failed her the few times she hadn't told him she needed protecting. Like their father, he couldn't seem to realize she had to make her own choices, her own decisions.

Ronan grimaced at the plea. "Five minutes," he finally bit out from between clenched teeth. "I'll go find Dad."

She waited until the front door closed before hurriedly crossing the room and checking the hall to be certain he left. Assured he was indeed outside, she turned back to Ilya slowly.

"How did you get past Dad?" She stared up at him, uncertain what to do, how she should act.

"The sheriff vouched for me, and Nik called him as I arrived." He shrugged as though it didn't matter. "I told him the same thing I told your brother. We were friends, we met at the job fair the week Nik hired you, and we've seen each other several times since. When I heard the report of trouble here, I rushed back to town with my friend Sawyer, in case you needed help. Sawyer's an agent with Brute Force, currently on medical leave."

"Have I met him before?" She hissed the question as she stalked back to the coffeepot. "God, don't get me in too deep with the stories here. I try real hard not to lie to my family."

"Omission is not the same?" he asked behind her with an edge of amusement.

"With my family, omission is self-preservation," she assured him. "Now, do I need to know anything else before they come back?"

His brow arched, and she didn't completely trust his suddenly curious expression. It reminded her of a male cat she once had, just before he swatted a bowl to the floor just to see her reaction.

"We're lovers, and I'll be staying here with you, along with Sawyer, to figure out why you were attacked. Can you handle that?"

She froze.

*Yep, cat.*

Emma could feel her knees weakening, her lungs trying to fill with air. Hell, it was all she could do not to pinch herself to make certain she was awake. Instead, she gave her head a quick, hard shake and made herself fix coffee.

"They'll never believe that," she all but wheezed out, the knowledge of certain destruction building in her chest. "I'd never take a lover without introducing him to my family first. Never. No way in hell can you lie like that."

She respected her family, respected the fact that they were family. Her parents and Ronan had always tried to protect her—they loved her. She'd never disrespect them like that. And they knew she would have never taken a lover before her divorce.

"Make them believe it." The order was made as though she had no other choice.

Emma poured the water into the back of the coffee-maker, replaced the pot beneath it, then turned to face him. Her hands fisted into the material of her dress as she glared back at him.

"I would never disrespect my parents and my brother by taking a secret lover, especially before my divorce," she hissed angrily. "Come up with something else and do it quickly."

Quickly because Ronan would demand answers. And oh Lord, her parents would see right through that lie.

"Very well," he stated as she turned at the sound of the front door opening. "We're going to become lovers."

Before she could disagree, before she could argue, she found herself swung into his arms, against that broad chest as one hand burrowed into her hair and his lips covered hers.

Where she had been cold, she was suddenly warm all over. Toasty warm. Her hands dug into his waist, because she had no idea what to do with them. She just knew she had to hold on to him.

With his lips, his tongue, he possessed her. It wasn't simply a kiss, a man didn't kiss a woman like this. He hadn't even kissed her like this the first time.

She'd never been kissed like this.

This wasn't a kiss. It was a sensual, carnal branding of her senses.

And Emma Jane melted beneath it.

She didn't hear the front door opening, forgetting where she was and even forgetting who she was, as she lost herself in pure, stark pleasure. The whole exploding-stars, heart-racing, breath-stealing kind of pleasure that even the books she read had never described properly.

One of those kisses.

Yeah, the kind she'd never even suspected might exist.

And all she could do was hold on as he gave her the most pleasure she'd ever known in her life.

With just a kiss.

And just as quickly as he'd stolen her senses, he released them. As he lifted his head and pressed hers to his chest, his arms, his warmth, surrounding her, she felt those incredible lips brush her forehead for an instant.

"I'll protect you, Emma Jane," he said as he brushed a kiss over the shell of her ear, the words causing her breath to catch. "Trust me. I won't let you be harmed."

"EJ, you didn't mention having a close friend." Her

father's voice shattered the illusion she'd allowed herself to become wrapped in and reminded her, quite clearly, Ilya had to have heard the front door open as well.

And now what the hell was she supposed to say?

# chapter four

It was Ilya who broke the silence.

"Forgive me, Mr. Preston." As he turned to her father, his voice was a little rougher, a little darker, than it had been. "It's been a while since I've seen Emma Jane. She refused to begin a relationship with me before her divorce was final. Now, after last night's events, I was unwilling to wait any longer to see her."

*Relationship? A relationship with him?* He wasn't just using her words to convince her father of a lie, but to convince her father of the ultimate lie.

This was so out of control now.

He released her slowly, ignoring the tightening of her body as he brushed a finger along her cheek.

"I'm sorry, Dad. Ronan." She turned and faced her father, her brother, and that smirking buffoon of a sheriff she'd once called a friend, Erik Quade. "I hadn't introduced him because he hadn't been back in town. I would have . . ." She lifted her hand, then dropped it helplessly. "Ilya and I need to discuss this. Alone."

Oh boy, did they need to discuss this.

She hated, hated, lying to her family this way.

But the truth would have been worse at this point.

She'd lost herself, again, in a kiss from a man she barely knew, one she'd only fantasized about for the past year. And even worse, she wanted nothing more than to have him kiss her again. And she knew better. She knew better than to think that kiss meant anything to anyone but her.

Definitely not the man who gave it.

And not for the reasons he had given it.

The kiss was no more than an illusion, and it was an illusion she had no choice but to allow for the moment.

Just for the moment.


Ilya was actually surprised at how quickly Emma Jane's father and brother, along with the sheriff, left after the introductions. From the kitchen window he watched two pickups and one sheriff's cruiser turn around in the driveway and drive off.

He almost grinned as he lifted the coffee cup to his lips and finished the cup of coffee he'd ended up fixing himself.

Emma Jane was a little overset, he thought, almost chuckling at the thought. She was flustered, flushed, and so damned fidgety while her family and Sheriff Quade had been there that he'd nearly allowed his amusement to escape at one point. And he hadn't been the only one. Even her father had fought to keep an amused grin off of his face.

The sound of the door snapping closed with a smack was his cue that she was displeased, he guessed. Was it just the night before he'd bemoaned the fact that no woman dared get angry with him or show any fire? He had rather been thinking more along the lines of a personal situation. Not one where said female's life was in danger.

Not when Emma Jane's life was in danger. Not when a threat existed to the only woman who had ever held him breathless, nearly spellbound as he watched her through a webcam when she stopped at Sheriff Quade's booth during that damned job fair.

Moving to the sink, he rinsed his cup, well aware Emma Jane was poised in the doorway and damned irritated. But she was cute when she was irritated. Those pretty gray eyes darkened like a snowstorm rolling in over the mountains. Her creamy cheeks reddened, her lips acquired the cutest little pout.

"If you have a better reason for my presence in your home, then now is the time to discuss it." He turned back to her and crossed his arms over his chest.

She had to be the only woman he knew who could stare him in the eye without her gaze constantly drifting to the tattoo.

"Well, don't you think it's just a little late to make that offer?" Yep, she was a bit irate. "I think that would have been sometime before that staged kiss you just had to display. Thank you by the way, because that's only going to create more problems."

That little edge of disgust in her tone didn't set well with him.

"Should I have told the truth then?" he asked, inserting just enough ice in his tone to ensure any normal female would take notice. "That would of course result in the contract we have with you becoming null and void."

A frown formed between her brows and her gray eyes gleamed with anger. "Don't use that tone with me, Dragon," she demanded with just enough fire that for a moment he wanted nothing more than to pull her against him again and taste the heat of it. "I'm not a child and I won't be spoken to as though I am."

No, she wasn't a child. But she was his far-too-innocent Emma Jane, and that innocence terrified him.

"Emma Jane, we are, you must agree, limited in excuses that would allow me to stay in your home, to both protect you as well as to learn why you were attacked," he pointed out, keeping his tone calm, his argument logical. "Our contract demands complete secrecy where your availability to our agents is concerned, as well as your cooperation in ensuring the security of your home."

She couldn't argue with that. That was exactly what the agreement stated. But she wanted to. He could see the need to argue burning in her expression, in the flush in one her cheeks, and in the brilliant anger burning in her eyes.

"You could have discussed this with me first," she argued, planting her hands firmly on her slender hips. "You ambushed me and you know it."

And she was calling him on it. How very intriguing.

"I merely did what was needed to convince those that were here that I couldn't be thrown from your home, or our discussion overseen by a protective father and brother." And to give him an idea if the attraction to him that he'd sensed a year ago was still there.

"They're my family," she muttered, as though that explained everything.

It explained very little to him actually. He was aware some families insisted on knowing every small detail of a grown child's life, but he hadn't thought this woman would allow herself to be so dictated to.

But he'd been wrong about women before.

"They don't live here, nor did they save your home as Ivan Resnova did," he pointed out. "My connection to you needed an excuse. I realized this when I first saw your father. I gave them what they needed, and what I believed they could accept quickest."

Her father wasn't stupid and neither was her brother. Ronan was already suspicious, and Ilya knew that to add to that suspicion could prove troublesome.

"Oh, stop being so cool and reasonable." The glare she flashed him was rather cute, despite her anger. "And do something about that damned tattoo if you don't mind. God, how does someone make a tattoo seem to move? . . ."

He watched as she swept past him, a subtle scent of spice teasing his nostrils.

"How do you suggest I handle it?" he questioned her, hiding the amusement he felt. "And the tattoo isn't moving, it is your imagination."

"I don't think so," she muttered. "And maybe if you'd given me a chance, I would have handled this situation far better."

"My dear, feel free to handle it however you please," he invited, hiding his amusement.

This woman had the ability to tease all his senses and make him hunger for things he hadn't realized his life lacked.

As he watched her rinse the coffeepot and replace it, he was taken aback by the comfort he felt here with her. In her pretty ankle-length dress with her deep brown hair falling about her shoulders, she looked tempting and innocent.

She fit here, in this house, he thought. The roomy, sun-splashed kitchen, the heavy wood table close to the window, the butterfly decorations and homey little plaques that hung on the wall.

"Well, our choices are rather limited now, aren't they?" The caustic tone of her voice had his brows lifting in surprise.

"Is the thought of others believing we're lovers that abhorrent to you?" He hadn't considered that. Perhaps he should have. No good woman would want to attach her name to a reputation like his.

She swung around, her expression flushed and faintly surprised before settling back into irritation.

"You don't understand." Her hands went to her hips once more and that frown settled back on her face. "It has nothing to do with you personally." Her blush deepened. "It has to do with the fact that my life will continue on here after you're gone. I don't want to have to explain a lover that wasn't after you walk away."

He tilted his head to the side as he regarded her for a moment. Since when did lovers or the lack thereof require an answer to others' curiosity? She acted as though having a lover was more than just relieving the sexual needs he was certain she had.

"Why would you have to explain anything?" he finally asked her. "You're a grown woman, Emma Jane. A very beautiful woman. No explanations should be required."

She gave a little roll of her eyes before training her gaze on his once again.

"I don't take lovers, Ilya," she finally said, her discomfort more alluring than it should have been. "My divorce was final only months ago. My parents, my friends, the people who are important to me, know I don't do casual sex, and convincing them that I've begun to do just that isn't something I would have done if I could have had a choice."

*Choice.*

Twice she'd pointed out that he'd taken that choice from her, and perhaps he had.

"I apologize for the necessity." He shrugged his shoulders, remembering Calvin Preston's protective stance. "Protecting the secrecy of the safe house is paramount, but when you signed with Brute Force you became one of our own as well. Your protection is just as important. Investigating the attempt on your life is going to be difficult enough. Don't make it more so by denying a connection we'll need to do our job."

Her jaw tightened. "You and your partner could get hurt . . ."

"Emma Jane." He hardened his tone. "Sawyer wasn't targeted, you were. He's here as backup only and to ensure we have advance notice of midnight visitors. You have no choice but to work with me and provide assistance on this. The belief that we're lovers ensures fewer questions will be asked and overt curiosity won't arise. Are we in agreement?"

Yes, he made it all sound very logical, and the truth of the matter? There were several different directions he could have gone to explain his presence. This one though gave him the greatest chance of getting into Emma Jane's bed.

And on the drive from New York he decided he very much wanted to get into Emma Jane's bed.

Though, he'd have to have Ivan keep the paparazzi away for as long as possible.

"Fine but . . ." She paused at a sound in the driveway. Impatiently, she turned to the kitchen window to see a large truck entering her drive, followed by several pickups and two closed vans.

"What the hell," she muttered.

"Ah, the construction company I called." Ilya's pronouncement caused her to swing back to him. "They're here to fix your bedroom. I'd better get out there."

Crossing her arms over her breasts, Emma watched Ilya turn and stride from the room as though they weren't involved in a perfectly serious discussion.

He must think she was a moron. Staring back at Ilya through the window, she took in the cool expression, and the imposing strength he possessed, as he began talking to the men pouring out of the vehicles.

Even a year ago she'd been smart enough to know he was attracted to her, even before that kiss the night they signed the agreement. Just as she had been, and still was, attracted to him. She'd also learned over the course of those three days the previous summer that he was an incredibly calculating man.

If he could go around a problem and attack it from behind, then that was what he did. He never did anything directly.

Oh, he didn't bother to lie, but neither did he bother to tell the complete truth. When he'd wanted to take her to dinner, he'd informed her they'd have to discuss her partnership with Brute Force while he ate. He was on a tight schedule. Then he'd given her three hours to get ready before he picked her up.

When she'd informed him the first time that she was married, he'd assured her he was well aware of her husband and would be happy to suggest a better attorney than the one she had at the time.

He'd already known of her separation, that she'd filed

for divorce. When he'd handed her the attorney's card, he'd already made an appointment for her. Because if she was going to be part of Brute Force, she needed to get rid of the trash first. But she'd seen something more in his eyes, something personal. Something hot and filled with intent.

Now here he was again, trying to ambush her rather than facing her with his intentions. Whatever they might be.

At least he'd taken care of getting the bedroom repaired. She hadn't been looking forward to that at all. The fact that he planned to share that bedroom with her at some point was disconcerting though. Letting Ilya into her life was one thing. Letting him into her bed would be disastrous.

# chapter five

Emma Jane was wary, Ilya acknowledged the next day as he watched her move about the house. She was also impatient, though she projected patience. If a man didn't know better, he'd believe she missed most of what was going on around her. If she wasn't ready to tackle a problem, then she let it brew inside her instead.

The fact that she believed she wasn't ready to deal with him wasn't something he missed. Unfortunately for her, Ilya was done with being patient or wary of the attraction that had flared between them the summer before.

A part of him had decided then that once her divorce was finalized he'd return. The depth of his hunger for her was uncommon, and no matter the wariness either of them felt, he knew it would be impossible to ignore.

Hell, he didn't want to ignore it.

He wanted to lay her down and taste every delectable inch of that curvy little body. The things he wanted to do to her should be outlawed in every country. Some of them probably were.

He wanted her, more than he'd ever wanted another woman, but he wanted her safe as well. To keep her safe, he had to have a direction to go in order to uncover who was behind the attempt on her life.

A professional hit team was sent after one little female who supposedly had no enemies? According to the information coming in, even her ex-husband, for all his petty abuses, spoke highly of her.

A professional hit team sent after one untrained, unprotected woman. Such things simply did not happen in this world. Professional hit teams were fucking expensive. One didn't waste them on someone who wasn't a strategic threat.

As he stood next to the kitchen counter sipping at a cup of coffee, his gaze found Emma Jane once again as she polished an obviously old piece of furniture.

Kneeling before the piece of intricately carved furniture, she rubbed at the detailed loops and ridges slowly, lovingly. Dressed in cutoff jeans again that hugged her delectable ass, a tank top, and sneakers, her brown hair caught up in a clip at the top of her head, she looked more like a teenager than the woman he knew her to be.

One untrained, unprotected woman.

They hadn't expected her to be alone.

She wouldn't have been alone if he'd gone to her when he was in town earlier that day. He'd come in silently though; he hadn't even told Ivan until hours later that he'd be in the area. Only one man had known, Nik Steele. And Ilya knew Nik wouldn't have told anyone.

If he hadn't forced himself to leave, she wouldn't have been alone. He would have been in that bed with her.

"Did you tell anyone what happened between the two

of us last summer?" He watched her closely, the way she suddenly tensed and jerked around to face him in surprise before rising slowly to her feet.

"What happened between the two of us?" Graceful hands went to her hips as she frowned back at him. "We went to dinner and you kissed me. Big deal. And it was no one's business."

*Big deal. Just how many men did she go to dinner with and kiss anyway?*

"If you hadn't still been married, I'd have fucked you, Emma Jane," he reminded her, and the thought of it had him rock hard. Hell, rock harder, he'd already been fully engorged before he ever made the statement.

A delicate flush worked over her cheeks as a flare of remembered pleasure crossed her expression.

"And that is why I told you to go back where you belonged." The snap in her tone did nothing to help him rein in his wayward thoughts. "And why would I even mention you to anyone? The Russian Lothario? The dragon lover?" She gave a little roll of her eyes. "I don't want to be lumped in the same category as your other conquests, if you don't mind."

She was nervous. He could see it in the way she tucked her hands in the pockets of those raggedy jeans, unaware of how tempting her breasts looked. Even with a bra.

Setting the cup aside, he leaned into the counter, reminding himself he was there for far more than getting into Emma Jane's bed.

"Someone sent a four-man professional hit team after you," he mused, ignoring the fear that flashed in her eyes for now. "No one sends four men after one tiny, untrained female who should be sleeping peacefully in her bed. Not unless they expect to find a hell of a threat there instead."

She frowned at that. "Professionals would watch the house and make certain who they wanted was actually there. Four dumb-ass morons would just find a way in, decide to kill the homeowner, and steal whatever could be found."

"Dumb asses couldn't get through my security system," he pointed out, surprised by her quick response.

Pretty, kissable lips thinned. "Maybe one of them was smart," she fired back. "Look, as far as anyone knew, we just had dinner a year ago, and even then, that was with Nik and Mikayla. Big deal. You haven't been back, you don't call, I don't call you. So why attack me thinking you'd be here? All the evil in the world doesn't revolve around dragons."

There was something too alone and too isolated about the way he stood watching her, so certain he was the reason she was in danger. As though he weren't permitted to have friends or lovers. The thought of that made her hurt for him, made her soften even more and that could be disastrous.

"Not all the world's evil," he agreed, the rough rasp of his voice stroking over her senses. "Which doesn't solve our problem. Why you?"

Why her? That question haunted her as well. Deep into the night, into her nightmares, it haunted her.

"I can't imagine having an enemy that vicious, let alone four of them." She shook her head at the question, her heart racing as the fear she fought to keep back rose inside her. "I'm nobody."

Her ex-husband had thrown that truth up to her for the better part of their marriage. She didn't excel, she

was complacent, too comfortable just being Emma Jane
Preston. And in a way he was right.

She'd just wanted to be herself, a wife, one day a
mother. She'd wanted children during that first year, before she'd seen the inner part of the man she'd married.

"Is that what you think, Emma Jane?" His head tilted
to the side as he stared back at her. "That is far from the
truth, but beside the point. So, you have no enemies."
He straightened, moving into the living room where she
stood slowly, each step deliberate. "Yet four men broke
into your home to kill you. You have not just arrived in
town, so it couldn't be mistaken identity. You have no
powerful relatives, nor did you witness a heinous crime.
That leaves few other options."

It left one common denominator. Ilya himself.

"And you think I haven't considered that?" She'd
thought of little else. "I've thought of every day of my
life that I remember, Ilya, trying to figure out what I
could have seen, what I could have done, to make someone want to hurt me. Especially like that."

To come in, guns blazing, bullets tearing into her
bed. She remembered the shape her room had been left
in, shredded, the mattress stuffing littering the room.

"You woke before they entered your room," he stated,
throwing her off guard. "How did you know to leave
your bedroom and hide in the bathtub?"

How had she known something was wrong?

Rubbing at her arms, she could only shake her head,
her gaze meeting his once again. "I don't know. I woke
frightened. It was like I knew someone was in the
house."

A chill raced over her flesh once again as she remembered the panic that had filled her, but before she could
rub her hands over her upper arms once again, Ilya was

there. His hands stroked up her arms and back down, the pale green of his gaze threatening to mesmerize her.

Heat rushed through her body. She could feel it prickling over her flesh and destroying her determination to resist the need for his touch. She'd learned the hard way what unrequited sexual need did to her. She'd lived with the shameful knowledge that the needs she sometimes ached for weren't natural.

"I would have been here." His head lowered, his lips almost brushing hers. "I would have been in your bed had I not forced myself to leave town that day, Emma Jane."

He'd been there? He'd been there and he hadn't come to see her? The thought of that hurt.

"Dragon," she sighed as his lips continued to hover just out of reach.

He was her dragon. So strong, so warm, that the heat of him seemed to sink inside her flesh and sensitize every cell in her body.

The effect he had on her was like nothing she'd known before.

She fought to breathe through the excitement of his touch, of his palms sliding from her shoulders, down her back, to her hips. Her heart raced out of control as she stared up at his lips, desperate for his kiss now.

The effect he had on her senses was devastating.

Then his lips touched hers.

The need that had been a part of her since their first meeting flared, exploded. Her hands grabbed at his biceps, felt the power beneath them, and luxuriated in it. Her nails bit into the material of his shirt and she went to her tiptoes to get closer, to experience his kiss deeper. Harder.

She wanted his kiss harder. She needed it. The broken moan that left her throat was a plea for it. And when his hands slid from her hips to beneath her tank top to caress her back as the kiss hardened and grew hungrier, she was certain she would orgasm from that alone.

The taste of his kiss, the stroke of his tongue against hers, stoked the flames of arousal she'd been forcing herself to bank and threatened to pull free the desires that she feared would leave her begging.

Only this man, her dragon, had ever threatened the desires that had only been vague fantasies until him. Until that first kiss, that first taste of a pleasure she hadn't known existed.

"That's it, baby. Burn for me," he groaned as he pulled back, then took her lips again in short, hard kisses that had her straining to get closer to him.

Burn for him? She was going to become an inferno.

The feel of his palms rasping over her back, stroking and caressing the sensitive flesh, sent bolts of sensation racing to her breasts and her clit. She could feel the moisture gathering between her thighs, the hardening of her nipples, and a ravenous hunger building in her womb.

Only with him. She had only felt this with him, she had only hungered for this harder, harder touch and those unnamed needs with him.

And she was definitely burning for him. So much so that when she felt his hand stroke to between her breasts and the clip of her bra loosen, she didn't even think to protest.

It was the middle of the day, right there in her living room where he backed her into the wall, lifted her to him, and through the thin tank top covered the hard tip of her nipple with his mouth as his teeth closed on it.

"Oh God!" Her head hit the wall, her body jerking as his knee pressed between her thighs and the heated strike of ecstasy shot from the tender point to her clit.

She was going to climax. Just a little bit more and she was going to come apart in his arms from just the pressure of that delicate bite and the press of his knee between her thighs.

"Give me more," he muttered, drawing back despite the press of her hands against the back of his head. "Let me see those pretty nipples."

The material of her shirt cleared her breasts at the same time he cupped one mound with his hand and lowered his head again.

Emma Jane froze at the swipe of his tongue on the hardened tip. The rasping caress short-circuited nerve endings and left her barely able to breathe, held suspended as she stared down at him.

She couldn't help it. She had to see his face, had to preserve this memory. Only to realize he was watching her as well.

As she fought to just breathe, he lowered his hands to her rear, lifted her again, and before she realized his intent she found herself sitting on the bureau she'd been cleaning. With one hand he pulled her hips forward as he pushed her back, driving his erection against the sensitive folds barely covered by the denim shorts she wore.

As he still watched her, his head lowered, lips parted, and as she watched he covered the other nipple with the heat of his mouth.

Her vagina pulsed, spilling her moisture to the silk panties she wore. Her hips jerked, arched, riding against the hard ridge of flesh tormenting her as his mouth drew on her nipple.

His tongue licked. Teeth rasped. Nibbled.

Bit with just enough pressure—then suckled the tip again.

Small, mewling whimpers escaped her lips. Her legs

curled around his hips, her hips moving against the hard ridge he'd pressed against her pussy in desperation.

His head lifted again, moved to the opposite breast, and his teeth nipped at the straining tip.

Emma Jane cried out from the sharp sensation that exploded in her nipple and raced to her clitoris. At the same time his hips rolled between hers, pushing his cock hard against her, the pressure hitting her clit in a way that had her mind nearly exploding with a dizzying array of sensations.

"No!"

Panic tore through her as she felt the sharp bite of sensation racing through her body build and threaten to explode. It was a sensation unlike anything she'd known, anything she'd imagined.

It was terrifying.

Ilya froze, his head still lowered, pale green eyes watching her closely.

"Please . . ." Her voice shook, and she wasn't certain if the plea was for him to stop or to ignore the objection.

She was trembling all over, uncertain, frightened. Not of Ilya, but of the response still racing through her with a strength she didn't know how to combat.

Slowly, so slowly, he pulled back as he slid the material of her tank top over her breasts.

"I'm sorry." The sob tore from her, the conflicting needs tearing at her as he slowly released her.

He watched her too intently, too closely.

"Don't be sorry, *draga*." He brushed back a fringe of hair that had fallen loose from her ponytail before stepping back farther.

Emma Jane shook her head, her fingers covering her trembling lips to hide them before she rushed away from him, before she begged him to ignore her, to take her.

The rasp of her nipples against the shirt was torturous, the need throbbing in her clit almost painful. And the fear of actually falling apart in his arms overwhelming because she couldn't control it.

Racing to her bedroom, she closed the door behind her, leaned against it, and let a single, sobbing breath free.

What was she going to do now? There was no way in hell she could fight this. She couldn't hold him and she knew it. Just as she knew he was going to own her heart before it was over.

Ilya stared at his hands, his lips kicking up in a momentary grin as he realized they were shaking.

Hell, she'd almost blown apart on him just with the act of his taking her nipple into his mouth. What would she do when he actually got his lips on her pussy?

And he would get there. He'd decided it was his new purpose in life. He was going to make Emma Jane come apart in his arms.

As soon as he got her past whatever demons haunted those pretty eyes when she pulled back on him.

Lowering his hands, he shoved them in the pockets of his slacks before turning to the doorway where she'd disappeared up the stairs. She was a woman fighting her needs as well as her perceptions of herself, he thought. She thought she was a nobody. Not just where the would-be assassins were concerned, but where life was concerned. She didn't see herself as exceptional and he knew she was far more than that. Now he'd just have to convince her of it.

# chapter six

It was after three in the morning when Ilya made his way downstairs, careful to ensure he didn't waken Emma Jane. She'd lain and tossed and turned for hours in her bed. And he knew she had, because the small audio-equipped camera he'd installed himself in her room had displayed it clearly on the smartphone he carried.

Watching her restlessness, her obvious nerves in sleeping in her own room, the anger that had begun burning inside him at the news of her attack only increased. The woman had a steel spine, there was no doubt of that, and when her shoulders straightened and that little chin lifted, then he'd already learned it was time to prepare for a battle.

Because of that, he hadn't informed her of the meeting in the early hours of the morning with Sawyer and the sheriff, Eric Quade.

The sheriff was amused as hell when Ilya had shown up, and despite the lie Ilya had given Emma Jane's father, he'd gone along with it. The mocking amusement in Eric's eyes hadn't been lost on Ilya though.

Making his way to the kitchen, he input the code on the security system and opened the back door. Both Sawyer as well as Eric were already there.

"Coffee," Eric hissed on a whisper. "Damn, Ilya, could you pick a more miserable hour?"

His brows lifted. "I've found this time of the morning to work best for such meetings," he responded, turning back into the room and heading for the table on the other side.

"No coffee?" Eric sighed.

"I'd prefer not to wake Emma Jane and I'm certain the smell of coffee will do just that." He'd debated the coffee himself for long moments as he made his way from his room.

"Won't matter," the sheriff grunted, his tone rueful. "She'll be down here chewing all our asses before we're done anyway. Might as well enjoy a cup of coffee first."

Ilya's brow arched.

"I was quiet coming down," he informed the sheriff. "As long as we keep our voices low, Emma Jane will be none the wiser."

"I bet that's what her midnight assassins thought too." Eric sprawled in one of the kitchen chairs as they all took their seats. "You see how well that worked for them."

Ilya had to admit that one confused him. How had Emma Jane known her home had been invaded?

"You say that like you're aware of how she knew," Sawyer said quietly as he took the chair between the sheriff and Ilya.

"Same way her momma would know. Same way my

mother would." His grin was almost smug, knowing. "They know their homes and lives just that intimately. Women like that make the best mothers too. They always seem to know when their young'uns are slipping around or getting into trouble."

Ilya simply stared at him, fighting to ignore whatever that was tightening in his chest at the thought of Emma Jane as a mother.

"Wasn't exactly children sneaking around her house," Sawyer pointed out.

"True." Eric nodded, his expression somber. "But this has been Emma Jane's home all her life. She was raised here. Her momma and daddy gave it to her when they built the new place a few miles away. She knows every nook, cranny, and creak, or lack thereof."

Now that made more sense, Ilya thought. He and Ivan both had that same sense of their surroundings, at both the estate in Colorado and the one on Long Island.

"That knowledge saved her life," Ilya agreed. "But it won't save her a second time. That's why Sawyer and I are here. To make certain Emma Jane isn't harmed."

"Well, you'll have to learn more than I have so far," Eric sighed at that. "There wasn't a fingerprint or tire tread and there's not so much as a whisper of a rumor as to why she was attacked. Even the movers and shakers among the criminal world are scratching their heads over this one."

And that was what he didn't want to hear.

"Her ex-husband?" Ilya asked.

Eric shook his head immediately. "Matt Lauren doesn't have it in him. Besides, he's too determined to prove he can get her back once she gets over her mad, as he calls it."

The disgust in the other man's voice was heavy.

"No chance?" Ilya hated to have to kill a man over a woman.

"No chance in hell even," Eric stated, leaning forward in his chair and propping his arms on the top of the table. "She was done with him even before she threw his ass out and filed for divorce. The man screwed around on her from the first days of their marriage till she actually caught him doing it. To make matters worse, she caught him in her bed rather than the one he used in a spare bedroom."

He'd brought another woman not just into Emma Jane's home but into her bed. The ultimate humiliation, and how he believed she would get "over her mad" Ilya had no idea.

"What about any enemies he may have?" Ilya asked, though he knew the answer himself.

"Matt doesn't have enemies like that," Eric blew out heavily. "EJ doesn't have enemies, period. She's well liked, always nice, and goes out of her way to help people. She didn't even throw a fit when Matt got her fired from her job last year. He's driving himself crazy trying to figure out who paid off her house, and why though. Even his parents have checked with the bank to see if they could learn who took over the mortgage."

*Good luck,* Ilya thought silently. There would be no tracing Ivan's part ownership on the home until the time came to sign off on the private agreement between him and Emma Jane.

"Any report from the Crime Scene Unit?" Ilya asked the other man.

"They're still running whatever they found. I know there were no fingerprints or DNA though." Eric concluded, "I don't know what to tell you, it's just a dead end."

"There's never a dead end," Ilya pointed out, considering other areas of investigation rather than the obvious. "Simply other routes to take. Sawyer's watching the house at night, I'll have Ivan send Maxine out to work with you. You can expect her within forty-eight hours. Ivan's working on the investigation on his end."

"And which angle will you be working?" Amusement crossed Eric's face, though his voice sounded suspicious. "EJ?"

Ilya's brow lifted. "That's between Emma Jane and myself."

He wasn't fond of her nickname. Her name suited her so much better.

"Well, at least I'm included somewhere," sounding sarcastic, put out, Emma Jane's voice spoke softly from the darkness of the hall outside the kitchen before she stepped forward.

Dressed in snug leggings and a loose T-shirt, she didn't look the least bit sleepy as she leaned against the kitchen doorway and regarded the three men disdainfully.

"Eric, you forgot to make coffee." The reminder sounded like an order.

"I didn't forget." The sheriff smirked. "He wouldn't let me. Said it would wake you. I warned him though."

A feminine little snort of disgust was her answer. But she merely watched as Eric rose to his feet and moved for the coffeemaker.

Ilya sat back in his chair and watched her curiously as her gaze met his. The fact that she'd been left out of this little meeting wasn't setting well with her.

"You were tired." He shrugged at her continued silence, wondering why he bothered to do so. "It wasn't worth waking you for."

Eric's muffled laugh had him sliding the other man a

withering look. Not that the sheriff bothered to look back at him.

"It's my home, it's worth waking me for." Her voice didn't rise, wasn't exactly sharp, but damn if he didn't feel chastised as hell.

Unfortunately, it might have the opposite effect than she'd intended. Rather than chastised, he was horny. Damned horny. Any woman who could so effectively berate a man without appearing to do so needed to be fucked. A woman that strong of will would no doubt challenge a man in bed and out, but it was the "in bed" part of that thought that had his senses engaged.

"True, it is," he finally answered. "I promise to make certain I wake you next time."

He couldn't blame Sawyer for the quick, surprised look on his face.

"I hate liars," she sighed, then turned back to the sheriff. "The next time you're in my home in the middle of the night, I'm telling Ronan. Maybe he can convince you to be polite."

Ilya glanced over at the almost desperate look the sheriff sent him.

"Come on, EJ," he wheedled. "I'm sure my agreement with him isn't so different from yours. I'm obligated till death or I agree to give up my firstborn." He gave Ilya look of mocking confusion. "I'm still not certain which one I signed away."

"Your firstborn would hold no appeal for me." Ilya shrugged. "I'm certain it would be impossible to control."

He and Eric had actually known each other for a decade or so. Their friendship was steady and went far beyond the sheriff's contract with Brute Force.

"And you think I wouldn't be?" Emma Jane's lazy tone belied the trap she laid with that particular question.

"Well, you'd be more reasonable." It was then he glimpsed the small handgun she gripped at her thigh. "Perhaps."

"You wish," Eric muttered behind him before placing a cup of coffee in front of him, then Sawyer, before turning to Emma Jane. "Coffee, EJ?"

Her lips thinned in obvious displeasure. "You make yourself at home when you're here far too often, Eric."

Ilya watched the easy, familiar smile the sheriff shot her before he placed a cup of coffee for her in front of the empty chair.

"That's your fault, sis," the other man pointed out affectionately. "Treat a man like a brother long enough and he'll start acting like one."

"Enough," Ilya stated softly when he glimpsed not just the anger but also the fear in Emma Jane's expression before she hid it. "Join us if you wish, Emma Jane. Not that there's much information to be found. The Crime Scene Unit is still processing whatever they collected after the attack, though we know there were no fingerprints or DNA."

She eased toward the table, pausing only long enough to lay the weapon carefully on the center island as she passed it.

As she neared the table he stood and pulled her chair out for her, waiting patiently until she was taking her seat to ease it closer to the table. He ignored the look of distrust she gave him as he did so.

"Stop or she'll expect me and Ronan to find our manners as well." Eric chuckled, his affection for her readily apparent.

"You'd have to learn some first," she reminded him quietly as Ilya returned to his seat and the coffee.

She sat stiff, uncertain. The violence she'd experienced had changed her world far too much. She was off balance, and Ilya guessed it would take her a while to find her balance once again.

"Keeping you safe is our only objective as we attempt to learn who tried to harm you," he assured her as he laid his arms on the table and watched her closely, the darkness shadowing her features. "You're not alone, Emma Jane. Nor will you be undefended, I promise you this."

"This had nothing to do with Brute Force . . ." she began, still holding to the thought that she was somehow the target rather than him.

"I keep my promises," he told her firmly. "No matter the reason, no matter the enemy. I will not leave you undefended."

He caught Sawyer's surprised look before he could cover it, as well as the sheriff's suspicion. He couldn't blame Sawyer's surprise, simply because Sawyer knew him. But there was something about the sheriff's expression as his gaze lingered on Emma Jane's sudden stillness that had Ilya wondering what she was revealing to the other man.

If it weren't for the fact he knew the sheriff saw her as no more than a sister of sorts, then he'd be planning ways to ensure the other man was completely out of her life. Ilya had never been given a chance to pretend he was anything other than what he was: a cold, hard, killer. And from the moment he'd first lain eyes on Emma Jane, he'd recognized her for the weakness she could be where he was concerned.

Unfortunately, she was a weakness he hadn't been able to walk away from completely.

He didn't bother to hide any part of the conversation from her. It was information he would have given her later in the morning anyway. Unfortunately, there just weren't enough answers as of yet.

"Why would anyone want to kill me?" she asked, nearly an hour later, looking to the sheriff rather than to him, and that just pissed him off, Ilya admitted.

"That's what I'm here to learn." Ilya rose to his feet, a silent signal to Sawyer and to Quade that this meeting was over. "Until then, I'm here to ensure you stay alive." He turned his gaze back to the sheriff. "Until we have more, we will concentrate on ensuring they have no opportunity to attack you again."

The two men wasted little time leaving, but as he activated the security system once more he noticed Emma Jane remained in her chair, silently watching him.

"You should try to rest," he told her as he returned to the table and gathered the coffee cups together. "I promise not to disturb you further."

She needed to sleep. He had seen the strain on her face earlier from the lack of rest and cursed himself for that meeting. He should have known his Emma Jane was one of those rare women who could detect even the slightest change in her home.

He'd heard his grandmother was such a woman.

Still was perhaps.

"I wasn't sleeping anyway." He caught the shake of her head in the dim light of the moon as it spilled through the partially opened shades that covered the windows.

Rinsing the coffee cups, he placed them in the dishwasher, aware she was watching him closely.

Closing the appliance door, he stepped back to her and held out a hand.

"Come. I'll walk you up. Sawyer and Eric are watching the house from two different locations and I've adjusted your security system to ensure it can't be breached without setting off an alarm guaranteed to wake everyone within a mile of the house. You're safe tonight, Emma Jane," he promised her. "And come tomorrow night, you'll be even safer."

"That doesn't tell me why." The quiet uncertainty and fear in her voice as she took his hand caused his chest to clench with regret and anger.

She should never feel so uncertain, so frightened of the dark and what the shadowed places in her own home might hold.

Closing his fingers around her much more delicate ones, he drew her from her chair.

"We'll learn why. It's just a matter of time." Staring into her face, he saw her lips tremble for a moment only before she breathed in heavily before tightening them.

She handled the fear with a strength he wouldn't have expected from her but found himself unsurprised by. He'd learned the year before during the negotiations she'd hammered out with him that she had a steel spine. Not many could stare Ilya down and demand, rather than plead for, what she required in the agreement.

"Until we learn why, anyone around me is at risk," she stated, pulling her hand from his, her tone showing little of the fear he'd glimpsed for a second in her expression.

*Steel spine.*

Son of a bitch, he had the hard-on from hell.

"I'd worry about them more than anyone else at the moment," he assured her with a mocking little snort. "Trust me when I say, they have no idea who they threaten if they make the mistake of coming against me."

He'd been honed in the fires of hell and beneath the

demonic hand of an uncle who should have been drowned at birth. For far too many years he'd endured hell, and he'd learned how to survive. Not just to survive but also to meet hell with a fire of his own.

"You're one man . . ."

He laid a finger against those pretty, soft lips.

"One man who knows what the hell he's doing. And trust me, they have no idea who they're facing now. They may think they do. They may want to believe they do, but in the end, they'll learn the error of it." God, her lips were soft, warm. For one insane moment he wanted nothing more than to immerse himself in her kiss again.

He let his thumb caress the soft, pouty curve, watched as her lips parted, her gaze softening, and arousal replaced fear.

He couldn't get the taste of her, the feel of her, out of his head, and he knew if he dared to take more, he'd never be able to stop as he had the last time.

"You should run, pretty girl," he whispered. "The big bad wolf will get a taste of you otherwise."

"He'll get indigestion," she teased, but he saw that she thought she could hide from him. Her desire for more and her battle against it.

"It's not indigestion the wolf fears," he assured her. "I believe he fears addiction far more. But the lure of the sweetest honey, the tastiest flesh, will prove to be his downfall I fear."

Her breathing was harder, harsher, much the same as his, but she stood still beneath the touch to her lips, parting them as he exerted just enough pressure, then allowed his thumb to press inside, closing on it with heated moisture.

"Do you know, I dream of fucking those lips?" He kept his voice low, gentle, watching the effect of his words on her as her eyes darkened further. "There could be few things more erotic than watching you take me with your mouth."

Her expression softened, became drugged with the sweet fever he knew was rushing through her.

"Would you take me, my Emma Jane?" he asked, barely holding back a groan as her tongue swiped over the end of his thumb. "Let me watch your pretty lips suckle me?"

He pressed his thumb against her tongue and a second later his cock nearly burst through the zipper of his jeans as she began to suckle him.

"Bad girl," he whispered, the rasp of his voice impossible to control as hunger began to fray at his control. "Should I spank you for teasing me in the dark, Emma Jane?"

She jerked back, but not before he watched her face flush with such need it was all he could do to let her go.

"This is crazy," she gasped, looking everywhere but at him. "You have to stop this, Ilya."

His brow arched. "I? Sweet, I'm man enough to know your pussy is as slick and wet as I am hard. If that wasn't true, we wouldn't have near the problem, now would we?"

She shook her head.

"Don't lie to me, Emma Jane." He jerked her to him, arching her hips, lifting her until she couldn't help but feel the rigid proof of his erection against the soft swell of her lower belly. "Lie to me, and I'll strip you here and show you exactly what you're fighting to deny yourself."

Her nails dug into his forearms, a gasping little groan falling from her lips.

Just as quickly, he released her. He'd be damned if he'd take her like that, like an animal intent only on his own release.

"Go to bed, Emma Jane," he ordered, desperate to escape the hunger he glimpsed in her eyes. "We'll talk when daylight adds a bit of sanity to my hunger,"

"I'm going back to work." The words tumbled from her lips, causing him to stop in the act of turning from her to watch her closely, his gaze narrowed on her flushed face.

"When?" He kept his voice quiet, controlled.

"Day after tomorrow." She watched him closely, and she would do well to be very, very wary, Ilya thought. "I'm just vegetating here. Nothing else has happened and you haven't found any evidence to support a threat. I have to get back to work."

She had to run away. She was running scared, and that was his fault.

"I called Nik earlier," she revealed.

"Very well," he agreed, never letting her see the anger or the need to convince her otherwise.

He and Nik should be able to keep her safe. He'd let her run, at least for a few more days. Until his hunger refused to allow her to run further. Then, he'd show her the difference between a man, and the little boy her husband had been.

"Good night, Emma Jane," he told her softly. "Sleep well."

She didn't answer, likely because she knew the same thing he did. Neither of them would get much sleep that night.

# chapter seven

Returning to work two days later wasn't easy, but being replaced wasn't something Emma wanted either. Though she was certain when she showed up, her cousin's husband, Nik Steele, would let her go anyway. He wasn't a man who tolerated problems in his life. Her cousin Mikayla had told her how the tall, blond motorcycle-riding Nik had ridden into town, taken one look at her, and set about eliminating the danger in her life.

At the time, Emma had thought how romantic that must be and how certain she would be that such a man would make her insane. She was even more certain of it after she'd gotten to know Nik.

But Mikayla's assessment had been right. Nik eliminated problems in his and his family's lives. And now she would no doubt be deemed a problem. She was just a cousin, not a sister, and only in the past year had she really spent any time around him.

The tall, blond owner of the electronic security firm she worked at as a receptionist had been quiet when she'd explained the situation over the phone to him the morning after the attack and asked for a few days off. He'd given her a week

She couldn't afford a week off, but her nerves and her senses had been too off balance to sit still and do her job and she'd known it. Not that she was much better after arriving at the office that morning, but at least she'd managed some sleep.

Ilya didn't make rest easy though. He was a prowler, Emma had decided. He moved through the house silent as a breath of air, and that very silence seemed to have the ability to bring her awake.

Either he hadn't prowled the night before or she'd been just too tired to care. He'd promised he'd wake her no matter what if he even thought trouble was coming. Not that she thought he'd actually keep that promise, but somehow she knew he wouldn't allow her to sleep if he thought she'd be in danger. How she knew that she didn't question too deeply. But as she'd stared into his green eyes as he made the promise, the overriding fear had eased marginally.

If she wasn't careful, Ilya Dragonovich would end up messing her hormones up bad. He possessed an intensity that drew her, and a certain sexual aura of knowledge that made a woman's heart race and her body strain to be closer. And that tattoo he carried had been created to move with his facial muscles or something, because sometimes it was just funny as hell.

And Emma wasn't immune to Ilya, especially after the other night. Her response to him still had the power to have her shying away from him in wariness. He did things to her that she couldn't explain, made her want things she'd only read about. Things she knew weren't normal, weren't acceptable.

At least her parents and her brother had finally stopped objecting to him being in the house with her. They'd prefer she come home, her father had told her, but at least he knew she wasn't undefended.

Knowing her normally suspicious family was swallowing his explanation of a relationship fully had her questioning their suspicious natures. Her family had known her ex-husband, Matt Lauren, for most of his life, and they still hadn't trusted him when she married him.

Of course, Matt had been an unapologetic bastard. She just hadn't been smart enough to heed the disquiet she'd felt even before their marriage. Now she was on the lookout for it.

Working steadily on the files her boss had stacked in several piles on her desk over the past days, she grimly promised herself she'd never make the mistake her marriage had been again. She'd let her youth and her need for her own family convince her that she loved Matt. She'd known before the second year was out what a mistake she'd made, but she'd taken the vows. She'd given her word. And that hadn't been easy to walk away from.

But it was fear that held her there in the last year of the marriage she'd had such hopes for. Fear and the growing hatred for a man she'd once loved as a friend and wanted to love as a husband.

Hindsight, she thought as she closed the file cabinet drawer she'd placed the last of the last of the files in. Staring out the window beside it, she watched as traffic and pedestrians moved slowly outside and let a sigh past her lips.

She should have listened to her father when he'd warned her that he felt she and Matt might not be suited for marriage. Her mother and her brother had made similar arguments at the time, and she hadn't listened to them either.

Now, two years after she'd walked away from her husband, she found that the anger and feelings of betrayal were no longer the cold knot of bitterness they'd been even before she'd left Matt. And if any anger was left, it was at herself rather than him.

Or maybe it had just been pushed back by the sound of gunfire and the taste of her own terror filling her senses.

"Emma." The smooth, cool tone of her boss had her turning to him, nervousness now overriding the memories and the fear.

She couldn't afford to lose this job, but she couldn't blame Nik for firing her either or, at the very least, letting her go until whatever reason she'd been attacked was taken care of. Maybe she shouldn't have been so eager to return. Distance could have changed Nik's mind if she'd waited.

"Yes?" She clasped her hands in front of her and restrained the need to take a deep, fortifying breath.

"Come into my office." He moved back from the doorway, waiting, his gaze as cool as his tone.

*Well, hell.* This was going to suck.

She'd barely worked there for a year, and she liked this job. She liked this job much better than the one she'd had when she left Matt. The one he'd ensured she'd lost.

Resigning herself to the inevitable, she moved across the reception area and into the office. Standing next to the heavy leather chairs, she waited until Nik passed her and stepped behind his desk.

"Nik, I'm certain there will be no repercussions toward you because of my employment here." She kept the statement calm, steady. "I really don't believe anyone would try to attack me here."

She wasn't going to beg, but dammit, she didn't want to lose this job.

"Sit down, Emma," he ordered, though not unkindly, as he extended his hand toward one of the comfortable chairs.

It was then her gaze was caught by the child sleeping on the sofa along the wall next to where her boss sat. The little girl lay on her stomach, long white-blond curls trailing over her shoulder as she clutched a ragged, stuffed Tigger.

The little girl was the image of her mother, Nik's wife, but with her father's light blue eyes and white-blond hair.

Nikita Steele, little Niki, her mother, Mikayla, called her.

Emma Jane lowered her head as Nik sat down, and tried not to allow herself to show the anger she felt at the situation.

"I talked to Ilya and Ivan earlier." His statement and familiarity with the two men had her head jerking up in surprise. His lips quirked in amusement. "I wouldn't leave you to deal with this alone after helping to set up the safe house. You're family, girl, and I know what family means."

Frowning, she stared back at him, trying to make sense of that one.

"It was you that had Ilya consider the house?" She

hadn't expected that, even though he'd been a part of the negotiations.

"Of course, like I said, you're family, and Matt was pressing where your home was concerned. I was merely waiting for them to activate their lease and begin your training. As they hadn't begun using the house or ordered that training yet, I'll let them live for now," he stated.

He smiled, kind of, but the look in his eyes reminded her of Ilya when he first arrived at her house and saw the destruction of her bedroom. A promise of violence.

"It wasn't their fault," she assured him, wishing he'd just fire her and get it over with. "I know Ilya's trying to take the blame for it. I can't imagine why anyone would believe he was there that night . . ." In her bed, in her body.

"Be that as it may." He shuffled a few papers on his desk until he seemed to have the right one before him. "When you come in tomorrow, you'll find the front glass of the office replaced. The opaque bullet-resistant glass was something I was having done soon anyway, I merely sped up the schedule on it. And I'll be at your home later this evening with a crew to overhaul the security. I can't allow assholes to cost me my best employee or one of Mikayla's favorite cousins, now can I?"

*A new security system?* She knew the types of fees Nik charged and there was no way she could afford it.

Emma stared back at him suspiciously. "Ilya wants the security changed, right?"

Nik was a good man, but he was still a business owner. He didn't provide such a job for free when it would cost him thousands in equipment and labor.

He laughed at that, though the sound was low, careful of the sleeping child.

"Let's say I informed both Ilya as well as Ivan of the price and the fact that they were paying it," he informed her, daring her to object with a single firm look. "Sorry, Emma, but quiet little receptionists aren't ever attacked in such a way for no reason. And I'm a damned nosy man. You know that. I want to know why my reception-ist was attacked."

Yes, he was a nosy man, but now her debt to Ivan Resnova had only gone higher. Nik's security services weren't cheap, as she well knew. It would add a hefty amount to the already large lien against her home.

At least she still had a job, she thought dismally.

"Thank you, Nik, but I would prefer that you send me a bill instead," she said quietly.

He grunted at that. "Stop looking so morose. Ivan won't tack the bill toward your home, I promise you that. He's an ass, but he doesn't go back on his word or his deals."

"But he didn't expect this . . ." she tried to protest.

"He should have," Nik cut the protest off firmly. "I should have secured the house myself last year. Ilya's good at what he does, but I'm here and I know a few tricks he might not have thought of. Had I done the work, the hounds of hell would have heard those alarms at the first attempt to breach the door. Mikayla and I don't live that far from you, either. I'd have been there within minutes. When Ilya and I put our heads together and get this system installed, a draft won't be able to sneak in."

This was so out of control. She didn't want her family or her friends endangered.

Emma pushed her fingers through her hair, fighting to make sense of this new reality.

"You shouldn't be involved . . ." she tried to speak again.

"Don't make me fire you," he stated, his voice hardening. "You're not just an employee, Emma, you're family, and a friend as well. We'll figure this out, and I have no doubt in my mind this has nothing to do with you personally."

*How could it not?*

"No one knew about my agreement with Brute Force or Mr. Resnova," she protested. "It had to be personal."

"You keep telling yourself that." He stared back at her, his expression concerned now. "But trust me in this, Emma, if one of those two is involved, you can bet, someway, somehow, it's their fault."

As he spoke, the door to the front office opened and Ilya entered the room.

"And I thought we were friends, Nik," Ilya stated, his expression mocking, his light green eyes stroking over her before they went once again to Nik.

Immediately, Emma felt breathless.

The air in the office felt heavier, warmer, and her body felt the change. It sensitized and the memory of that single kiss slammed into her senses.

She'd felt for certain that some time away from him and his effect on her would prove that it wasn't really as intense as she'd felt it. The hours away from him had only increased it though.

*Damn it.*

*Damn him.*

Because she couldn't afford to allow her senses to become so immersed in him. She couldn't allow herself to give in to the attraction to him. She knew herself far too well, and she knew he was a risk to her heart.

Just as she'd known it a year ago.

There would be no maintaining a careful distance where it came to Ilya.

"Of course we're friends." Nik grinned as he rose to his towering six and a half feet tall to shake hands with Ilya. "As long as you keep my assistant and one of my wife's favorite cousins safe. She gets hurt, I'm gonna get pissed."

*Assistant?* The last she'd heard, she was still a receptionist. Did a promotion in name only come with a pay raise? she wondered. And since when was her cousin ever dangerous?

"Of course," Ilya agreed. "I never imagined differently."

The look he gave her caressed her, warmed her, reminded her of the wicked, sensual dreams and his habit of throwing her senses into chaos.

"I'll leave the two of you to talk." Rising quickly to her feet, Emma moved to escape the office.

She had to get away from him. She hadn't even noticed a testosterone abundance in the air until he stepped into the room. Now her femininity felt embraced, surrounded by it. She'd never felt this before, never felt so much a woman nor so very in need of a man's touch.

"Emma Jane." The lowering of his voice stopped her, but the gentle hand on her upper arm held her. "I'm having lunch with Sawyer after this meeting if you'd like to join me."

She paused, her eyes narrowing on him. It was smooth, it was subtle, but she heard the order in his tone. He wasn't suggesting or asking for a damned thing. He was demanding it.

"Lucky for you, that's a meeting I wouldn't want to miss," she assured him. "So, I believe I will join you."

His lips twitched, but before he could comment she

pulled free of him and swept from the office to return to her own desk.

The snap of the door wasn't loud and it didn't disturb the child sleeping on the sofa, but Ilya knew it was no accident. Emma Jane was just giving him a hint of her displeasure. Not quite a taste, but enough to have anticipation stirring in places it hadn't stirred in years.

"Mess my assistant's heart up and I'll shoot you," Nik threatened as Ilya took the chair that still held Emma Jane's heat.

The other man was actually glaring at him, rather like her overprotective brother had done. The threat wasn't one Ilya could discount though. In the years since Nik Steele had been a soldier in the Russian Army, under a different name and in a different life, the threat he could be had only grown stronger.

They had never been enemies, thankfully, but they'd never been friends either in those days.

"I'll guard her with my own life, I've already assured you of this," Ilya reminded him.

Nik merely narrowed his eyes on him for a moment before a vaguely uncomfortable look of amused knowledge crossed his expression.

"I'll accept that." Nik nodded rather than saying anything more or threatening him further. "I'll be at the house with my men this evening to install the system if you sign off on it." He pushed a file across his desk. "She's under the impression Ivan's paying for it. I'd suggest you not tell her any differently for a while."

Ivan wasn't paying for the system, though he'd offered to. Unfortunately, according to the contract that cost would have been added to the lien should it be proven the threat had nothing to do with her agreement with them. Ilya had taken the cost himself, rather than risk that. Not that he believed for a moment that Emma Jane had such enemies. The fact of the matter was, he took her security quite personally and would handle it himself. Ivan could just pay him back later.

"I would have already discussed it with her had that been my intent," he informed Nik before opening the file and turning his attention to it. "She's an independent little thing. She'd be upset."

Nik snorted at that.

"'Independent' is a mild description. Emma is determined that no one will ever take advantage of her heart, her reputation, or her family name ever again. Her ex-husband did both while they were together, and he still makes the occasional attempt."

Ilya didn't bother to look up from the proposal Nik had put together. "He won't make that mistake again. I'll ensure it."

That was next on his to-do list. The visit he had planned would ensure Matt Lauren never again shadowed his ex-wife's life. Not by the mention of her name or by anyone she associated with.

The man had managed to gain credit with various businesses and managed to ensure that debt with Emma Jane's name before their divorce. She owed thousands because of him. The only reason her credit hadn't been ruined was because those bills were all local and Emma made regular payments on them.

Ilya had already arranged to pay off the creditors and secure their silence in that regard. He'd make a visit himself to see Matt Lauren and to make sure the other man knew where and when to begin repayment. Emma

Jane would no longer receive balances on those debts or demands for payment. It was ridiculous that her father or brother had allowed it to begin with.

She demanded they stay out of it, Ronan Preston had told Ilya. She had begged to be allowed to deal with her own problems, her father had explained.

He wasn't about to discuss it with her. And in the future he'd make certain no one else took such advantage of her.

"You do know she's liable to shoot you with that gun of hers if she catches you interfering in her life. Don't you?" The amusement in Nik's voice grated. Mostly because he was right.

"Then don't tell her." Looking up from the file long enough to give the other man one of the blank stares others found so intimidating, he was met with a low chuckle rather than fear.

"Oh, I won't say a word," Nik promised. "That doesn't mean she won't find out."

She wouldn't find out.

Ilya had that covered. He knew how to intimidate. He'd been taught when he was no more than a boy how to make certain his wishes were carried out.

Emma Jane could maintain her independence and be none the wiser.

# chapter eight

It took her boss and two of his installers several hours to replace her security system with one Ilya felt would ensure her safety. A new door on her bedroom, one complete with a dead bolt of all things. An alarm would go to the sheriff, Nik, and Ilya's cell phone and her parents' home phone.

By time they left, the mental tally of the expense of the system, new doors in her bedroom and at the front and back, had her ready to hyperventilate.

She remained silent, refusing to quarrel with Ilya in front of Nik and his men, but the minute they drove from the house, she turned to him slowly as they stood on the porch. Staring up at him, she let herself pay attention to the dragon's head as it rested at his brow.

At the moment, it merely watched as though waiting to be amused.

"My children, if I ever have any, will be repaying this debt to Mr. Resnova," she informed him, irritation raking at her senses. "And don't tell me they won't be, because I don't believe you."

She placed her hands at her hips, trying to appear more intimidating than she actually was. Short and round did not make for an imposing presence.

"Emma Jane." The placating tone of his voice set a flame to her temper that she was certain would burn out of control. "All this would have been done once your home was activated as a safe house and placed in the system our agents can access. We simply hadn't gotten around to it."

They simply hadn't gotten around to it yet?

"We signed the papers last year," she reminded him, watching him through narrowed eyes now. "I should have already been in the system."

And here she'd wondered why no one had arrived to hide in her home. Not that she'd been particularly eager to have such dangerous company. She wasn't. But she'd made the commitment to do it. Having her home not listed for use smacked of charity, and she wanted no one's charity.

She watched as he shrugged negligently, his broad shoulders tensing and shifting beneath the fine white cotton shirt he wore.

His expression was just bland as hell, his green eyes gazing back at her calmly as she glared at him.

"Sometimes these things take time, and I have been a rather busy man in the past months," he finally said calmly. "Are you ready to go in now? We can warm up the food I had delivered earlier."

The food he had delivered her ass. Oh, it had been delivered all right, from a restaurant she knew for a fact did not deliver. And it smelled divine.

"You're being manipulative, Ilya," she told him as

she entered the house ahead of him. "I don't like it. And I won't warn you again."

Stepping into the kitchen, she moved for the refrigerator where the Styrofoam containers waited. Before she'd done more than reach the center island, she found herself pulled to a stop and swung around to face him.

"Your mistake is in warning me the first time." His voice was still low, calm, but something seethed in his expression and seemed to darken the tattoo at the side of his face.

Her lips parted, her intent to inform him just how little she appreciated his high-handedness rising angrily to her lips.

Until his lips covered hers in a kiss.

She hadn't known how much she'd craved his touch, craved it so deep, so desperately, that the moment his lips covered hers the anger dissipated and need rose instead. Her hands gripped his shoulders, nails digging in, and she lifted to her toes to get closer, to take his kiss deeper.

He tasted of coffee and male hunger. His tongue licked against hers, teased her, tempted her. He made her forget the fact that he was dangerous, that he could be criminal. All she cared about was the pleasure.

She was only barely aware of him lifting her to the kitchen island and sliding between her thighs. The full skirt of her dress was no hindrance at all, bunching easily at her thighs and spilling over them. It bared the thin cotton of her panties and enabled the hard ridge of his cock behind the material of his slacks to press, to rub . . .

It was exquisite.

*Oh God*. It was so good. She'd never known so much pleasure as Ilya's kiss, as the feel of his hardened flesh pressing into her.

"Damn, the taste of you," he muttered, his lips releasing hers, sliding along her jaw, her neck.

Tiny bursts of electric pleasure sizzled beneath the sensitive skin of her neck. They wreaked havoc with her senses, with the sensitive nerve endings. Each rake of his teeth, lick of his tongue, and fiery kisses spread along the column of her tongue left her crying out at the unfamiliar sensations.

She'd never known pleasure like this with any other touch.

She'd never reacted to her husband so easily and with such heat.

"Emma Jane, how sweet you are." The rasp of his voice and the stroke of her lips along her shoulder, the valley between her breasts, had her shaking and gasping for air.

"The taste of you . . ."

Emma jerked, crying out as Ilya's lips covered her nipple, surrounded it with heat, and began sucking it heatedly.

Her breasts were bare, the buttons on the bodice of her dress parted, the material spread open, and her bra unclasped. She only barely felt the material surrendering to his fingers, and now she was surrendering to his marauding lips and tongue.

"Ilya . . ." She needed to protest this, she did. "Oh God, Ilya . . ."

Her fingers flexed in his hair, tightened, holding him to her.

The feel of his lips tugging at her nipple, his tongue lashing it, was too much. Between her thighs, the rasp of material against the swollen flesh of her clit was a torment she couldn't resist.

She felt empty, hot.

She felt surrounded by pleasure. Wicked, carnal hunger and pleasure unlike any she'd ever known. Sensual, erotic, the sensations would become addictive.

And he'd leave.

She knew he'd leave.

A sob tore from her lips as his lips moved to her other nipple and one hand to her thigh. So close to that aching, swollen flesh. She was slick and hot, and she wanted nothing more than to be taken. Right there, on her kitchen island, where she'd never be able to forget . . .

"Please, Ilya . . ." The sob in her voice was humiliating because she knew she wanted nothing more than to be taken, to be owned by him.

"Sweet Emma Jane," he groaned, the sound of his voice, his accent thicker, rougher, had her womb spasming in need.

His lips released her, but she could still feel his breath against the sensitive bud as his forehead pressed against her shoulder.

"Get away from me, *draga*," he groaned, one hand clenched on her thigh, the other tightening on her hip. "God help me, get away from me before I take you here, in your kitchen, like an animal and destroy both of us."

The image that invoked had moisture spilling between her thighs as they tightened against his hips. She'd never been taken like that. Like nothing mattered but the passion and the promise of chaos.

And she knew it was something she should never allow. She shouldn't have allowed it to go this far.

"Ilya . . ." She didn't know if it was a protest or a plea.

Whichever it was, he slowly released her and moved back. With deliberate movements he pulled the cups of her bra in place and latched them, then slid the material of her dress back in place, though he didn't attempt to rebutton it.

Stepping from her, he gripped her hips and lowered her until her feet were on the floor once again before lowering his forehead to hers and staring back at her.

His expression was tormented.

Why?

"Go, pretty girl," he ordered her again, his voice a roughened rasp. "Go now. While I can still let you go. Warm dinner. I'll . . . walk or something . . ."

He turned and disappeared from the kitchen. Emma Jane watched him leave, wondering what the hell had just happened.

Fury vibrated inside Ilya's skull like a temperamental child kicking and screaming at the unfairness of the world.

If there were a wall he could punch that didn't belong to Emma Jane, then he'd have no doubt broken his fist by now.

Instead, he stood on her back porch, a willing target for anyone dumb enough to take a bead on him, the sound of Emma Jane's hungry cries still ringing in his ears, and contemplated another sleepless night. He was doing nothing more than napping through the night since arriving at Emma Jane's home.

He didn't bother pacing the floors, because it didn't matter how quiet he was, he invariably woke her. He'd be slipping from his room or back upstairs, and there she'd stand in the doorway of her room, leaning against the frame, arms crossed, her expression too intent to suit him. It was as though she knew the restless hunger plaguing him and shared it.

There was no way she could know this hunger. This

need to have her beneath him, arching to his driving thrusts and crying out for more. And he knew the price she could pay for the pleasure they would share if he wasn't extremely careful. More careful than he could possibly be and still have her.

Pressing his fists against the banister surrounding the porch, he fought the need to return to the kitchen and take her.

Never in his life had he fought such a battle to turn away from a woman. Not to take what he hungered for. But he'd never hungered for anything as he did Emma Jane.

His lovers never lasted more than a few nights, he never formed relationships, and he never let himself become emotionally involved.

He never let himself forget he was a liability if he ever allowed himself to care for any woman. Or allowed any woman to care for him.

He'd walked away from Emma Jane the year before without ever allowing her to guess how just her smile affected him. She'd never known how her laughter touched him or just how bad he'd needed to fuck her.

*God damn . . .*

Straightening, he ran his hand over his face. He stilled at the action, pausing at his jaw before moving his fingers slowly to the point above his brow where the tattoo of the dragon began. The flesh tingled, that damned almost itch.

Several times associates had questioned why he didn't remove the dragon once he was away from Russia. He found that suggestion rather funny. There was no removing the dragon, even if it was what he wanted. The dragon. Not just protective but vengeful, wreaking havoc and blood when needed. Powerful, intuitive, the ink and design unique from any others. It wasn't just a tattoo, it was his legacy, the only thing he had that linked him to anything good.

Dropping his hand back to the porch, he clenched his fists, with memories better left forgotten. They would be forgotten were it not for the dragon on his face and a past he knew better than to forget. Even for the time it took to immerse himself in a pleasure unlike any he'd known before Emma Jane.

Dragonovich. The Dragon's son.

Years after his uncle and Ivan's father had carved the side of his face because he was the image of his father, Ilya could still recall the pain, the betrayal. He bore his formidable father's dark looks, pale green eyes, and build. From birth he'd been the image of a man he'd never had a chance to know.

It wasn't his birth, the dragon, or the reason for it that ensured Ilya never made the mistake of calling any woman his own. It wasn't even the half brother his mother had given birth to later and who had tried to protect Ilya at one time. No, it was his uncle and Ivan's father who had decided Ilya's fate. A fate Ilya had learned the hard way not to fight.

He was still amazed Ivan had not just braved forming a committed relationship to a woman but actually married her when he'd learned she was pregnant as well. Their pasts were bathed in blood and their present would be as well if they weren't extremely careful.

Just because the danger Ivan's wife, Journey, had faced had come from an unexpected enemy didn't mean that the monsters from the past weren't waiting.

Breathing out roughly, he contemplated calling Ivan and demanding to know if there was more information. All that stopped him was the knowledge that the other man would have called had he learned anything new regarding the attempt on Emma Jane.

It wasn't possible that she'd been targeted by anyone other than one of his or Ivan's enemies. Most likely one of his own.

But how could anyone know of Emma Jane or guess that he hungered for her as he'd never hungered for another woman?

Ilya had learned long ago the price that awaited should he allow himself to love, to claim something for his own. The loss of that love was too great a price to bear and it was one he wasn't willing to pay.

Until his heart thawed for Emma Jane's smile, for her laughter, and it had been far too late when he'd realized it was happening.

And now there was no way to claw back his hunger for her.

# chapter nine

The weekend arrived with little fanfare and no further drugging kisses or mind-destroying caresses. That didn't mean Emma had forgotten that taste of the erotic delight Ilya had given her. And even if she'd wanted to forget, the tension growing between them each day and the heated dreams each night refused to allow it.

She wanted him.

No, it went beyond simple want. She ached for him, and that ache was growing by the night in a way she hadn't imagined possible.

She'd been a virgin when she'd married Matt, and despite his accusations during their marriage, she hadn't cheated on him. There hadn't been anyone else in the years since she'd left him either. And she suspected the reason there hadn't been anyone else was Ilya.

Acknowledging that didn't make the situation any easier, and it didn't change the fact that once he'd eliminated the threat against her, he'd leave and return to his own life.

The fact that she needed his touch wouldn't matter, and it wouldn't change the outcome.

"I think I'll turn in early," she said quietly as she put the last of the dishes away after dinner and glanced around the kitchen to be certain no further cleaning was required. "It's been a long week."

He stood at the bar watching her silently for long moments.

"We need to talk first." Hs announcement had her gaze swinging back to him quickly.

Leaning against the island, his arms crossed over his chest, he watched her intently. The dragon tattooed on the side of his face seemed to flex dangerously as his jaw clenched. He looked bold, dangerous. Strong.

This man was rumored to be a criminal, he'd definitely killed before, and he was known for his determined bachelor status.

There was no future with him and she knew it, just as she had known the year before that she didn't have a chance of touching his heart.

"What do we need to talk about?" Suspicion sharpened as he straightened, something dark and far too knowing flashing in his expression.

A week had gone by with no further incidents. No one had tried to kill her either, a definite plus. Ilya hadn't touched her, hadn't kissed her since the night before. He hadn't even been close enough to touch.

Nothing may have happened, but the tension was growing to a point that Emma Jane felt the threat anyway.

"About what?" She couldn't stand there and talk to him. It was all she could do to get through the evenings with him.

"Stop running from me, Emma Jane." It was a warning if she'd ever heard one. "You come in from work, prepare dinner, then spend the evenings in your room. Do you think that's going to work for much longer?"

She was actually praying it would.

"And how is that running from you?" she demanded, though she knew that was exactly what she was doing. "From what I understand you had me investigated pretty thoroughly before deciding to make that offer last year. I work, I come home, I eat dinner, and I go to bed, Ilya. You'll have to return to wherever you came from for the nightlife you're no doubt used to."

That single brow lifted, causing the dragon arched above it to rear its head back in a gesture of arrogance.

"Emma Jane, do you truly want to push me this way?" If the look was a warning, then his voice was a dare. "Because I promise you, it's a one-way trip to the very place you seem determined to avoid. My bed."

Her womb actually clenched. Moisture spilled from her vagina and Emma was certain she was on the verge of an instantaneous orgasm.

"And how would you know what I want?" Tossing the dish towel she realized she was clenching between her fingers to the sink, she glared back at him. "Sorry, Ilya, but even dragons aren't all-knowing."

God, what was wrong with her? She wasn't like this. She wasn't a bitch, she wasn't a confrontational person. What she was, she decided, was a crazy woman.

"I'm sorry." She gave her a head a hard shake, unable to stare into those pale eyes or the dark arousal on his face. "I'm tired, Ilya. I'm just really tired." And she ran from him.

He was wrong, she hadn't been hiding, she was running, and not from him but herself.

The depth of whatever brewed between them was frightening. She'd never felt another person's presence as she did Ilya's. She didn't even have to be in the room with him, as though the tormented lust that roiled in his gaze reached out to her no matter where she was or how far away he was.

Hurrying to her room and the adjacent bathroom, Emma forced herself into the shower. Showers didn't help, she knew that, but it gave her time to think. It gave her a chance to find some distance. Placing the damp towel on a towel rack after drying, she collected the bottle of lotion she preferred and moved into the bedroom.

Perched on the side of her bed, she poured a generous amount into her palm and began spreading it over her body. As she did so, she couldn't help but wonder how it would feel if Ilya's hands were stroking over her. They were warm, callused, the slight rasp over her arms and against her thighs had made her ache for more.

She would have given herself to him that last night he'd touched her, she realized as she pulled on the loose pajama pants and matching top. Right there, on the center island counter, she would have willingly let him take her. And she would have reveled in the pleasure as she did so.

What would she do when he left though? And she knew the day would come when he walked away. It was there in the regret that lingered in his gaze. He wasn't a man who would allow himself to love a woman with nothing to offer him but her love in return.

But then, men didn't look at love the same way women did. Some men were able to compartmentalize emotion, where many women couldn't. Especially men whose lives had been as filled with violence as she'd read Ilya's and his employer Ivan Resnova's had been.

As she turned down the quilts on her bed, a sigh slipped from her. It was actually early for her to go to bed, even on a work night. Weekend nights she stayed up later after returning from her parents' or a night out with friends. She'd asked her friends to stay away for the time being, though, and she'd elected not to go to her parents'.

Now, ten days after the attempted assault, she found herself reluctant to go to bed, but almost just as reluctant to leave her bedroom.

If she went downstairs, Ilya would hear her and he'd follow. Just as she knew when he left his room, he knew if she left hers. That sense of combined awareness of each other was both confusing and oddly comforting as well.

Staring at the bedroom door, she actually considered leaving the room, just to once again test the theory. It wouldn't be the first time she'd tested it. She had a feeling she'd be testing more than just their awareness of each other though. So far, Ilya had remained aloof since that night in the kitchen, though she knew it wasn't forgotten by him, any more than it was by her.

And neither of them seemed willing to face it.

Had she ever seen such tormented lust in another man's eyes? she wondered. She knew she hadn't. There was no doubt Ilya wanted her, just as there was no doubt that eventually he would take her.

Flipping off the lamp on her bedside table, she leaned back against her pillows and contemplated the darkening ceiling and the man who fascinated her in ways she couldn't explain. From the day he'd arrived on her doorstep offering her a solution to losing her home, she'd been drawn to him.

He was dangerous. He was hard. And when he looked

at her, she could sense the hunger he felt for her and denied himself. That was something she'd never known before.

Closing her eyes, she let herself remember the look on his face. The lust and dark need that had filled his eyes even as he ordered her away from him. The warmth of his body against her, the pleasure in his touch.

As she did so, her hand lifted, her fingers drifting over the side of her breast, rasping the cotton of her top against her sensitive flesh.

Her breath caught at the sensation.

How long had it been since she'd been touched before Ilya? Too long, she thought as she brushed her finger against the hard point of her nipple. Her eyes closed, her body softening as she felt heated moisture gathering between her thighs. The thought of Ilya touching her, taking her, had her breathing growing ragged, her body flushed.

He wouldn't be an easy lover, but how often had she wondered what it would be like to be taken with such intense hunger?

Smothering a moan, she let her hand drop to the bed, refusing to attempt to ease the arousal burning through her. She knew masturbating would only make things worse. It only made the need to be touched burn brighter. Not just the need to be touch, but the need to be touched by Ilya.

*Dammit.* This wasn't what she needed in her life.

She hadn't asked to be tormented by a man. She hadn't asked to have someone attempt to kill her or for her life to be turned upside down.

After the years she'd spent constantly attempting to placate Matt's childish temper tantrums or to hide his growing abusive nature, she'd hoped for a little peace.

She didn't think that was uncalled for in the least, but evidently, she was wrong, because the current state of affairs was anything but peaceful.

Rising from the bed with the intent of going downstairs for a glass of water or maybe that rest of the wine in the bottle she'd opened a few days before, she slid her feet into her slippers, then froze.

Her head jerked up as the alarm began shrieking through the house, the sound loud enough to wake the dead.

Quickly retrieving the handgun from her bedside table, Emma rushed for the door of her bedroom.

Before she could reach it, Ilya was there, pushing it open and gripping her arm to pull her behind him. He didn't say a word before pushing her into his room at the other end of the hall.

"Stay put!" The order was as harsh as his expression before he closed the door in her face.

She stared at the door as it closed in her face, her mouth dropping open at his order.

*Stay put?*

That wasn't what they had agreed to.

That wasn't what she was doing. This was her home, and she'd promised herself she wouldn't hide again if it was invaded. She wasn't a coward and she had no intentions of pretending to be one. And she wouldn't let Ilya die for her.

Pulling the door open, Emma slid from the bedroom and started down the stairs. When she was halfway down, the siren abruptly halted and a heartbeat later a blood-curdling scream was abruptly cut off.

A male scream, and she knew neither Ilya nor that shadow Sawyer would dare make such a sound. That only left the intruder.

Rushing down the stairs, she paused just outside the kitchen.

"Ilya?" she called out his name before stepping into the kitchen and coming to an abrupt stop.

The tableau laid out in front of her was unbelievable. In a million years she would have never come up with this one in her wildest imagination.

The lights were off, but the light of a full moon was bright enough to illuminate the kitchen. Still, Emma moved her free hand to the light switches and flicked on the dimmer counter light next to the sink.

The light wasn't bright enough to blind, but the soft glow clearly bathed the two men who stared back at her silently. One in abject horror, the other with icy, murderous intent.

Her ex-husband, Matt, was splayed out in the floor, blood welling from his busted lips, one eye already swelling shut. Ilya was crouched over him, powerful legs bent and resting on Matt's arms as one hand gripped his neck; the other pressed the barrel of his handgun to Matt's temple.

Tears welled from Matt's eyes and the plea to save him was clear in his expression.

"Are you going to kill him?" she asked softly, gazing back at Ilya as her heart prepared itself to break into so many pieces it would never be the same again.

How had she grown to care about this man to the point that the realization that he wasn't who, what, she believed he was could hurt so bad?

"Do you want him to live so bad?" The Russian accent was thicker, his voice harder than she'd ever heard it.

Her eyes narrowed on him and anger began to churn inside her.

"Do you really want to disappoint me in such a way?"

she asked him softly instead. "Really, Ilya? Because you won't like how I deal with it. Not at all. Do it if that's your intent though. Don't hide it from me."

She could hear the sirens in the distance and knew without a doubt that along with Eric, her family, and probably her boss as well were only seconds away.

His expression tightened for a moment before he suddenly released Matt and launched to his feet. In the same movement he shoved his weapon in the back of his black slacks and turned to Sawyer.

"Get him out of here . . ." he began to order.

"I don't think so." Emma stepped closer, aware of the explosive tension radiating in the room as Sawyer helped Matt to his feet. "Put him in a chair. Now!" she snapped when the other man didn't move fast enough to suit her.

*Men.*

*Had there ever been a day where they weren't making a woman completely crazy?*

Thankfully, Sawyer didn't argue or test her precarious temper.

"EJ, I need a doctor," Matt whined. "He broke my nose, EJ."

He slumped in the chair Sawyer all but threw him into. "EJ, I need . . ."

"You need to shut the hell up, Matt," she ordered, laying her own weapon carefully on the kitchen island before pushing her fingers through her hair and glaring at Ilya. "Please deal with Eric and . . ."

"Sawyer!" he snapped, jerking his head to the lights and vehicles that could be seen pulling into her drive from the window on the far side of the room.

Sawyer didn't argue but hurried for the front door, and once again Emma turned her attention to Matt.

*Childish, entitled.* She hadn't realized how shallow

and immature he was when she married him. Or how immature she had been herself. She'd learned how to grow up though. Life and Matt had left her little choice.

Breathing out heavily, she shook her head as she watched him, realizing how little Matt had changed over the years. With his classic blond good looks and bright blue eyes, he drew attention when he wasn't whining and bleeding all over himself.

"Why are you here, Matt?" A little boy in a grown man's body. It was such a shame.

"EJ, I just wanted to check on you," Matt mumbled as he laid his head on the table. Blood was dripping to her floor. "I was just worried." He sobbed. "Oh God, what are you doing with him? He's a killer, EJ. Did you get so desperate for the pain that you had to take a killer?—"

"Shut up, Matt." But she had a feeling it was too late. *So desperate for the pain.*

It had a been a steady accusation after he'd found the books she'd tried to keep hidden from him. The romances, so filled with lust, with pleasure, with women's journeys into something more than a missionary position.

"God, EJ, what's wrong with you? It's just sick . . . I wanted to love you, not hurt you . . ." Matt's whine reminded her of a spoiled teenager. One whose cruelties and pettiness were out of control. But still, just a teenager. One who wanted only to hurt others.

And he was destroying her, because Ilya and Eric heard every word. The humiliation was decimating.

"Emma Jane, go to the front room and Eric and I will deal with this." Ilya stood, demanded, cool and in complete control of himself.

Except for his eyes. The pale green seemed to glow with rage. He'd kill Matt and she knew it. And that was something she did not want on her conscience.

The difference between the two men couldn't be more striking than it was at that moment. And she couldn't imagine being more angry at both of them as well as herself.

Compressing her lips, she glared back at him, receiving that cool stare in return.

Not taking her eyes off Ilya, she moved to the sink, jerked a dish towel from beside it, and turned on the cold water before breaking the stare.

"Shut up before I kill you myself, Matt." She'd sign the house over to Resnova before she'd have Matt's death on her conscience. Or before she'd suffer further humiliation. Matt could run his mouth to his cronies all he wanted, they didn't know her, not like Eric did and possibly Ilya.

"Emma Jane, get away from him," Ilya all but growled, and though she knew he wasn't in the least possessive of her, his tone, the tension in his body, both screamed possession.

She shook her head at the order.

"I suggest you give your employer your report before I make my call to him," she stated, hating the knowledge that once again her life was out of her control. "But whether you do or not, it won't matter. This won't happen again."

Wringing out the towel, she moved to where Matt sat. Thankfully, she glimpsed an ambulance pulling in the drive, right behind her brother's truck. She wondered who called them, then pushed the thought away as she pressed the damp towel into Matt's hands.

"EJ . . ." Sincere blue eyes stared up at her in appeal. "He's crazy. You see that, don't you? You have to make him go . . . I'll forgive you . . ."

"I still have a gun," Ilya growled, suddenly behind

her as Matt's gaze jerked to him in fear. "And it's still loaded."

What little color was left in Matt's gaze bled away. At the same time, men began pouring into her kitchen.

The shouted questions, amazement, anger, and her family's fear rushed around her like a tidal wave that threated to drown her beneath their concern.

"Enough." It was her brother Ronan's voice that cut through the shouted questions and press of bodies surrounding her.

The room silenced immediately, and all eyes turned to him.

"Emma Jane should join Mikayla and her mother in the front room," Ilya took over seamlessly as Ronan pressed her gently away from Matt and his muttered accusations.

Accusations her brother heard.

Not that any of it could be hidden now. Ilya had heard it all . . .

She should pity Matt, she thought.

Ronan and Eric might well kill him after this. Matt knew better than to attempt to break into her house again just to begin with. She'd warned him the year before that she had a security system in place, yet he'd done just that, and now he was destroying her.

Emma let her brother ease her into the front room though, simply because she wanted to go, not because it was what he wanted. She'd had enough for the time being.

Ilya remained silent as Nik Steele sidled over to him, his expression bland. Pausing next to him, the other man watched, as Ilya did, as the paramedics worked to take stock of Matt Lauren's injuries.

Thankfully, the bastard had stopped running his

mouth when Emma Jane left the room. But not before everyone there had heard him accuse Emma Jane of having "deviant desires."

If he were in a better mood, Ilya might have helped and given the paramedics a list of damages.

The bastard had a broken nose, a cracked rib, and several bruised ones. And it was possible his arm was fractured. Not probable, merely possible.

"He's crazy," Matt whimpered as Ronan moved in behind the paramedics. "I just wanted to talk to EJ, Ronan. She's letting him hurt her when he gets in her bed . . ."

"One more word and you're going to be missing a tongue, you little bastard," Ilya bit out furiously, aware of Emma Jane's brother as he moved to block the sight of them from where his sister now stood with their mother. "What made you believe you could slip into her home without notice? You knew I was here with her."

Matt swallowed tightly. "Someone got in before without the alarm going off. I just figured something was wrong with it. I was just going to talk to her."

*Talk to her? In the middle of the night?*

"Do you take me for a fucking fool?" Ilya didn't bother to attempt to hide his sneer or the cold, murderous fury brewing in him.

Emma Jane's ex-husband missed none of the threat Ilya posed.

"I swear . . ."

"That's enough, Matt." Emma Jane chose that moment to step into the room once again as Ilya's and Ronan's attention was focused on her ex-husband. "Get him out of here, Ronan, while you still can." She turned to her brother, her expression once more calm, though in her gaze he could see the shame burning inside her.

Ronan seemed to shrug at her look. "He's lucky to be alive. Something me or Dad, either one, would have taken care of if we were here."

The disgust in Ronan's voice drew Ilya's attention. The younger man's expression was tight with anger and fear for his sister.

"You and Dad might believe you had reason. Ilya can't make that claim," she stated, pride tightening her expression.

And for some insane reason, that look made his dick so damned hard it was agony.

Thankfully, his shirt had come untucked in the tussle with her ex-husband. Ilya had merely finished pulling it free rather than taking time to fix it.

"Stop harassing him, Ronan, and let the paramedics get him out of here," Emma Jane ordered her brother with the ease and comfort of a woman used to being heard. "Mom's not going to leave as long as he's here, and I'd like at least a few hours' sleep tonight."

She turned her back on them and moved to her parents once again. Ilya was aware of her father drawing her farther into the living room, as though in hopes of keeping her attention from Ilya and her brother.

"Want some advice?" Nik asked softly from his side.

"Not particularly," Ilya answered, his tone just as low.

He'd be damned if he needed anyone to tell him how to handle his woman.

"Convince her that you wouldn't have killed in cold blood before making the decision I can see brewing in your expression. Don't destroy her trust completely, Ilya, or she'll make you regret it." And with that, Nik walked to the front room where his delicate little blond wife awaited him.

They left moments later, right behind the paramedics and the stretcher they had that son of a bitch exhusband on.

Ilya remained in the kitchen, keeping an eye on Sawyer as he adjusted the security system on the panel next to the door.

He didn't like this attempt Matt Lauren had made to get to Emma Jane. It smacked of an attack to gauge the security rather than an attempt to discuss anything else with Emma Jane.

Had Emma Jane waited just upstairs as she was told to do, the bastard would have a bullet in his brain now rather than telling Emma Jane's secrets.

*Goddammit.*

Pushing his fingers through his hair, he breathed out roughly at the confrontation that was no doubt coming. His self-control was already shot. He was harder than hell and far past just the simple need to fuck.

At this point, the thought of touching her, of having her, was becoming an obsession.

# chapter ten

She knew there was no avoiding Ilya once everyone had left, so she didn't even try. She gave Eric's deputy her statement, filed charges against Matt for breaking and entering, and gave an affidavit that Ilya was there as a friend and heard the alarm as she had before rushing downstairs.

There was no hiding the fact that Ilya was living with her now. Ilya, Ronan, and Eric had managed to keep Sawyer's name out of the reports, though she assumed it was deliberate. Wouldn't do for the killers to know someone was watching, waiting. Someone other than the dragon suspected to be her lover.

A man who knew how to hurt her, as her ex-husband had claimed. Because obviously only the most dangerous sort of man could satisfy her deviant desires.

*God.* This was a fiasco.

Even in her wildest nightmares she couldn't have imagined this happening. Matt knew better than to attempt to break into her home again. Even Ronan had threatened dire consequences should he try. Her father had outright promised to kill him.

Pushing her hands through her hair, she wondered how she could possibly salvage the situation, even though she knew it wasn't possible. There wasn't a single omission or lie that could cover this one.

Not that she did good with out-and-out lies.

The problem was, she'd seen the look Ilya had shot her way when Matt had been throwing her secrets out to the room. The lust, pure and white hot, that flared in his eyes had mixed with intent.

It wasn't curiosity or suspicion, it was pure knowledge. As though he well understood her desires and knew exactly how to sate them. And perhaps that was the part that truly terrified her. Because that part of her nature had always confused her.

She hadn't wanted to delve into that side of her nature. That was why she'd fought Matt at every turn after he'd found the explicit romances she'd been reading the summer of their third anniversary. Missionary position with her husband suited her fine. By then, she wouldn't have dared allowed him to know where her fantasies veered. Because those fantasies had never included him.

Until she'd met Ilya, they'd stayed confined to the heroes of those books.

But now those fantasies had a face, a name, a man she craved. And there was no convincing the need rising inside her that dragons were dangerous and shouldn't be played with.

A firm knock at the door had her flinching before she turned to face it, just in time to watch Ilya step into the room. The door snapped closed behind him, and if ever a man had a predatory look on his face, then it was her dragon. Even his dragon looked sexually intent.

He leaned back against the door, his gaze narrowed on her, his expression inscrutable. She had no idea what he was thinking, and that fact made her nervous.

"You know." He crossed his arms over his chest, his head tilting a bit thoughtfully as he watched her. "I had a rather intensive background check done on you, as well as your ex. And not so much as a whisper of deviant behavior could be found." His head straightened and she was certain there was a glimmer of amusement in his pale green eyes. "Why is that do you think?"

He found this amusing?

Her ex-husband had sat in her kitchen and accused her of begging him to spank her while he fucked her and Ilya found it amusing?

"I guess you neglected to ask the ex-husband." She couldn't hold back the twinge of hurt that he was laughing at her. "He just proved he's more than willing to run his mouth."

Just what she hadn't envisioned in her darkest fantasies.

"Ex-husbands aren't normally so reliable." That hint of an accent in his voice had heat curling through her despite her complete mortification. "I rather doubt Mathew Lauren kept his mouth shut where his accusations are concerned. What he likely didn't take into account was the honor of the woman he was maligning and the fact that her friends so wisely kept their mouths shut about his accusations." His look became more somber. "No matter his attempts to shame you, he couldn't succeed. You value yourself far too well to allow others to have the opportunity to gossip about you."

She hadn't dared. She couldn't have borne the shame

of her brother having to fight because she'd made the wrong choice. Or her parents enduring such shameful gossip. They were a close family, not just with one another but with their aunts, uncles, and cousins as well.

"Even the lovers you've taken after your marriage never spoke of it or admitted to a relationship with you," he continued. "A rare circumstance indeed."

"What lovers?" she muttered, still staring at him resentfully.

She hated that he'd heard Matt's filth.

He blinked back at her before pinning her with his gaze.

"Emma Jane, surely you have had other lovers." He said it as though she'd broken some law.

"Ilya, you were here a year ago and I refused you because my divorce wasn't final. The ink is barely dry on the papers now," she reminded him. "Sorry, no other lovers. And not in a million years would I have begged Matt for anything."

That would have been sheer idiocy.

He just stared at her.

Ilya had refused to believe there had been no other lovers. No woman he knew went a year without a lover. Women were delicate, meant to be touched, to be pleasured. Especially one such as his Emma Jane.

"A year is a long time," he pointed out, watching her expression carefully.

There was shame, resentment, and beneath that a woman's hunger, her needs.

"It didn't matter." She shrugged, breaking eye contact and staring at the floor for a moment. "I'm not very good at the whole sex thing anyway. Just ask Matt," she all but sneered.

Some men should not be allowed to live for what they

did to an innocent woman's dreams and her budding sexuality.

Emma Jane had barely been twenty when she'd married and, from what he learned, still yet a virgin. Five years later, the innocent heart had been scarred, her once-natural needs hidden, frightened of exposure.

"Do you believe a woman's need for more sensation, for adventure and the ultimate pleasure in her sexuality is somehow wrong, Emma Jane?" he asked her softly, and in her quick look saw her desperation and her fears. "That you wanted to feel your lover deeper, more dominantly is somehow wrong? Do you believe that your lover's need to watch your pretty ass blush for him could be so unusual? Or that screaming in pleasure as he works his cock up your ass is so deviant? Do you believe women read such material because that *isn't* what they want?"

His Emma Jane wanted, she ached and needed, and she was so very frightened of all those pleasures.

"It doesn't matter." She was breathless, flushed, her body so very needy.

Beneath her sleep shirt, her nipples were hard, tight. And he bet her clit was throbbing.

"Doesn't matter, love?" he crooned. "It matters very much to me." And he wanted to show her why it would matter to her.

She had no idea how to decipher what her sexy body was dying for. She had found the acts in the pages of books and reading them had ignited a hunger deep inside her imagination. She wanted his teeth on her nipples, wanted his lips sucking at her neck, leaving his mark on that slender column. She wanted to be spanked. She wanted his hard dick stretching her, showing her the pleasure and the pain. And he would stretch her. She was tiny, delicate, and he was large, and so much stronger.

His dick was iron hard, his need to touch her clawing at his guts, and she looked as unconcerned as the most perfect ice princess.

The thing about ice princesses though, they had such a heart of fire that once revealed melted all hints of icy cold. He'd never had the pleasure of melting one though, until now. Until his fiery, so uncertain, Emma Jane.

"What you think does matter, Emma Jane," he assured her. "It will always matter to a man who truly wants to be a lover, and not just an empty fuck. And I am your lover, baby. We're just going to make it official tonight."

She couldn't speak.

She couldn't breathe.

He lifted his hands to the buttons of his shirt and began releasing them. Emma Jane watched wide-eyed as Ilya freed each button of that damned shirt, taking a step toward her as they released.

"Ilya, this might not be wise . . ." Yet she was breathless, excitement riding her hard and filling her.

"It's very wise, honey," he assured her. "And it will be oh-so-good."

A woman could never hope to control a man like Ilya, let alone tame him. Once he took her, nothing in her life would be the same. She wouldn't be the same.

"Don't worry, we'll take it slow and easy," he murmured, a dragon's voice, mesmerizing and seductive.

*Slow and easy?*

She shook her head, barely aware she was doing it.

"Yes, love, slow and easy the first time," he crooned, the shirt sliding from hard, muscled shoulders to reveal an upper body that was all corded strength. "A chance to feel each other, to know the limits your body has."

Tight, tanned flesh rippling over muscle that came naturally and not from a gym. A light mat of black hair over his chest that arrowed down beneath jeans. There was a tattoo she made a mental note to check later, right in the center of his chest.

Later . . .

He released the black belt he wore, paused, and toed the short, scarred boots from his feet.

"I want your mouth, Emma Jane," said the dragon's voice. She shuddered at the sound of it. "I want you on your knees, my dick parting those beautiful lips as you learn the flesh that will bring you such pleasure."

The belt hung free, and a moment later denim was pushed down hard thighs and kicked free, revealing the dark length of his cock. Thick, pulsing with heavy veins, the engorged crest damp.

"Come, love." He stepped in front of her, his fingers gripping the hem of her sleep shirt. "Let me see the beauty I've dreamed of for a year now. Let me show you, Emma Jane, what you hunger for."

Emma Jane felt entranced. Power shimmered on bronze flesh, gleamed in his pale green eyes. It wrapped around her, pulled at her, until she knew that resisting him was impossible. She didn't want to resist. Not this.

Her arms lifted and she allowed him to toss away the sleeveless sleep shirt she wore. A second later, the pajama bottoms and her panties slid down her legs. And all she could do was stare into the heavy-lidded, lust-laden gaze holding hers.

"There we are," he murmured, pleasure filling his voice, his expression, as his palm flattened on her stomach.

He stroked up to her breast, cupped one swollen curve, his thumb flicking over her nipple before moving to her shoulder, to her neck, where he curved his fingers against it.

"I'm not an easy lover, Emma Jane." If that was a warning, then she took very little notice of it. "When we're finished, you'll carry my marks."

*Okay, fine.* He needed to get on with it though. Now, while she was immersed in the spell he was weaving around her.

Still holding her neck in his grip, she watched, transfixed, as his head lowered.

She expected the coming kiss to be gentle. Slow and easy, he'd said.

The hold on her neck was firm, his fingers curling against it, gripping her in place without her feeling threatened. She understood why a second later. His lips didn't settle on hers, they didn't seduce or cajole—they possessed her.

His tongue pushed past as his lips slanted over hers. His free hand tangled in her hair, the friction of his grip sending tiny flares of sensation racing over her scalp like the scratch of tiny claws.

Emma Jane clutched at his shoulders, feeling the muscles shifting beneath her hands as he edged her toward the bed, tiny step by tiny step, his lips and tongue stealing her senses as he did so.

A second later, a nip to her lips, just sharp enough to drag a mewl of shock from her, and he was consuming her kiss again. Over and over, lips, tongue, his teeth raking against the kiss-swollen curves until her senses were so immersed in that kiss when his lips moved she would have followed. The hand holding her hair tightened, the one at her neck held firm before sliding away and trailing to her breasts.

Emma Jane whimpered at the sensation, poised on an

edge that made little sense, with no idea which direction she should go.

"That's it, *balaur pereche*." He whispered the unfamiliar words against her neck, the accent thick, heavy. So heavy she wasn't even certain if the words she heard were correct.

And a second later, she didn't care.

His lips, teeth, and tongue found an area on her neck so sensitive, so laden with overexcited nerve endings, that she came to her toes, shuddering at the roughened caresses. Sharp kisses, heated, a tasting of her flesh as he murmured in another language, words that stroked her senses even if she couldn't understand them.

Her head fell back into the grip he had on her hair, tilted, her fingers tightening on his shoulders as her knees weakened. The sharp little bites, heated tastes, and strokes of his tongue were so good. Too good. Her entire body was too hot, too sensitive. She ached as she never had, needed something just out of reach. She was so focused on it, so desperate, that she wasn't aware the bed was at the back of her legs until she toppled onto it with a gasp.

"Fuck me, you're a beauty." The accent was thicker, his expression harsh, the dragon flexing at the side of his face as he stared down at her.

He leaned forward, one hand bracing on the bed at her shoulder as his gaze trained on her breasts. Emma Jane swore her nipples hardened further, the sensual heat exquisite. Her fingers bunched in the blankets beneath her.

She fought just to breathe as his head lowered, lips parting a second before they touched her flesh.

Emma Jane's back bowed. The instant, suckling heat of his mouth surrounding her nipple shocked her, seared her. A bolt of sensation raced from her nipple to her clit, threatening to push her past the edge she was teetering on as her clit pulsed in nearing ecstasy.

Sexual need burned through her bloodstream, sensitized her flesh to a level she'd never known, and had her crying out, pleading for things she had no idea how to put into words.

He didn't seem to need the words though.

He took her nipples, one at a time, just as he'd taken her lips, as he'd marked her neck. Nipping, sucking firmly as his hands caressed and stroked until Emma Jane knew the whimpering cries she heard were her own but could do nothing to stop them.

She was burning alive in sensation. The little sparks of heat from his teeth, a soothing lick of his tongue, a muttered groan, foreign words whispered against her flesh.

His tongue lashed at her sensitive nipples, his teeth raked over them, and his mouth sucked at them firmly. He wasn't afraid she'd feel the drawing motions of his mouth. To the contrary, he was going to make certain she felt it all the way to her womb.

His caresses moved from her breasts, lower, stroking over her stomach as he pushed her legs apart and knelt between them.

And he destroyed her mind.

He had no mercy on her as his tongue parted the slick folds, licked, thrust inside her. Heated kisses, firm licks. Each stroke, each caress, pushed her higher, yet never allowed her to find that edge she was so desperate for. He sucked her clit firmly, but it was never enough, never lasted long enough for her to slip over that edge.

"You taste like sunshine." The words were muttered a second before strong, white teeth gripped her thigh and a finger pressed inside her.

Her hips jerked at the hard intrusion of his finger. The muscles of her vagina clamped around it, rippling desperately as pleasure tore through her in a heated rush.

Sensation tightened and roiled inside her, clenching her muscles, her vagina. She was so close . . .

"Ah, not yet, my Emma Jane." The rasp of his dark voice stroked over her as his teeth released her thigh and his fingers eased back.

Ilya straightened, gripping her hands as he did so, he pulled her up until she was sitting in front of him. "Take me now. Give to me . . ."

Her lips parted as she stared up at him. Along the perspiration gleaming on his abs, what looked to be a dragon's claws closed over an emerald in the center of his chest, to the pale, pale green of his eyes as the broad crest of his cock touched her lips.

Ilya had known the year before what this woman was to him. She was his. His woman. As he stared into the dark gray of her eyes and watched her lips cover the crest of his cock, he knew not just his heart was hers, his soul was hers.

Pleasure tore through him as her mouth touched him, then became hungry, taking him, sucking him, as her tongue so shyly caressed him. With silken fingers she explored his erection, the taut sac of his testicles, stroking as she sucked him, tongued him, made him crazy with pleasure.

It was exquisite. Her mouth was shy but hungry, taking him by small degrees and loving each inch she filled her mouth with. It was like seeing a part of her sexuality be born, as he watched her face. It wasn't lust that filled her expression, but hunger, overwhelming need. It was the look of a woman learning her freedom and reveling in it.

There was nothing practiced or experienced in how she took him, but it was all the more destructive for the fact that her sexuality was still her own. It wasn't marked by what others had taught her or forced upon her. Her sensuality was coming into its own at this moment, and the knowledge that he was the man to share it was a pleasure all its own.

He didn't tell her what to do, didn't guide her. He gave her the same as she gave him, allowed her to see, to feel, his pleasure. With guttural moans he let her know when it was so damned good it was all he could do to hold on. His fingers clenched in her hair, loosened, and tightened, keeping the heated sensation she needed spiking her senses.

And he knew what she was doing. Everything she may have read, every word that had aroused her in whatever book she read . . .

"Ah fuck!" The roughened sound of his voice shocked him as she took him deeper, stroking the shaft with one hand as she loved every inch she tasted of him, all the way to the back of her heated little mouth. Then she moaned, her gray eyes dazed, and she swallowed against the bulging head of his cock. "Ah yes, baby, show me all those books taught you."

He stared down at her, demanding, jaw clenching on a shattered groan as her tongue worked the sensitive flesh beneath the head of his cock. Damn her, he was going to blow if she kept this up.

He wasn't going to last long, not like this. The feel of her mouth working over his cockhead, her tongue lashing beneath it, rolling against it, licking him like a fucking dream.

"Emma Jane, sweet . . ." His hands tightened in his

hair, pulling her back as his balls tightened and he nearly came in her mouth.

"Dragon . . ." she whispered, her gaze still locked with his and drugged with pleasure.

Control was a thing of the past. It was lost, torn from him at the dazed, sensual sound of her voice.

Emma Jane gasped in surprise as Ilya lifted her farther up the mattress, coming over her, his knees spreading her thighs apart as he covered her.

The heat of his cock pressed between her thighs, the width beginning to stretch her, to part her entrance with a blaze of sensation before he stilled.

The engorged crest was lodged inside her, making her crazy, the stretch, the throb, of his cock pushing her higher, giving her a glimpse of what was to come.

"Look at me." One hand tightened in her hair, pulling her head back. "Open your eyes, Emma Jane. Look at me."

She forced her eyes open, staring up at him in dazed pleasure.

"Slow and easy?" He all but snarled the words. "Tell me. Slow and easy?"

*No.*

*No.* He'd brought her this far, he couldn't stop now.

She was shaking her head as he asked the second time.

"Don't stop. Please . . ."

The sudden thrust inside her didn't bury him full length, but the sensual pain had her arching, screaming for him as the first orgasm tore through her senses. Oh God, that was what it had to be. She jerked, shuddered, and such incredible pleasure exploded inside her again.

"Ilya!" She tried to scream his name, to form the

words to plead for just a moment to catch her breath, staring up at him, his features savage, the gleam of such pleasure, such hunger in his eyes.

He wasn't going to take her easy, not for anything.

No, not her dragon.

On the third thrust he buried full length inside the gripping, clenching depths of her vagina.

"Please, Ilya . . ." She could feel him throbbing inside her, like a heartbeat, like life. "I need you . . . I need . . ." God, she had no idea what she needed.

She was sobbing with the intensity of needs she had no idea how to satisfy as they built inside her. Her pussy rippled around his erection, the heavy, stretching presence inside her tearing aside any shyness or embarrassment. But spearing straight into the dark, unfulfilled desires she fought. Ilya shook his head to disperse the perspiration that dripped into his eyes. With him buried inside his Emma Jane, the feel of her pussy sucking at him, tightening around him like the tightest fist as she came again, stole that last thread he had on his own hunger.

He spilled inside her, when he'd never spilled himself inside another woman.

She was his, he'd known that all along. Locked in his heart, his soul.

His semen shot inside her as a growl ripped from his chest and he opened that last part of himself to her.

She was his.

She held all of him.

God help them both.

She was her dragon's mate . . .

In her life, Emma Jane had never known the complete, boneless sleep she fell into when Ilya dragged himself beside her and pulled her into his arms.

"Sleep, *pereche*." She was certain that wasn't exactly what he said, that last word wasn't easy to understand. *Balaur pereche. Something.* She might not be able to figure out the pronunciation, but it sounded possessive.

It sounded like it meant more than just a word. When he said it, she felt something tug at her heart, at her dreams, that made little sense.

She'd feared just falling in love with him, but she was learning it could go far deeper than that.

The last thing she remembered was her hand resting over the dragon's claws on his chest, right over his heart.

There was something about that tattoo that lingered in her mind. Other than the fact that it was unique, she knew it meant something to him, just as the tattoo at the side of his face did. The one she'd glimpsed on his back. The marks on the backs of his shoulders. Ink she never knew he had.

"Dragon," she whispered as exhaustion overtook her and she gave in to the comforting darkness overtaking her as strong arms held her, her head pillowed on her dragon's heart.

# chapter eleven

Emma Jane awoke to the feel of Ilya's hand smoothing down her bare back, taking the sheet with it and baring her skin.

"You have lovely skin," he stated, drawing the sheet over her butt. "It would take ink like canvas does paint. The image would shimmer with a light of its own."

She turned her head to stare back at him curiously as he lay next to her propped on his side.

"What sort of image?" she couldn't help but ask, wondering at the somber look on his face.

"It wouldn't matter," he said, though she knew he was lying. "Perhaps it is best left unmarred. It is always best to leave the past behind with no ink or scars to remind you of things better forgotten."

Was he talking about when he walked away from her? As though she believed he'd ever stay.

She'd mark him, she decided. In a place where he wouldn't have a choice but to see it every day of his life and he'd have to think of her. She didn't want to forget him, and she didn't want him to ever forget her.

"I have a very good memory," she assured him as his fingers caressed from her shoulder to her hip, then the rise of her rear.

The rasp of his callused flesh had her heart racing in excitement, her body preparing for his possession again. She wanted him again, all that wild, untamed power moving inside her, taking her.

"As do I," he whispered. "Sometimes it's far too good."

Emma Jane parted her lips to drag in more air as his head lowered. He was within a breath, just a single breath, of kissing her again when the sound of his cell phone on the bed table ringing imperatively had him pausing.

On the second ring he grimaced, twisted around on the bed, and grabbed the device before reclining on his back and bringing the phone to his ear.

"Yes?" he answered, that husky growl in his voice far too sexy.

Sitting up as she dragged the sheet around her, she let herself stare at the tattoos along his side and the center of his chest.

*Dare ye not awaken the dragon, for he rides hell-fires, wields Heaven's sword, and slay you he shall . . .* The words were in two lines along his right side at his ribs.

The most impressive one, though, was almost a 3-D image. Ghostly scaled dragon's claws, blood dripping from the sharpened tip, held a beautiful, faceted emerald. Beneath the emerald words were inscribed in the leathery palm below the gem. The Russian script was unfamiliar to her, but it meant something important to him, she thought. The tattoo was right over his heart and beside the emerald . . . She leaned closer, frowning, paying little attention to the one-sided conversation.

That was a bullet wound, and it wasn't an old one. That scar was fairly recent.

Her gaze lifted to Ilya's, meeting it in the realization that he'd been watching her all along.

"I'll be there momentarily," Ivan stated to whomever he was talking to.

When he disconnected the call, before she could speak he dragged her to him, his lips landing on hers with a hunger that was more than simple lust.

His fingers tangled in her hair, held her to him, and destroyed her senses once again. She loved his kisses. Loved the male hunger and strength in them, the way he kissed her like she was a woman, not like a doll that might break.

Even when she surprised him and jerked her lips back to nip at his lower lip, there was no anger, nothing that could make her feel shame or cause her to hesitate. No, his eyes narrowed, a grin kicking up at the corner of his lips as he took the challenge.

When his lips returned to hers it was to deliver hard, heated kisses that didn't give her a chance to catch her balance or find other ways to dare him. The hand in her hair tightened when he pulled back, his features taut with male hunger.

What she did to him tore at his soul. Equal parts lust and pure overriding hunger for just the taste of her filled him. Staring into those dark, slumberous gray eyes, he knew after his Emma Jane no other woman would ever do.

If he didn't convince her that she loved him or find a way to stay when this was over, it might kill him. No dragon wanted to lose his mate, and Ilya more than any wanted to keep his.

To keep her, he'd have to show her all the ways she could be free with him. That she could burn with him and let a dragon become more than just a bodyguard, far more than just a lover.

"You have to be somewhere," she gasped as his lips moved to her neck, his teeth raking against the sensitive cord at the side.

"Momentarily," he growled, his breathing harsh, heavy, even as he tried to control it. "I have other things to do first. As do you. Come, love, ride your dragon."

Ride her dragon.

Emma Jane lost her breath as he muttered the words against her neck.

Oh yes, she wanted to ride her dragon.

One hand gripped her hip, the other the opposite thigh as he guided her over him.

He didn't enter her immediately. Instead, he settled her until the slick folds of her pussy cushioned the hot flesh instead.

Emma Jane rocked against the pressure against her clit, her head tipping back, eyes closing at the pleasure surrounding her. A second later a whimpering cry left her lips as Ilya's lips covered a nipple and sucked it inside the head of his mouth.

What was it about his touch? she thought hazily. Why did she respond to him, want things with him that she would have never wanted with another man?

This hard, tattooed, dangerous dragon. What made her open to him when she'd been able to open to no other?

Her hands clenched his shoulders as his lips drew at first one nipple, then the other. He gave her the sensation she needed, that erotic bite of a pleasure bordering pain. The lash of fire, the scrape of his teeth.

His hands caressed her back, hips, the callused palms moving over the curves of her rear before he gripped them, holding her still, letting her feel the throb of his cock against her clit.

Excitement raced through Emma Jane. Her heart beat almost painfully in her chest and blood thundered through her veins. Each time he touched her he lit a need inside her that she couldn't deny or turn away from.

And with each touch it only grew stronger. He was filling parts of her that weren't physical, branding himself on to her soul and ensuring when he was gone he left her forever longing for him.

"Ilya, this is killing me," she whimpered, her fingers tightening on his shoulders as the suckling pressure on her nipple became hungrier. "It's so good. And not enough . . ." His teeth raked her nipple, causing her to jerk at the flash of sharp sensation and the moisture gathering between her pussy and his cock to increase.

Ilya was certain he was going to spill his seed between their bodies. The undulation of her hips, the slick, hot flesh sliding against his dick, her naked body his to stroke, kiss, or mark, however he pleased. She was like no other woman he'd ever known in his life.

How the hell was he going to walk away from her when the time came that she decided his bloodstained past was far too dark for her? She was so deep inside his soul he couldn't imagine being without her now. This, this moment in time, was life, it was living.

Holding her, feeling her need for him like he'd felt no other woman's. She warmed the parts of his soul that had never been warmed.

Just holding her, seeing her smile, feeling her kiss, reminded him of dreams he'd never dared allow himself.

"Ilya," she murmured against his lips when he drew her to him for a kiss. "Please, I need you inside me now."

She rarely spoke while he was taking her. She still held parts of herself from him. But like sunlight through the clouds, she was slowly emerging, slowly testing her own limits.

"Then take what you need, baby," he dared her, staring into her drowsy, sensually drugged eyes. "I'm here for your pleasure. Whatever that may be."

Something bright and wild flared in her gaze, but that shadow of uncertainty still lingered. Still, she lifted herself, one graceful hand moving between their bodies until she gripped his erection and slid the swollen head through the slick folds of her pussy.

He'd have a fucking stroke waiting.

A man could only bear so much pleasure at one time.

The nerve-laden crest pressed against her entrance, felt the head, the snug muscles parting, and never had he had to fight so hard to hold back his release. He could feel the perspiration beginning to film his forehead as sexual heat rushed through him, stoked by her innocence and her sensuality.

The slow degrees that she took him in had him groaning at the pleasure. Tighter than a fist, her inner flesh rippled over his cock, inch by inch as she stared back at him. Rising and lowering herself, she took more and more of him, pleasure and excitement rising in her expression.

Watching her, gauging each response, he caressed her back, her hips, then lower until he could grip the curves of her ass. He didn't lead her, didn't change whatever pace she set. He didn't want to take control of the movements, he wanted to increase her pleasure.

As her fingers dug into his shoulders, he let his fingers delve into the narrow crevice of her rear, stroking, caressing, until he found the sensitive entrance located there. He let his fingers linger over it, stroke it, until he'd managed to draw back the excess moisture spilling from her pussy.

Ilya watched her carefully for any hint of uncertainty or denial, but all he saw was the increased pleasure and need.

His courageous, adventurous Emma Jane. She hadn't been meant to live without pleasure, without excitement.

As her pace increased and her pussy became slicker, hotter, Ilya drove her higher by giving what many would think forbidden, depraved. With his finger slick with the juices spilling from her pussy, he entered that other, snugger entrance and watched her go wild.

Her orgasm rushed over her, her movements becoming jerky, her slick heat tightening further and throwing him over that edge he'd sworn he'd resist this time. He spilled inside her, again. Ah God, the pleasure of her, the clenching caress around his dick as he shot his release inside her, destroyed him.

Her fingers flexed against his shoulders, nails digging in, then her lips went to his neck, and Ilya couldn't throttle the wrenching groan that came from his throat as she marked him. His Emma Jane, sweet, shy, so very hungry for all things sensual, marked her dragon as her own.

They showered together, and his Emma Jane, he found, could be as playful as a little mink as they washed each other. Her soft laughter during those stolen moments was a memory he tucked close to his heart. Just in case.

When Emma Jane was finally dried and nearly dressed, her mother called. Ilya left her to talk to her mother and made his way from the house to meet Sawyer in the tree line at the back of the house.

The other man was waiting, relaxed and silent as Ilya approached him.

John Sawyer was one of the agency's best. He'd been a SEAL before bad intel had caused him to lose half his team and left him sour on the command structure. A wound six months before had put him on recovery until only weeks ago. Not that anyone could have guessed he'd been wounded.

He was a stubborn son of a bitch who took zero bullshit and was as quick to kill as he was to breathe if the situation required it. His brown eyes were cold and hard, his expression rarely showing any expression. He wasn't big on mercy, and trust was low on his list of priorities. But he and Ilya understood each other. One killer to another.

"You were right last night," Sawyer stated as Ilya stepped to the tree the other man leaned casually against. "Matt Lauren was testing the security." He looked up and Ilya followed his gaze, narrowing his eyes at the flash of metal he saw hidden close to the trunk.

"What is it?" Ilya asked him.

"I didn't get too close, didn't want to let anyone know it was spotted." His eyes moved around the perimeter, always watching, always aware. "But from what I saw, it's locked on the security plate at the back door. I'm going to guess it's analyzing the protocols each time anyone enters or exits, looking for the passcode in. Someone's gone to a hell of a lot of trouble here, Ilya."

Ilya moved around the tree, his gaze trained on the camouflaged box.

"Any sign of audio or video?" he asked the agent.

"Not according to my inspection of it. My equipment isn't detecting anything either. What I did detect though, and that's in the security system itself, are very brief intervals, some less than a second, hitting the electronics every hour or so, or when the back doors were used." Sawyer nodded toward the house. "I'd say when her ex-husband entered and set off the security, that bad boy was locked on to the security plate the whole time. Someone's looking to come in and catch you unaware."

*Good luck there.* Ilya wasn't an easy man to catch unaware.

"I'll contact the sheriff and arrange a little talk with Matt Lauren," Ilya decided.

"Good luck there," Sawyer grunted, drawing Ilya's gaze back to him. "I called Eric when I found it. Lauren's parents had him out before daybreak, and he's no place to be found now."

He was hiding because he knew Ilya would come after him. *Smart man,* Ilya thought mockingly. A dead man walking, but he'd be walking a bit longer than he would have been if he hadn't found a place to hide.

"Want me to find him?" Sawyer asked, no anticipation or judgement either way in his tone.

Sawyer knew Ilya would kill the other man, though, and he was offering to remove the cost of that action from between Ilya and Emma Jane.

"I want you to do exactly what you're doing." Ilya shook his head. "You're my backup while we're sleeping. This is the wrong time to take the chance that those bastards will return while you're busy with something else."

Sawyer nodded slowly before turning back to him. "I want my team," he stated then. "Max, Elizaveta, Grisha, and Tobias. There's four of them, two of us, and one little girl caught in the cross fire. Doesn't give her very good odds if you ask me."

And he was right. If it was just him and Sawyer when the attack came, then Ilya would look forward to the fight. But he knew fate's capricious ways and he didn't want to risk Emma Jane to fate.

"I'll contact Ivan immediately and have them on a flight within an hour." It was an action he'd already considered.

"Whoever it is, is patient. That means a hell of a lot of money is backing them," Sawyer observed. "They don't want to fuck up again. The fact that they haven't gone after her since we arrived bothers me, Ilya. That bothers me real bad."

It bothered him as well, Ilya thought. Complacency wasn't the problem, and if Emma Jane's would-be assassins had even checked into who he was, they'd know that. Ilya wasn't just well trained. He'd been a hardened soldier by twelve and each year of his life had only added to it.

He'd never been a child, never known innocence, so there wasn't a chance either chimera would affect his protection of Emma Jane. He was a dragon. No, he was the Dragon Heir, whether he had wanted the title or not. Perhaps it was time to wield what little power he had in that circle of cutthroats, thieves, and assassins.

If he was very, very lucky, the ones trying to move against Emma Jane had no idea the death they were facing if so much as a scratch marred her skin in their endeavors.

It would mean calling his grandparents and meeting

with them. The last time he'd done that, he'd left with the ink over his heart. God only knew what they'd ink next.

"Get some rest," he told Sawyer as he turned away. "Your team will be here before dark."

Sawyer nodded at that and, rather than walking away, pulled a small black digital box from the backpack next to the tree and began fiddling with the controls again. Sawyer's idea of rest. If the man ever slept, Ilya hadn't caught him doing it.

Meanwhile, Ilya had calls to make.

It had been two weeks since the first attack, an almost unheard-of amount of time considering the fact that Emma Jane wasn't hiding and only one man, possibly two, was guarding her.

That told him at the very least, they knew who he was and they knew what awaited them if they killed him. The last man who had tried had died screaming. Ivan had actually been merciful. But Ivan had only been one step ahead of the brother Ilya refused to claim and the grandparents who demanded the blood of the shooter's family as well.

Try talking a Romanian dragon out the blood he was lusting for? That hadn't been fun.

They were still upset that Ivan hadn't saved the shooter for them to kill.

He and Ivan were brothers of a different sort. Their loyalties had been honed in the fires of hell amid the fiery lash of the whip. And in some cases, he thought, reaching up to touch the scars beneath the dragon ink, the knife. Ivan's father and Ilya's dam's brother had especially enjoyed using a whip and a knife.

*Little bastard is too fucking pretty. Like a little girl. We're going to make you look like a boy . . .*

They'd carved the side of his face with such joy that the boy Ilya might have been at one time had been forgotten. And it had been done as the bitch who gave birth to him had looked on with a sneer.

As far back as he could remember, even then, he'd known Lorena Stefanova, the woman who gave birth to him, hated the sight of him. It had been years later that he'd learned the reason why. Learned that the name Dragonovich was one she couldn't withhold from him and it wasn't the name of the husband she'd taken in the first months of her pregnancy.

She hated the boy she gave birth to because she couldn't kill him. To do so would bring a wrath upon her that she'd only barely escaped in the Dragonovich family's vengeance for the death of Ilya's father.

The Dragonoviches weren't powerful in the way of oligarchs. It wasn't money or family name that made them powerful, though they had plenty of that. It wasn't even one of the criminally corrupt names. It damned sure wasn't an old name that came with prestige or power.

The Dragonovich, son of the Dragon, or the Dragon as the head of the family was called, would always stand as the head of a Romanian clan of cutthroats, thieves, and assassins who due to their strength, vengeance, and loyalty were whispered of in tones of fear and awe.

And Ilya was the Dragon Heir, born to take the title of Dragon from the moment of his father's death. The Dragon heir, long descended from a clan said to have earned the protection of the great beasts that once ruled the mountains and skies of a little known province in Romania so long ago. It was said that the ink used to mark the Dragon Heirs carried the blood of those last surviving dragons.

He was both cursed and revered in certain circles. Feared and respected. He'd been raised in hell, beaten, scarred, and nearly killed more than once before the Dragonovich clan managed to locate him. By then, he was truly a dragon of war, of stealth and death.

And dragons only mate once, his grandmother had told him years ago. When the dragon heir carried the heart mark and the dragon's woman carried his ink, then any who thought to harm them would know a vengeance that had only grown over the generations.

His grandfather had placed the mark over his heart because Ilya had told him that he knew Emma Jane was the only woman to have touched his heart, the only woman he'd not just kill for but die to protect.

The old man swore he'd heard the dragon's song and was given the image of the stone to place in the dragon's claws.

He'd had no intentions of claiming her. No one should have even learned she existed.

Stepping into the house once again, Ilya stared around the sun-filled, cheerful kitchen.

Emma Jane loved her home, her family. She understood loyalty, and honor. He'd met so few women who did. And he very much feared the reason she was a target was due to the fact that somehow, someway, either his mother's family or her husband's had learned that the Dragon heir had taken a mate.

If there was one thing Lorena Vasilyev would not be able to tolerate, it would be that the son of the man she'd had murdered had found a mate. A woman he gave his heart to willingly, when even trickery couldn't gain his father's.

Pulling out his phone, he made his call to Ivan to request the team Sawyer required. As he'd promised the other man, they'd be on a jet heading to Hagerstown within the hour.

Then he turned and headed to the front room where he'd left Emma Jane earlier. The only chance he had of finding Matt Lauren was the knowledge she might have of where he'd hide or whom he would run to. At the moment, he was the only connection Ilya had to Emma Jane's assailants. The only chance Ilya had of striking at them first and ensuring he never had to explain the shame of his past or the danger he may have brought on her.

# chapter twelve

Emma Jane sat, still and silent, and listened as Ilya told her what Sawyer had found and they suspected had been placed there before Matt had broken into the house. A device that analyzed Ilya's security protocols and had the ability to possibly hack the codes he and Sawyer were changing every day.

If that weren't bad enough, frightening enough, then he told her that Matt had been bailed from jail before daybreak by his parents and had completely disappeared.

That sounded like Matt, she thought as Ilya sat quiet now, waiting for her to give him the information he needed. As she watched him, her gaze slid to the mark on his face, and even the dragon's image was filled with demand.

Where would Matt go? Who would hide him?

How could he and Sawyer find him?

They'd kill him.

As she stared back at Ilya, she knew in that moment if he got his hands on Matt, then her ex-husband was dead. Sawyer wouldn't stop him either. He wasn't just a Brute Force agent working with Ilya. She'd watched them talking several times, not that she'd heard what they were talking about, but she'd watched their body language, their expression.

Sawyer was just as hard core as Ilya. They were the type of men who had killed before and, according to the limitations of their particular code of honor, would kill again. And killing Matt for attempting to help whoever wanted her dead would be within the limits those two had set for themselves.

"Emma Jane." Something gentle, compassionate, flashed in his gaze as he lifted his hand and cupped her cheek. "This is your life. There's no doubt he was helping your assailants."

From where she sat facing him on the couch, their knees nearly touching, she could see the scars she'd learned lay beneath the tattoo of the dragon. They were carefully disguised by the ink but still there all the same.

She knew from what she'd read about him that the dragon was documented as far back as his teen years, which meant the scars had come even sooner.

What kind of life had her dragon led that had made him this hard? That had made it so easy to decide to kill a man, for any reason, let alone a woman.

"What proof do you have that he was helping them?" She twisted her fingers together as her gaze lowered from Ilya's. "Matt isn't a violent person, Ilya. Not like that. A bully, yes. But not violent."

Or was he?

How many times had Matt told her he'd kill her or

have her killed if she divorced him? The only thing his parents liked about him was the fact that she was his wife. Even they had no idea how to deal with him as the years had passed.

"Do you want to see the video the cameras we placed around the tree line recorded?" His voice was still low, filled with understanding. "There was at least one other person with him, though he was smart enough to keep his face from being recorded. The moment Matt started toward the house, the bursts of interference to the security began. He knew."

Ilya was trying not to hurt her, she thought, almost amused. It was obvious he had no idea how to be consoling, because that was definitely a gleam of murder in his gaze.

"You'll kill him." She lifted her gaze to him, staring back at him painfully. "If you find him, you won't return him in shape to stand trial or to be questioned by Eric. You'll get whatever information you can beat out of him before you kill him."

It wasn't a question and they both knew it.

His features turned implacable, sharper. This was her Ilya, her dragon. The man who would kill because of her.

Tears filled her eyes. She didn't want him to kill because of her. There was so much more to him than the dragon who believed he had to protect everyone he took responsibility for. And that was her Ilya. He wasn't a man who enjoyed killing, but he did it, when he felt it was needed.

"Emma Jane, he was willing to aid the men who came into your home with the intent of doing you harm," he reminded her, his tone carefully modulated, gentle. "Have you forgotten that somehow?"

She jerked to her feet, offended by not just his tone but his words as well.

"I'm no imbecile, Ilya, so don't speak to me as though I am." She stabbed her finger back at him before clenching her teeth and pacing away from him.

She was scared for him, not of him. She was scared for herself and what lengths this man would go to ensure her safety, her life. There had to be limits, didn't there?

"You are a very intelligent woman," he stated, his tone neither angry nor frustrated. "Even more, you're very perceptive, and I won't try to lie to you. Ever. Will I kill him?" He inhaled slowly. "If not over this, then I have no doubt he will push me to that point eventually." He shrugged as though now was as good as anytime. "The now is what concerns me though. Now he's working with professionals determined to take you from me, Emma Jane. I won't allow that."

It was like a core of pure titanium suddenly flashed in his gaze, in his expression.

"Swear to me you won't kill him," she whispered. "You won't order Sawyer to. Tell me you'll bring him back alive."

Silence stretched between them and it was telling.

Tears filled her eyes and she fought the sob aching to be released. The pain that welled inside her was almost impossible to push back.

She loved this man. She loved him so much that she'd be damned if she'd allow him to kill a man in cold blood for her.

"No." She had to force the word out while choking back a cry. "No."

His head tilted to the side, a frown hovering over his brow, causing the tattoo to lower its scaled head imperceptibly as though it too were confused.

"Why, Emma Jane?" He shook his head as his fingers seemed to curl as though to fist before relaxing once more. "Do you want to die, baby? Do you think I'll allow that?"

Three quick, jerky breaths pulled the tears and sobs back far enough that she could talk without breaking down.

"If I cry before we arrive at Mom and Dad's for lunch, then Daddy will be cross with you and Ronan will probably try to hit you or something," she said, her breath hitching. "And I'm a very ugly crier. I wail and my face goes all splotchy . . ."

A tear slipped free and her lips trembled as she stared back at his suddenly panicked expression.

"No. Baby, no." He rushed to her and pulled her into his arms, one hand at the back of her head as his other arm held her close. "I'm sorry. Please, you can't cry, Emma Jane."

Clasping her face between his palms, he kissed the tear from her cheek, kissed her trembling lips.

"You are right. He'll show up eventually and Eric will catch him. You're right," he swore to her.

Ilya knew she wasn't right. Matt would be looking for a way out of the area so he could disappear for good. He knew he was dead if Ronan got his hands on him, let alone Ilya.

"I told Mom and Dad we'd be there . . ." Her voice still trembled and he couldn't bear it.

In the weeks he'd been with her, she hadn't cried once, though she deserved hours of tears if that was what she wanted.

She'd straightened her spine and argued where she felt it was needed, ignored what didn't have to be addressed, and tried to take one day at a time as they waited for the enemy to make their next move.

She was the strongest woman he knew, and he'd be damned if he was going to be the one to make her cry. He wouldn't let it happen.

"Then we should leave," he agreed quickly, staring down at her distressed expression though, thankfully, no further tears were falling.

*Please, God, don't let her cry, not over this,* he thought as she gathered her purse and laced sneakers over her white socks.

She wore jeans and one of those little tank tops she liked. Soft, satiny skin shimmered like the tears had in her eyes.

The thought of those tears had disgust crawling up his spine as he helped her into the truck he'd acquired for his stay before moving quickly to the driver's side.

She kept her head down, her fingers picking at the strap of her purse as he drove toward her family's home. She hadn't been joining them for Sunday dinners until today, and he had a feeling the only reason she was insisting on it was to avoid what she feared would be the pressure he'd exert for her to give him what he wanted.

She did not have to worry about that. Those tears were his breaking point, and he'd never imagined he'd be so weak in the face of them.

His hands still weren't quite steady from glimpsing them. They'd shaken like a toddler's when he'd seen that tear fall and heard the sob in her voice that she was trying so hard to hold back.

"Would you like me to wait for you in the truck?" he asked as they neared the house.

He hated letting her out of his sight, but he wasn't

part of the family or really a part of her life outside her protection.

When she looked up at him, the gray of her eyes still showed a hint of tears.

"You don't want to go in with me?" Was that hurt in her voice?

Another hurt he had caused.

"Emma Jane," he groaned, pulling to the side of the driveway and putting the vehicle in park before reaching out to cup her face as gently as possible. "I never want you out of my sight. I would wrap you in tissue wrap and tuck you in my pocket to keep you with me always if I could. Why would I not want to go into your parents' home with you?"

She swallowed, obviously still upset from earlier. He fought to find a way to fix it, to clear the tears and bring back her smiles.

"I swear to you, Emma Jane, I will not kill Matt Lauren," he swore, though it galled him, making that vow. "You don't know the person I am, but my vow is my bond. I will not break it. I can understand how he can still be important to you."

And that was bullshit. He just hated the bastard

He'd give his word though and mean it. A man's word was all he had to call his own, and only he could make it of worth, or of no worth at all.

"You think I don't know the man you are or the dragon you can become, Ilya?" she asked him softly. "And Matt doesn't mean anything to me one way or the other. It's one impossibly stubborn, far too protective dragon I care about. And I don't want you to kill because of me. I don't want to be just another weight on your soul."

Had she lost her mind somehow? There was no better

reason to kill than her. To protect the woman who held his heart and soul, he'd take his own life if needed.

"Weight on my soul?" His fingers trailed over her brow, her jaw. "Emma Jane, you make my soul lighter. You could never be a weight."

He touched her lips with his own, a gentle kiss filled with all the emotion he couldn't express with words, only with his touch.

He couldn't tell her she was his heart, his soul, and every dream he'd been unaware he'd been harboring within him. She was the light to his darkness, the one person in the world he couldn't exist without. He could bear a separation, there would be hope then. If her life was lost though, he would quickly follow. A man didn't survive if his heart withered away inside his chest.

"We better go in," she whispered when his head lifted.

From the corner of his eye he could see her father standing on the porch of the farmhouse frowning at them, hands on his hips, his eyes narrowed.

A father. Emma Jane had a father, a loving mother, and a brother. Her dragon could ensure she had a future to enjoy with them, even if that future didn't include him.

He held her hand after helping her from the truck, Emma Jane realized. As they walked the rest of the way to the house, he released her, but only to place his hand at the small of her back.

He wasn't an easy man to understand or to read. And sometimes she had to fight to keep up with the schemes she swore were brewing in his head. Things as simple as fixing the AC when it began rattling several days before or keeping her out of her flower beds outside and in the house.

His pale green eyes would narrow, and though his expression wouldn't change, the tattoo would shift, the dragon's head would tilt and appear conniving. And she didn't dare tell him why she was laughing when that happened.

"'Bout time you got here," her father grumbled as they stepped to the porch. "That fool brother of yours is threatening to go hunting for Matt. I wouldn't worry if him and Nik weren't cleaning Nik's rifles while talking about it."

Emma Jane laughed. "He's just trying to impress Nik. That's his new hero after he learned Nik had that sniper rifle. Ronan's a puppy."

Ilya came to a hard, complete stop, as did her father, but she just breezed by them and stepped into the house as she called out to her mother.

Ilya turned slowly to meet her father's gaze as the older man shook his head pitifully. "We love her, but I swear when God was giving out street smarts that girl musta been playin' with the butterflies."

Ilya laughed. He simply couldn't help it. A deep, caught-by-surprise laugh at the image of God giving out street smarts to punk-dressed kids while sweet little Emma Jane chased butterflies.

Suddenly, she was at the door staring at him and her father with narrowed eyes.

"Stop laughing at me. I know you are." She gave both of them a fierce, perturbed look as she wagged her finger at them, but the someberness of the moment passed.

And he'd actually managed to laugh.

"Come on, son." David Preston slapped him on the shoulder, gripped it companionably, and pushed him toward the door. "Her momma made the best dinner you'll ever eat. Besides, someone needs to tell her brother to chill his blood lust. EJ and her momma are too sweet for some things. Just way too sweet."

And there was a message in there, but it was one Ilya knew he couldn't allow himself to hear. Some men never allowed their women to really know them, all the way to their souls. They expected those same women to trust them though.

Trust began with trust, Emma Jane knew that. But he knew the day was coming when trust wouldn't be enough. The past would catch up with him if he stayed and she'd learn the depths of the darkness in his soul.

What would that do to the little girl who chased butterflies and consorted with a dragon?

# chapter thirteen

The list of places Matt might actually go to wasn't long, or at least the one Emma Jane gave him wasn't. The one Ronan came up with was another story.

The younger man had that list waiting the minute Emma Jane and her mother had begun cleaning dinner from the table with Nik's wife Mikayla's help. With a tilt of his head, Emma Jane's father directed Ilya to the garage while Emma Jane, her mother, and Mikayla remained in the kitchen.

Nik and Mikayla had left their daughter with Mikayla's parents so she wouldn't overhear anything she shouldn't, since they were certain where the conversation would go and where little Nikita would insist on being. Right in her daddy's tall shadow.

And this was a conversation a child had no business hearing.

Relating the promise Emma Jane had managed to get

out of him, Ilya watched his brother roll his eyes in disgust as he turned to his father.

"I told you, pay up," Ronan demanded from both Nik and his father.

Ilya lifted a brow as he caught Nik's eye, seeing the ten-dollar bill he handed over to Ronan.

"You could have held out just a few more days, so we could get his money." Calvin Preston shook his head in despair. "Thought you were made of sterner stuff, boy."

Behind the feigned disappointment was a gleam of satisfaction in the older man's expression.

"She was going to cry," he stated ominously. "Besides, men such as Matt Lauren rarely skate by untested for long."

And Emma Jane had no idea the shadowed force making their way to his location. Once they learned about Matt's abuse and his attempts to hurt her after the divorce, they'd take care of it without a word from Ilya.

She was his match, his mate. He carried her in his soul, and her protection was uppermost until Ilya's grandfather could arrive. This little town was getting ready to get busy, as much as he hated it.

Glancing back in Nik's direction, he noticed the other man watching him thoughtfully while Calvin and Ronan argued over the best way to deal with Matt Lauren.

"I'm not going to tolerate much more of this, Dad," Ronan snapped, as his father warned him to patience. "Do you know he was hitting her?" he hissed into his father's surprised expression.

Calvin sat down wearily in one of the plastic chairs they'd arranged to talk.

"She would have told us," her father said, his voice hoarse. "She wouldn't keep that from us."

"Yes, she would have," Ilya stated, keeping his voice low as he glimpsed the retribution gleaming in Nik's arctic gaze before he lowered it to study the label on his beer. "According to my investigation into Lauren, he admitted it to several of his so-called friends when he did so."

He owed the bastard for that, too.

"I'll let the family know," Calvin stated, his expression hardening as he rubbed the back of his neck. "That little bastard."

"Keep it under wraps for now, Cal." It was Nik who made the suggestion. "When he turns up dead, we don't want the authorities looking at the family. And men like that tend to meet with bad accidents." Nik shrugged as though he wasn't plotting just that.

"He'll try again," Ronan predicted, turning to Ilya. "I want to go back to the house. I'll keep watch with Sawyer. I didn't make any promises to EJ. I can kill him and get away with it." And Ilya believed Ronan would actually do it, if he had the chance. Unfortunately, he couldn't allow the younger man to do so. It would break her heart to know her brother had killed for her.

The thought of having Ronan there taking turns with him through the night inside the house while Sawyer and Tobias covered the outside had Ilya breathing a little easier.

The more Ilya thought about Matt's breaching of the house and the device being used to hack their security, the more certain he was that another attack was coming soon.

Sitting in the darkened living room after Emma Jane went to bed, Ilya stared through the crack he'd made between the curtains, eyes narrowed against the darkness he could feel coming.

They could block the bursts of activity it generated, but the effort was wasted. It wouldn't break the adjustments he and Sawyer made, and other than an out-and-out assault they weren't getting in tonight.

They were patient, as Sawyer had pointed out. Patience equaled a nearly unlimited budget. But whether it was mercenaries or an in-house security force, it cost money to just sit around, wait, and watch. And that was what they were doing.

Men who had that kind of time had the advantage. And Ilya didn't accept anyone having an advantage over him. Especially not where Emma Jane was concerned.

As he sat there he was aware of Ronan entering the room. Emma Jane's brother was quiet, he gave him that. But Ilya knew a lot of men who were quieter and a few no man could slip up on.

"You should be sleeping," he told the other man as he eased back from the window.

"No one else is," Ronan grunted. "Don't think EJ is sleeping either. As long as you're up prowling the house, she won't be sleeping."

No, she wasn't sleeping he knew. The light laughter of that afternoon had eased away when they returned to the house and darkness began to fall. She was too quiet, her gaze touched by sorrow. The knowledge that the attempt to harm her wasn't a mistake or a misunderstanding was hurting her more than anyone could guess.

"She'll insist on working in the morning," Ronan pointed out, his voice resigned. "Go to bed, man. I know where you're sleeping, I'm not stupid."

There was an edge of censure in the younger man's voice though. Just enough that before Ilya could stop himself, he had the edge of the knife he kept tucked in his boot at Ronan's jugular.

"Where I sleep is no man's concern. But brother or no, you'll not blame her for it. Blame the one at fault," Ilya warned him.

Ronan glanced at the knife. Lifting his hand, he carefully placed two fingers against the blade and pushed it away from his throat as his gaze snapped with disgust.

"Listen, you Russian bastard," he snarled with a hiss, his chin tilted pugnaciously. "As far as I'm concerned, my baby sister is a virgin for life. I helped raise her, fixed up the strays she brought around, and dried her tears when she cried over them. You on the other hand"—he shot Ilya a disgusted look—"when you leave, she'll do more than cry. Her heart will never be the same again. And men like you never hang around, do they? You blow into town, save the girl, and ride away before she knows you took her heart with you."

Staring back at the brother, he realized where the censure was directed, not at his sister but at the man sharing her bed.

Flipping the knife, he caught it easily and tucked it back in his boot.

"Long as we understand each other," Ilya muttered, turning back to the window. "Now go get some rest."

"Emma's the best thing that ever came into your life and I bet you don't even know how to deal with it," Ronan sneered behind him, his voice low. "Men like you don't know how to love anymore, do you, Ilya?"

If it had been fury in the brother's censure, or even a hint of disgust, Ilya could have flipped him off and never looked back. But it wasn't. It was the brother who would dry her tears, who would have to see the pain Ilya left behind.

He didn't turn back to Ronan, he stared out the window, but it wasn't the yard or the tree line he saw. It was the past, bleak and filled with blood, without hope, without Emma Jane.

"*Balaur pereche*," he murmured. "It's Romanian for 'dragon's mate.'" He rubbed his chest where the emerald, where hope, rested. "Emma Jane is *balaur pereche*. The light to my darkness. My hope." He wiped his hand over his face before shaking his head. "All the light in the world can't change what made me. I would cut my own throat to protect her, if it would ensure her protection, but once the hound gets the scent, it never lets up, does it? And I have a feeling hell's hound is exactly who's determined to take her from me."

He could feel Ronan behind him, tense, waiting.

"Was my sister attacked because of you, Ilya?" He could hear the suspicion, the fury threatening to explode.

"I don't know," he breathed out roughly. "I lied when I showed up here, Ronan. There was no relationship. Your sister and I had a simple business transaction a year ago. Nothing more. As far as she knew, there was nothing more. For my part, I knew who she was to me. There's no intel that suggests it's because of me, no whispers of it. But neither is there a whisper of why, no matter how we search."

"If you lied, then why come back when she was attacked? Why lie to her family?" The confusion in Ronan's voice was understandable.

"I saw her at that job fair," he told Emma Jane's brother. "On Eric's surveillance display. She knew he was there, she didn't know I was." He laid his hand against his heart. "Shadows filled her pretty eyes, but she stopped at the camera, made a goofy face at Eric. 'Hey, punk.'" He wanted to smile at the memory. "She said that, thinking it was Eric, and I found myself wishing she would smile at me like that. Then her smile turned sad and she looked away. 'Gotta run. Save home and hearth.' And I saw her pain. And that was when Eric told me her estranged husband had cost her a job and was trying to make sure that she didn't get another. She was losing her home in her divorce, she had lost friends and wasn't certain who to trust any longer."

He had seen a loss of hope, of dreams, in her soft gray eyes and something inside him had melted for her.

"Despite all she had against her, hope still lived in her gaze, and despite her fears, she was still fighting for what was hers. I wanted only to make certain she never lost that glimmer of hope, or that valiant courage. I would give all I own to ensure she always keeps it."

"It was bad," Ronan agreed. "I didn't think we had a chance. Dad was trying to take out a second mortgage. She wouldn't let Nik give her the money."

"So Nik called me," he admitted. "When she lost her job he gave her a job, and I secured her mortgage. And for three days she negotiated like a shark for that place. And I saw a woman's love for her home."

And in those three days he'd fallen more and more in love with her.

"Are you going to walk away from her, Ilya?" Ronan asked then. "Because that would be the biggest mistake of your life."

"Would it?" Ilya asked. "Russia is not America. And just because we're citizens here now, it doesn't mean the ocean is so vast that the past can't follow. I'm the Dragon heir, the living legacy of blood, death, thieves, cutthroats, and assassins. Emma Jane is the light, innocence, laughter. I'd only bring darkness to her life, Ronan. She deserves far more than that."

He'd wanted to stay. For a small amount of time he'd told himself that if Emma Jane could accept his past then he had a chance.

If.

A lot to place on one delicate little woman's shoulders.

It wouldn't take long before the innocence dimmed in her eyes, before she stopped smiling, stopped laughing. Before the dreams were lost forever.

"I fucking hate you, Ilya," Ronan said softly. "Watching my baby sister live with a broken heart when you're gone will make me hate your ass."

The face of a mother's hatred flashed before his eyes. As Petrov, her brother, and Ivan's father held him down, he'd stared at the woman with the cold blue eyes as he screamed in agony, the blade slicing his face open, over and over again.

Years later, walking into his apartment to find his mistress dead, her flesh carved open, her blood staining the floors, he'd known who had ordered it. Ilya had killed her brother in front of her, the bastard who had cut him open, beaten him mercilessly for years.

And still, she'd have any woman he cared for murdered. She had hated his father for not making her his *matcha,* and she hated the son she'd tricked that dragon into giving her. The son could pay for the father's sins, she'd decided.

"Better your hatred, her pain, than her blood," Ilya told him quietly, aching for her touch, for her passion. "As long as she breathes, I breathe. If I stay, neither of us has a chance. But if blood could ensure a life with her, I would shed it. Over and over again."

"Fuck, Ilya," Ronan cursed in a whisper of a sound. "God damn. Go to bed, man. I got this, and I don't think we have to worry about me getting sleepy tonight."

Emma Jane turned from where she stood at the bottom of the steps and silently hurried back to her room as she lost the fight with her tears.

The sobs were contained. Ilya couldn't know she'd heard every word, every lost and broken dream that had echoed in his voice. Or the knowledge that he intended to leave her. He couldn't know her heart was already breaking in two and it would continue to break, over and over again.

Sliding back into the bed, she knew there was no way to hide her tears from him. He'd know the minute he was close. She hadn't cried in all the weeks since her attack. Tears didn't help her think, they didn't help her figure things out. They just gave her a headache.

A sob hitched her breath as she wrapped her arms around his pillow and held it to her. Her cries were silent, but her tears were slick and wet, dampening the pillow as they rolled from her. As her heart broke, over and over again, for her dragon.

She heard the door open and fought to stop the tears, the silent sobs. She had him for now. For now, he was here, and he was hers. Could she really ask for anything more from him? Did she have that right?

"Emma Jane? Baby?" He lifted her into his arms, holding her against his bare chest.

He must have undressed as soon as he came in, before he realized her heart was breaking.

"I'm sorry." She tried to halt the sobs, because she knew earlier that day he'd been willing to promise her anything to make them stop.

*Would he promise to stay? . . .*

*No!* She tightened her arms around his neck. She wouldn't do that to either of them.

"What's wrong?" Cradling her in his arms as he sat on the bed, he pushed her hair back from her face, kissed her lips.

She could only shake her head. She couldn't lie to him, she couldn't tell him the truth.

"I'm okay." She tried to stop the tears again, but they refused to stop. "You weren't here when I woke up." And she'd gone looking for him when she should have stayed in the bed.

"I'm here now." His lips brushed hers, lingered, then his teeth nipped at the lower curve. "You can sleep now, baby. Let me hold you. I promise not to let you go."

He wouldn't let her go until it came time for him to leave.

But that time wasn't now. He wasn't leaving tonight.

Gripping the hem of her pajama tank top, she pulled it off, rose in front of him. Tangling her fingers in his hair as he stared up at her, his green eyes gleaming with hunger, she licked her lips.

"Don't be easy, Ilya. Not even once," she whispered.

"God, baby," he groaned, burying his head between her breasts. "Your brother's prowling the damn house. He hears me make you scream and he'll slice my throat."

*Yeah.* There was that.

"Will you make me a promise?" she asked as he slid the pajama pants off her hips.

"Anything." His lips moved over her breasts, licking, stroking the short length of his beard over them. "Whatever you want."

"When my brother isn't in the house, will you make

me scream? Make me scream, Ilya, because it hurts so good I can't bear it."

She was on her back a second later and he was pushing her legs apart, coming between them.

"Fuck," he groaned. "If you let your brother hear you, I'll sleep in the guest room the next time."

She buried her lips against his chest, then clenched her teeth on a moan of ecstasy as his cock pushed inside her.

He stretched her, filled her. Pulling back, he thrust deeper, working his hard flesh inside her as she capped her hand over her mouth and fought back the moans.

She would not let him sleep in the guest room.

"You're tight, Emma Jane." The Russian in his voice thickened as his dark voice rasped over her senses. "Slick and sweet around my dick."

She lost her breath, forgot to breathe until he thrust fully inside her and she almost forgot not to scream.

A wicked chuckle vibrated at her ear.

"When I take you next, I'm going to spank that pretty bare pussy. Watch you come to the most erotic caresses."

He was thrusting inside her as he spoke, holding her to him, his lips at her ear as he pushed her higher with his words alone.

She didn't dare even whisper his name as he moved forcefully inside her, stroking across sensitive flesh, exciting her body to a fever pitch.

"Once you've come for me, I'll turn you over, watch your pretty ass turn pink as I spank it." Harder. He thrust harder, his hold on her tightening as image and sensation pushed her closer to the edge. "Once you're begging for me, screaming from the pleasure . . ." He gripped her hips, his own pumping hard and fast, stroking her to an orgasm she almost feared. "When you're pleading, Emma Jane, I'm going to take that pretty ass. Mark it. Fuck . . ." His voice was ragged as she shattered, lifting against him, her body tightening, shuddering as pure rapture raced through her senses. "Mine. Fucking mine."

Ilya buried deep, his cum pumping inside her as something in his chest pulled free and sank into her as well.

She was his. Fucking his. She was the Dragon heir's mate and he might have to leave, but he'd make damned sure she never forgot . . .

"Mine . . ." The word tore from him one last time as he felt her teeth clench against the tattoo inked just for her. Her mark covering the mark that was made for her.

God help him, he'd die without her.

# chapter fourteen

Despite the tears she'd shed the night before and the sleepless hours afterward as she just lay in Ilya's arms, Emma Jane woke before the alarm went off.

Ilya was awake. He was lying on his side, watching her, his gaze probing.

"Good morning, sweet," he said, his voice not in the least bit drowsy.

"How long have you been awake?" Turning on her side to face him, she cuddled closer to his broad chest, her hand stroking over his bicep, feeling the corded strength just below his flesh.

He was warm and naked against her, and aroused. His cock pressed against her lower stomach, iron hard and so very hot.

"Hmm, for a bit." His lips brushed over her forehead as he murmured the words. "I considered waking you, but that brother of yours keeps coming to the top of the

steps, then retreating as if the hounds of hell wait beyond this door."

The amusement that touched his voice roughened the
tone further and made her wish her brother had stayed at
home.

"You're the one that let him butt his nose in," she reminded him, pushing against his chest as the alarm began beeping. She rose from the bed.

Silencing the strident tone, she slid him a teasing
look, taking in the look of sexual frustration as he
watched her.

"Send him home today," she suggested, not bothering
to cover the nakedness of her body. "And tonight, maybe
I'll see if I can make you scream."

Pure, carnal anticipation lit his gaze as she turned
and hurried to the bathroom. She had just enough time
to get ready and get to work. If she was late, Nik would
give Ilya one of those knowing male looks and Emma
Jane would have to kick both of them.

She walked back into the bedroom nearly an hour
later, dressed in a black skirt that ended just above the
knee and a sleeveless white blouse. Pushing her feet
into the black pumps she'd put out the night before,
she stared at the man sitting on her bed, fully dressed
now. The short growth of beard only emphasized the
hard lines of his face and made his dragon more imposing. The red-eyed creature seemed to watch her
with the same, lazy interest as Ilya. "What are your
plans today?" she asked as he rose and met her at the
door.

Dressed in one of those white cotton shirts that made
him look too damned sexy, jeans, and scarred boots, he
looked dark and dangerous.

Exactly what he was.

"Ronan, Eric and I are going to see if we can run Matt to ground," he said, his gaze somber. "Two agents will be outside the offices. Don't leave unless you're with them or Nik until I return."

"I can handle that," she promised. It wasn't as though Nik would allow her out of the office without protection anyway.

"Before we leave, I think you should change clothes." He said it so seriously that she paused and looked down at the skirt.

"Why?" Lifting her head, she looked back at him as he stood staring at the garment in interest.

"Because you look far too beautiful to let out without me at your back. And I wouldn't last long before I had to fuck you. I could see Nik objecting should I run him from his office so I can take care of that little problem," he observed as her reached her, gripped her hips, and pulled her to him.

The hard shaft beneath his jeans pressed against her lower stomach, tempting her to say to hell with it and demand he take her back to bed.

"Do what you have to do," she whispered, staring up at him, her heartbeat accelerating at the thought. "We'll have tonight."

"Yes, we'll have tonight," he assured her, kissing her just enough to keep from messing up the light pink lipstick she wore before drawing away. "Come on, I'll drive you in. Ronan can follow us."

He caught her hand and held it all the way to the truck. Ronan didn't follow them though. He jumped in the back seat of the dual cab, uncharacteristically silent as Ilya pulled from the house.

"The two of you should get dinner before you pick me up," she told them when neither of them appeared to have anything to talk about.

"What would you like?" Ilya made the turn into town, staring straight ahead as Ronan remained silent.

"Mexican maybe, or Italian," she suggested. "It doesn't matter. I just didn't put anything in the slow cooker before we left."

Because she hadn't laid anything out the night before. It wasn't normal for her to forget that, especially with her brother around.

"Mexican it is," Ilya promised her. "Text me what you prefer and we'll pick it up before coming for you."

She nodded before glancing back at her brother.

He was leaning into the backrest, his hat pulled over his eyes, as though dozing.

His conversation with Ilya had upset him the night before. Once everything was over and Ilya was gone, she'd have to let him know that she'd gone into this with her eyes open. Everyday-girls-next-door didn't get to keep the dark knight, no matter how much they loved or how much they wished.

But she was certain no one would ever love Ilya more than she did. As dangerous as he was, as impossible to predict, and as arrogant as he could get, she loved him.

"Nik's waiting to walk in with you," Ilya stated as they parked behind Nik's pickup across from the front entrance. "Elizaveta and Maxine are in the parking lot, they'll be there till I pick you up." He gestured to the dark sedan with tinted windows parked beneath a tree in the lot on the other side of the sidewalk.

"I'll be fine," she promised him, even though she

crossed her fingers and prayed she was right. "I'll see you this evening."

His short nod and implacable expression almost caused her to grin.

"Kiss me goodbye," she murmured.

He glanced at Ronan in the back seat with a scowl.

Her brother shifted restlessly.

"For God's sake, kiss her and get it the hell over with so I can take this damned cap off my face!" Ronan snapped. "And be damned quiet about it."

Ilya slid one hand into her hair and pulled her to him for a quick, hard kiss.

"Am I allowed to kill your brother?" he growled against her lips.

"Not today." She wagged her finger at him as she drew back, fighting against the sadness that threatened to overtake her. "You two get along now, or I'm telling Daddy on you."

Ilya grimaced while her brother gave a mocking snort, straightened his cap, and opened his door to step out of the truck.

Opening her door, he helped her out, handed her over to a waiting Nik, then slid into the front seat.

"Those two will end up disagreeing," Nik murmured as he glanced in the truck to see Ronan shoot Ilya the finger.

"I think they already have," she sighed, remembering the conversation from the night before as Nik led her across the street. "I'm just hoping they don't come to blows."

"Keep hoping," Nik suggested, amused. "But don't bet on it."

Stepping to the door, he sheltered her with his own body as he unlocked it and stepped inside with her.

Checking the spacious outer office, he moved behind her as she strode to her desk.

She was halfway there when without warning hard hands grabbed her shoulders and Nik was throwing her to the floor as everything went to hell in a clash of violence that turned the world black. Her last thought was that she might not have tonight with her dragon after all.

Watching Emma Jane cross the street with Nik, Ilya couldn't shake off the heavy premonition filling him. He could feel it, like a malevolent force gathering around him.

Nik kept her carefully sheltered, even as he unlocked the door and escorted her inside. She was safe. He repeated that assurance, but still, he threw open the door, ignoring Ronan's sharp question, and took the first step to cross the street when his world shifted in an explosion of such force it blew the windows of the office out and threw Ilya back against the truck.

Reality faded before his horrified gaze.

Smoke, glass, and dust billowed from the gaping holes where windows had once been, just feet from where Emma Jane had stood inside the office.

He screamed her name.

He could hear himself screaming her name as his body jerked into action and he raced to the building.

There was no getting in through the front doors. Cement blocks, twisted metal, and debris blocked the entrance.

He didn't waste time fighting what he knew couldn't be moved. Instead, he raced down the sidewalk and up a short alley and went in through the back, followed by Ronan as well as several other men, along with Maxine and Elizaveta.

He had to get in there. He had to find Emma Jane.

God help him, what would he do without her?

She couldn't breathe.

Emma Jane fought to see through the dust and smoke burning her eyes and blocking her vision. Just forcing her eyes open hurt. She had to blink several times to get past the layer of dust that seemed to coat them as well as her throat.

Everything sounded distant, not quite right, as though she were trying to hear through water like she did as a kid in the bath.

She could hear sirens blaring, but the sound was muted, screams, animalistic and filled with rage. Even as she tried to make sense of the sudden change in reality, she fought to breathe, to drag in enough air that panic didn't overtake her.

The air was thick, gritty, and it felt like inches of it were coating her lungs. But even if it weren't, there was a weight on her back, pressing her tight to the floor and making it hard to pull oxygen into her lungs. And it hurt.

It hurt so bad.

She couldn't move, she couldn't breathe.

And she had no idea why.

What happened?

Fear was filling her instead of air, panic blooming in her mind as she fought against the pain and fear.

"Emma Jane," Nik groaned her name, his voice weaker than she'd ever heard it. "Stay still. Just for a bit."

*Stay still?* She had to move. She had to get out of there where she could breathe, where she could find Ilya. He was going to be upset that she was hurt.

She tried to move again, only to stop at the sound of Nik's pained groan. "Still. Stay still."

"Emma Jane!" Ilya sounded desperate, his voice rough as he screamed her name. "Emma Jane!"

"Ilya," she tried to call out to him, but the sound was low, barely a whisper as her lung fought to draw in air. "Ilya . . ."

She tried to move, stopping again at Nik's low, desperate moan.

Each time she moved, it hurt him. Was he lying on her? Something was, and it was damned heavy.

"Emma. Emma Jane. Baby." Ilya was suddenly there, crawling to her from the direction of Nik's office rather than the front door.

She tried to lift her hand, to reach out to him, but her whole body hurt. Moving seemed impossible. His hand gripped hers instead when he reached her and she held on to him for dear life. She could hold on now, her dragon was here. Ilya wouldn't let anything else happen.

"I've got you, baby." He moved closer, his hands going over her face, her neck.

"Nik's hurt." She fought to speak despite the lack of air. "I can't breathe . . ." She could feel the panic rising inside her again. "I can't breathe . . . I'm scared . . ."

"I know, *matcha*," he whispered.

*Mate*. He called her mate, just as he did the night before and every time he took her.

Dragon's mate.

She was her dragon's mate. A dragon's mate didn't panic.

Steadying the fear and the panic, she used short breaths as she gripped Ilya's hand and steadied herself.

"Nik's hurt," she whispered again. "I think I'm okay."

"Hold on." He touched her face where it lay against

the floor. "Ronan has a crew on the other side working to remove the debris. I'm going to ease up here and check Nik okay?"

"Kay." Short breaths. She wasn't smothering. Yet.

"I'm right here," he promised again. "I have to slide over to get in place. You won't be able to see me . . ."

"Dammit, Dragon, just do it." She needed to breathe. "I've got this."

Well, she didn't really have it, but he didn't know that. He wouldn't be disappointed in her because she gave in to her panic.

She closed her eyes and just concentrated on staying sane.

She could hear Ilya talking to Nik but couldn't make out what they were saying. That droning, buzzing noise was in her head again when she realized those short little breaths weren't working.

*Just concentrate,* she told herself. She couldn't panic, she had to concentrate. Ilya was working as fast as he could.

"Emma, get ready." Ilya was there again, his hands touching her face, forcing her to concentrate on him as he grabbed her outstretched arms just above her elbows. "Ready, baby?"

"Ready." She forced the croak out as she gripped his biceps with desperate hands.

She heard someone counting. "One. Two. Three . . ."

On "Three," she felt the weight lift from her back. Her first lungful of air had her choking, gasping as her lungs protested.

Ilya dragged her toward him only to have others pull her free while he yelled at someone to get ready. She couldn't see what was going on. Firm hands pulled her into Nik's office, then strapped her to a back brace.

The world spun around and fear struck at her as she felt unconsciousness trying to rush over her.

"Dragon," she whispered his name, thought it sounded more like a whimper as the black edged closer.

"I'm here, baby." He was there, his hand holding hers as she felt herself slip away. "I'm right here, baby."

The ambulances were gone, crime scene investigators and bomb squad just pulling out, when the dark figure stepped to the entrance of what had once been the outer office of Steele Electronic Security.

The upper floor had collapsed into the area, a wide steel beam had caught Nik Steele and pinned him and his receptionist to the floor, nearly killing both of them.

He surveyed the beam, whistling soundlessly at the weight Steele had managed to keep off the Dragon heir's woman. Had he not, the woman would have been crushed, her much smaller body unable to bear the weight.

And if she had died?

He rubbed at the side of his neck before lowering his arm once again.

Had the woman died, then the Dragon heir would have to be euthanized before he struck back.

Pulling his phone from his jacket pocket, he called the man who had sent him to keep an eye on this particular situation. He had a feeling he'd been sent far too late though.

"Report," the sharp, clipped voice answered immediately despite the time difference.

"Second strike was made," he reported. "They messed up. Nik Steele was caught in the explosion. From what I saw, the girl is fine, but he looked in pretty bad shape. Do you have any fucking idea the hell that's going to converge on this damned place now?"

Silence met his report.

He knew what was going on in the other man's mind. A war on two different fronts wasn't something they needed. And they sure as hell didn't want a war with the black-clad shadow group Steele was part of. And that wasn't even half as bad as what would be coming now to protect Ilya and his woman.

"He's a good man. Strong," the other man mused. "He'll pull through if he can. What of Ilya?"

"Unharmed," he stated. "He rode with the woman to the hospital. I should have a report on her condition as well as Steele's soon."

"Let me know when you have it," he was ordered. "I'm boarding the jet now and heading for Washington. I'll let you know when I land."

The line disconnected and he sighed heavily. He didn't believe his boss should interfere in this, but it wasn't often the other man heeded anyone's counsel but his own.

Pocketing the phone, he looked at the debris once more before leaving the building and moving unhurriedly to the area where he'd parked his car. He could feel the eyes on him, studying him. Whether they were enemy or friendly or merely curious he had no idea. They were nosy, that was enough for him to know it was time to wrap this the hell up. The situation was now out of control and an international incident wasn't what they needed.

It damned sure wasn't what his boss needed. But when had that ever mattered?

The call came over the secured lines located inside the underground operations center of a privately funded, government-backed investigative and strike force known as Elite Operations One.

"Commander," a voice called out to Nathan Malone,

commander of the elite division. Nathan stood tall as he went over several reports handed to him by scrambling operation techs. "We have Viper on the line."

Commander Malone turned, jerked the landline from its cradle with a barked, "Go."

"Renegade down, surgery required, possible internal bleeding. The woman's considered stable, he protected her by taking a steel beam to his back and somehow holding his weight from her. The dragon-heir is un-harmed. But we have a bigger problem." Viper paused. "An unknown was sighted several vehicles back from the two female bodyguards before the explosion and he was wearing a dragon mark on his neck. It looked pretty damned authentic to me too."

Malone looked down at one of the reports in his hand with a grimace. "Be advised, Viper," he growled. "We have mobilization in five of the known groups within minutes of the explosion. One is suspected to be elite guards. Report as you can but don't get burned."

The call disconnected.

"Get me reports on the grandfather," he yelled out at the techs. "Where the hell is that wily bastard?"

The dragon-son, the grandfather was called, and dragon-heir, his grandson, though many called him the dragon-son as well. The distinction was that "The" for some reason. The heir's father had died before taking the mantle of dragon-son, though he'd left a son as an heir to that title. Often, the commander had been told, the heir carried the title as well once he was fully trained and began placing dragons in ink on his own men.

Hell, the information they were pulling in on that damned clan was sketchy and confusing as hell. He'd been much happier before he received the message that came via a Russia contact the year before.

*"Meddle not in the affairs of Dragons,"* it had read. *"For you are crunchy and taste good with ketchup!"* The amusing phrase ended with the seal of the dragon families, a dragon in flight.

That message still had the power to make him want to grin, but he had a feeling it was far too close to the truth.

"Commander, we have the old dragon moving," his senior tech called out. "One RV, a bakers' dozen riding with it, and what looks like two other units riding on a path that intersects outside Hagerstown. Look out, we have our first known meeting of dragons."

Just what he needed.

He turned to his assistant. "Get Live Wire on the line. We have a situation . . ."

# chapter fifteen

Nik Steele had sustained two broken ribs, a fractured forearm that required surgery, internal bleeding, and a laceration to the top of his head requiring stitches. The fact that the Viking bastard was still alive amazed the hell out of Ilya.

When he'd seen the beam lying across the debris covering the area where he knew they should be, his heart had nearly stopped in his chest. Agony had gripped him, along with a horrifying rush of killing rage.

Because he knew only one person insane enough to strike at both Ilya as well as a former Russian rumored to have seriously covert friends.

And word would be reaching the families loyal to the dragon, Ilya's grandfather. Sons of those families marked as dragon warriors would be forming, preparing or already in the process of coming together to either protect the dragon-heir or support his protection.

Sitting on the uncomfortable plastic chair in the surgery waiting room with Nik's wife, Mikayla, and her friend Deidre, he stared at the floor morosely. Emma Jane's family was with her; the room so crowded there was little enough space for the nurse who kept a check on her vitals. When Ilya learned Mikayla was in the surgery waiting room alone with only her friend, her family having not arrived from a camping trip they'd been on, he'd decided to sit with her.

Hell, he wouldn't want his sister left alone right now, no matter where the bastard sitting with her wanted to be.

Emma Jane had family, he reminded himself. They loved her and they'd be there for her when he was gone. The kindest thing he could do for her was not allow either of them to get used to him being by her side.

Even if that was where he belonged.

"Ilya, why are you sitting here with me?" Mikayla questioned him from where she sat with her friend Deidre, on the chairs across from him. "Dr. Ron assured me Nik is going to be fine. It's just that it seems that's his favorite arm to break and the surgeon wants to make certain it heals properly." She grinned mischievously. "He keeps telling Nik he's getting too old for shenanigans that break bones. I think Nik's trying to prove otherwise."

"I should have been there, not him," he growled, hating the fact that he hadn't been the one to protect Emma Jane.

He was a stupid, possessive bastard, he thought, because who saved her shouldn't matter. She was fine, unharmed, just a few bruises.

"He reminds me of Nik when the two of you first met," her friend Deidre drawled. "All in love and unwilling to accept it. I love watching it." And that was pure glee in her expression too.

Redheads just had an odd sense of humor, he decided.

"Be nice, Deidre." Mikayla bumped her friend's arm with her elbow as she gave a little roll of her eyes. "I'm certain Ilya doesn't need to be told when he's in love. Not all men are as stubborn as Nik, you know. Are they, Ilya?"

The innocent, all-knowing expression was such a ruse, he thought. It would pay to never forget that this woman had made a tame housecat out of a man who had been called Russia's tiger in another life.

"I'm certain I would know if I were," he assured both of them.

Of course he knew he loved her, he just knew the man he was. Nik was able to walk away from the blood and death. Ilya didn't have that option. He would never have that option.

"Did you know that dragon on your face is kinda weird?" Deidre's voice was at least lower. "Watch it, Mikayla. I swear it's glaring at me."

Ilya tilted his head back and stared at the ceiling. Yes, he knew that sometimes the ink at the side of his face seemed to have a life of its own. Not that he had ever had proof of it. It was the skill of the artist who inked the iridescent scales, red eyes, and proud expression that gave the image such life. It was a talent that ran in the Dragonovich family.

His grandfather had taught his father and he'd taught Ilya. The proper muscles to target, the color added to each scale, the depth of the eyes and where they were placed. It was simply the tricks of master artists.

Gustov Dragonovich had cried when he'd inked Ilya's face, covering the scars that marred it and giving him the only protection left that he could claim. That was his place as the dragon-heir.

The families had searched for him, the old man had sworn, but Ilya's father was taken from life before he could return home and tell them the name of the woman who had tricked him into impregnating her.

She'd wanted to be the dragon's mate, but she'd refused to accept that her dragon felt no love for her. That much Ilya's grandparents had known. It was the identity of the woman they hadn't been able to learn. Until the old cook in his mother's employ had overheard Ilya's identity. Her son had wed a young girl from one of the Romany families many called gypsies, and she'd heard of the search for the missing heir. A boy suspected to carry a mark resembling a dragon in flight, on his lower back. And she had seen that mark.

Within days six men had slipped onto the grounds where Ilya was kept, and carried him away with them.

They couldn't strike against her though, no matter how much they wanted to. Only Ilya or the woman he marked as his own could take the life of the woman who gave birth to him.

*Fucking traditions. Multi-layered, often confusing to the logical mind, and a pain in the ass for the most part.* Yeah, so why hadn't he killed the woman who had given birth to him, who had condoned the hell he'd lived in for so long?

He wasn't insane enough to even think she'd suddenly find a mother's love. The woman was a rabid psychopath.

No, he had no illusions of motherly love, what he had was that voice that whispered that only a soulless man could kill the dam who whelped him. And he wasn't that man yet.

What would Emma Jane think of him, to know that even his mother had been unable to love him? When he'd seen the love her parents spilled over her, he'd been thankful, for her. To know she wouldn't be alone.

"Would you stop whatever you're thinking?" Deidre hissed, causing his head to jerk down to allow him to glare at her.

"What?" She made no sense.

"That dragon looks like it's going to take flight right off your face and bite me. Go back to Emma Jane before you completely freak me out," she demanded.

He turned to Mikayla as she fought to hide her grin.

"Nik warned me before I met you," she confided. "Said it only happened when you were really pissed off or upset."

He grunted at the information and rose to his feet to find a chair on the other side of the room. He just needed to keep them in sight, he told himself.

Maybe he should borrow Ronan's cap.

"Ilya." Mikayla followed him, sitting next to him now, petite and delicate, he understood why Nik called her his fairy. "Go be with Emma Jane. That's where your heart is. Deidre and I are fine. My parents and all the heathen brothers and one very outraged child will be here soon driving the hospital staff crazy. I promise, I won't feel the least abandoned."

"I know you wouldn't," he breathed out heavily. "Emma Jane's room is filled with family. She's safe with them."

"And it's so very hard to breathe with them crowding around," she answered for him. "Yes, very much like Nik."

He nodded slowly.

"I knew him, long ago," he said, the words only loud enough to reach her ears.

She watched him with interest, knowing there was

nothing about her husband that she wasn't already aware of.

He couldn't help but grin.

"Has he mentioned Dragon's Blood?" He lifted a brow as he asked the question.

"Very pricey vodka, very exclusive, and sold only to those the owner agrees to sell to," she recited the information. "He's been trying to find a bottle for years."

He pointed to his dragon. "When he comes around, tell him to be watching for a very special delivery. And even that doesn't pay the debt I owe him for keeping my Emma Jane safe. His name, those of his wife, their child, and her family, will be listed among those that all dragons, from now till the last one falls, will consider under our protection."

Tears filled her eyes.

"I know who you are, Ilya," she said just as softly. "And Nik would never ask for such a thing. One bottle of the vodka will suffice. He's been unable to get any from his sources."

Because Ilya hoarded it. Those with money bought enough to keep the business making the Russian alcohol that was so highly prized making more than it needed. The rest Ilya kept in storage, unwilling to allow his enemies to purchase it from him.

Dragon's Blood was a recipe centuries old. A merging of an old recipe held by the head of a family of Romanian gypsies and another rumored to have been stolen from a tsar. The name was newer, only a few centuries old, but more prized than ever before.

"He will never have such a problem again. And had I known, he would already be supplied. He saved my life, Mikayla, when he shielded Emma Jane and ensured hers. It won't be forgotten."

She touched his arm, the pressure light, comforting. "Would you do the same for me, Ilya?" she asked. "I believe you would, so no debt is owed."

"Regardless," he told her as the elevator opened and her family began pouring out, "your family's here now. Please, give my regards to your husband, as well as my message."

Shit, she had a lot of family too, he thought as the wave of parents, brothers, and cousins rushed toward her, filled with questions.

Ilya slipped away, to check on Emma Jane again, found the room empty but for Elizaveta and Maxine, and slipped to her bedside.

Maxine rose from her chair, her short, compact body and California blond prettiness deceptively unthreatening. As the door closed behind her, Elizaveta turned her gaze to him, watching him for long moments.

"The doctor is releasing her this evening," she told him then. "Her family went to find dinner while they await the paperwork."

Reaching out, he slid his hand beneath Emma Jane's, the warm silk of her palm resting within his much larger hand perfectly.

"She has a large family." Laughter teased at Elizaveta's voice. "They're very loud and the males are very flirtatious."

He cast her a teasing look despite the pain filling him.

"They flirted with you?" he asked.

He knew she often despaired because most men could sense the fact that she could kick their asses. That gave her few opportunities to practice her feminine wiles.

"They did." She nodded with a smile. "And her brother was actually quite good at it."

It was apparent she was impressed with Ronan's skills in that area.

"Ronan's a good man," he assured her. "Someone's trained him as well. He's no slouch at protecting himself."

"Nik often trains the men in the family, Emma Jane told us. He told them they needed to be men who could protect their women, not pussies needing protection." That was almost a giggle in her voice. "He does a have a way with words, does he not?"

"He does," Ilya agreed, but Nik had always been like that, even in his other life as a Russian soldier. "He's always been a damned good man too. An honorable man."

Even in the world of thieves, cutthroats, and assassins, there was a code. There had to be, or only anarchy would reign. Those who didn't respect that code found themselves cut out, permanently.

As he caressed Emma Jane's knuckles with his thumb, he marveled at the softness of her skin once again, the way it shimmered with life, almost begging for an ink master's art. He could see his dragon curled about her wrist, iridescent, scales gleaming, eyes warning, as though it would lift from her skin and sear anyone who would dare harm her. And around his wrist, he could see the image of her dragon, sinuous and filled with fire. Slate gray eyes would stare from an inquisitive face as it lay protected on the underside of his arm.

Others could ink dragons, many had tried to duplicate the dragon such as the one Ilya wore, or the one he would have placed on Emma Jane's wrist if it were a different world. They had tried, but only those of Ilya's line had known the proper ink, the needle, and the exact placement when forming the image to create that look of subtle life. It was an art the first Dragon son had created and passed down to his son until Ilya's grandfather had passed it to him.

"She loves you, Ilya," Elizaveta stated somberly. "She looked for you after you left. She was very sad you were gone."

"Nik's wife was in the waiting room alone waiting for him to come out of surgery." He gave her the excuse he had given himself. "I sat with her until her family arrived."

Elizaveta nodded. "That's what she said, and she understood your need to make sure Mikayla was safe. Still, she was frightened without you."

His head jerked around. "She was frightened? Her family was here with her."

*Why would she have been frightened?*

"You weren't with her, Ilya," Elizaveta pointed out as though to a child as she got to her feet. "It was not her father, her brother, or her cousins that make her feel safest. It is the arms of her dragon she needs."

With that, she left the hospital room, closing the door softly behind her and leaving him there with Emma Jane.

Moving the chair closer to her bed, he rested his head next to her fingers, closed his eyes, and let himself just feel her. He found himself drifting, found sleep sneaking up on him, his body relaxing in the chair, his head on her bed, hand gripping hers.

"Oh, Dragon," her soft whisper eased past slumber and wrapped around him like the warmest blanket. "I love you enough to let you go, but how I wish I could hold on to you . . ."

His hand tightened on her, his fingers sheltering hers, but he slept on. A moment out of time when gentle fingers sifted through his hair, stroked his brow, and the sound of love, not the words, the love, stroked the ragged pieces of his soul.

They released Emma Jane that evening just as Elizaveta had told him they would. With Sawyer and Tobias flanking him, he carried her from her room to the reinforced SUV waiting at an exit at the back of the hospital.

He slid into the back seat with her, buckled her in, and gave Tobias the order to pull out when Sawyer slid into the driver's seat of the vehicle behind them.

"Sawyer, pull ahead. You, Elizaveta, and Maxine secure the house, Ronan and Eric can cover us," he spoke into the speaker wand of the comm link as he kept his gaze on the traffic Tobias pulled into, and he kept Emma Jane in the middle of the seat, cushioned against him.

"It would take a dumb ass to attack right now," she observed, though she was tense, her fingers holding on to his wrist tightly.

"How does she expect you to impress her, Ilya?" Tobias snorted, flashing a grin in the rearview mirror. "She doesn't understand your need to show off yet?"

She slid the younger man a doubtful look but only gained a chuckle in response.

"Us younger agents are still in training?" he tried. "He likes to make sure we know what we're doing."

This time, Tobias kept his gaze on the road rather than the mirror until he took the exit and headed out of town. Traffic was reasonably light, flowing easily, a little above the speed limit. Nothing seemed to be following them other than Ronan and the sheriff in the vehicle behind them.

It was fully dark now, which actually made it easier

for Ilya to tell if they were being followed. Sometimes it felt as though the dark, the shadows, were his greatest strength. He moved through them with an ease few others could match.

"Take the exit ahead, Tobias, and take the next left," he told the agent. "We'll go in along a more direct route, see if everything stays clear."

The look Tobias flicked him showed the agent was feeling the same thing Ilya was. Not a sense of a coming attack, but a sense of something coming. And there was a difference. One was a surety that danger would touch them, the other was simply the possibility.

"What's wrong?" Emma Jane asked, her fingers gripping his tightly.

"Not wrong exactly," he assured her. "I'm just being careful, baby. It's just that easy."

It wasn't a lie, but it wasn't exactly the truth.

"House and grounds secured," Sawyer spoke in the link. "Nothing's disturbed, nothing's moving."

"Location secured, Tobias," he told the other man.

"Entrance is secured," Elizaveta reported from where she was parked in the other SUV at the entrance to Emma Jane's driveway.

"Route in secured," Maxine reported. The road to the house would be free of vehicles parked anywhere but where they should be.

"We have a clear," Ilya stated, feeling Emma Jane's hold relax marginally. "Proceed in. All converge."

They'd all meet in the drive leading to the front door, where he'd make damned sure she was covered like a baby in a blanket, into the house.

He could feel something nagging at him, a certainty that he was missing something now and couldn't figure out what. What could he have possibly forgotten or overlooked?

"Here we go," he told her as Tobias pulled into the driveway. "Hang on one minute, we have protocol for this when we have more than two agents on-site."

Yeah, that was true enough, but still, not the whole truth.

Once the agents as well as Ronan and Eric, who had been given directions before leaving, were at the back passenger door, he told Elizaveta to go ahead and open the door.

Maxine and Elizaveta helped Emma Jane from the seat and began rushing her to the door. Ilya and the male agents surrounded them, weapons drawn until they were all inside. From there, all but Ronan and Ilya broke off and began rechecking doors, windows, pulling shades and dark curtains to ensure no shadow appeared in the darkness beyond the house.

"What's going on, Ilya?" She sounded far too calm. "And don't bother to lie to me or give me some half-baked version of the truth."

Turning, she glared up at him, the dark gray of her eyes the color of newly minted steel.

"I'm not lying to you, Emma Jane," he assured her. "We've had no new intel, no answers, no hints, period. And I'm not taking chances, it's that simple. I won't lose you because I wasn't prepared."

He kept his expression implacable, but he noticed it was that damned tattoo she took in for long moments. What did she see? He never saw what others did in the tattoo, and most of the time he was damned glad of it.

"What's your gut telling you?" she asked then.

That was the one question he wished hadn't parted her lips.

"My gut? My gut's telling me to get ready, something's coming. I don't know what, I don't know how dangerous it is, but I damned sure am likely to get pissed over it," he growled. "Now, are you hungry, sleepy, or in the mood to watch TV? Because standing here in the entryway isn't one of those choices."

The second the sharp words left his lips guilt seared him even as fear and regret flashed in Emma Jane's eyes.

"Goddammit," he muttered.

Before she could make a choice, he picked her up and carried her up the stairs to her bedroom. There he laid her in the bed Elizaveta was turning down as he stepped into the room.

"Pillows." Elizaveta hurriedly propped pillows behind Emma Jane and Ilya eased her back against them.

"Ronan called moments ago. He is bringing her soup she likes from her favorite Mexican place. He will be here within the hour," Elizaveta told him as he let Emma Jane settle.

"Let me know when he arrives," Ilya ordered, staring into soft, filled-with-hurt, gray eyes. She was pale, tired, and he knew, carried so many bruises beneath her clothing that if he could weep, he would have already shed tears.

As the door closed behind the bodyguard, he touched Emma Jane's cheek, the bruise discoloring it causing his chest to clench.

"Who would do this to you?" he whispered, suspecting he already knew. "Matt Lauren is no explosives expert." His fingers trailed to her neck and her collarbone, where he traced another deep bruise. "Who do you know, Emma Jane, who would want to kill you in this manner and who has the skills?"

She shook her head, closing her eyes briefly to blink back her tears.

"This is my fault," he whispered. "I don't know how or why, love, but this isn't about you, or anything you have done. This is a strike against me. When I learn who has done this, you will not try to stay my hand. You will not allow your eyes to fill with tears until I fear for my sanity if you cry. Do you understand me?"

Emma Jane stared back at Ilya, seeing the shadows in his pale green eyes, as well as the regret and sorrow. He was breaking her heart. There was so much sorrow in his gaze, and above his left brow, in the dragon's face, she imagined she saw loneliness, sadness.

"I promise, Ilya," she answered, reaching out, her hand touching his face, the prickle of his short beard against her palm, rasping the flesh. "I won't cry. But if you find out who it is, you better strike fast because my gun shoots as well as anyone else's."

The thought that anyone would try to hurt him by using someone he had helped, because he might care for them, infuriated her. No one was allowed to hurt him. This strong, stubborn man, so determined to ensure no one was harmed because of him, was the man she loved.

She loved him. And she had never loved anyone as she did Ilya.

His expression softened at her words, a brow arching just a bit, the dragon's face shifting enough to watch her almost warily, as though uncertain whether or not she was telling the truth.

"My fierce little love," he drawled, lips lowering to touch hers, and despite the pain, despite the bruised state of her body, she felt herself responding to him.

As he eased back, she licked the taste of him from

her lips and watched as he rose from the bed, wishing that kiss had been longer, deeper.

"Rest for now. Elizaveta will let you know when your brother arrives," he promised her. "Goodnight, Emma Jane."

# chapter sixteen

Ilya was pulling away from her, Emma Jane acknowledged the next several nights later.

He didn't come to bed until nearly daylight and he was up and gone before she woke. He'd stayed busy all day, stopping in the living room where she channel-surfed, napped on the couch, or pretended to read, only occasionally.

The bruising, though deep enough in certain areas that moving could still be uncomfortable, was healing.

Rest would cure it, her doctor had promised, and she took the advice seriously. If anything else happened she wanted to be able to run, fight, or shoot, whatever she needed to do.

The night she had stood outside the living room and listened to Ilya and Ronan talk in the darkness almost seemed like a dream now. His voice hollow, filled with bitterness and echoing with loneliness, still had the power to tighten her throat with the need to cry. Her proud, fierce dragon forced himself into the loneliness that she often saw in his gaze. He was so determined that no one he loved be hurt that he had made the decision to simply not love.

That wasn't the man who faced her after the explosion, nor was it the man who sat at a desk across the room that evening, phone and laptop both in use.

He'd told Ronan she was *balaur pereche*, dragon mate. His mate. That incredible tattoo on his chest, layered to appear to sink inside his flesh, the gem floating in those ghostly claws, held safely against his heart, was for her. Her birthstone.

Her dragon.

And he was just going to walk away from her when all this was over.

She picked at the throw blanket covering her legs as she stared at some nature program on the television. The lights were low, the lamp Ilya had on the desk illuminating his features in perfect detail.

He was so handsome.

The tattoo and scars merely emphasized the danger that emanated from him and added to the arrogant cut of his features.

The iridescent scales of the dragon seemed ever changing, shifting or flexing with the slightest shift of his facial muscles. Watching it now, she swore it stared back at her in loneliness, as though aching to join her.

*Pure fancy,* she thought. It amazed her, though, how that dragon could give the impression of emotion that Ilya's face usually lacked.

It was a tattoo, it wasn't alive.

But when she glanced back, it hadn't changed, the head seemed tilted just enough to keep its eyes on her, its scaled features locked in somber isolation.

*Poor Dragon,* she thought. *So stubborn and proud.* And she had no idea how to get past that stubbornness or that pride. How to tell him without revealing what she knew that she ached to be the light to his darkness. That she wanted nothing more than to spend her days, her nights, showing him what love really was.

She finally gave up on the television and just watched that tattoo, letting fancy take her as Ilya's head shifted to look at the laptop. The scaled features and red eyes of the dragon seemed to peer at the laptop as well, in complete boredom now.

Then the dragon gave the impression of drowsiness.

She grinned at the fanciful thought.

A second later Ilya's brow arched, lifting the dragon's head until it looked back at her arrogantly.

"You should be resting," he reminded her, his attention still on the laptop.

"Your dragon is bored," she drawled. "You know, Mikayla and I used to sit around after seeing you in the news or society pages and talk about how interesting that dragon was. Whoever did the work was a master. I agree with her—it seems alive at times."

Ilya seemed to freeze for a moment before he sat back in his chair and watched her curiously.

"Alive? How so?" he asked.

She grinned at the question. "Ilya, sometimes the dragon seems amused, or curious, sometimes angry. With me, he's incredibly flirtatious."

It seemed fanciful, but she couldn't help noticing when it happened.

"You rarely show emotion on your face, but sometimes the dragon does." She remembered Ronan's amused disbelief when she mentioned it to him.

He'd actually laughed at her.

"A strange phenomena indeed." The gentle mockery in his voice almost made her laugh.

"Maybe it's just me." She shrugged. "Or maybe your dragon just really likes impressing me."

His brow lifted again. "I have no doubt he does," he agreed. "He has rather good taste."

Emma Jane's soft laughter stroked over Ilya's senses, calming them, arousing them, making his skin ache for her touch. It was soft and warm, everything he wasn't. Everything he had never had in his life until his Emma Jane. And keeping his distance from her was killing him. He literally ached for her touch and it wasn't just the lust that rose inside him for her. He wanted to feel her warmth, just feel her against him longer than the few hours he was allowing himself at night.

As he watched her, ached for her, he rolled her to her back and propped the pillows beneath her shoulders. She watched him fully now.

"Who did the work? They were amazing in their artistry," she said, her gray eyes stroking over him.

"My grandfather," he answered, remembering the old man's tears as they ran over his craggy face while he did the work. "Sometimes Grandmother will draw a design if something or someone touches her, but Grandfather always does the work."

She bit at her lip, questions burning in her eyes, Ilya thought. She wasn't adept at hiding her curiosity.

"What?" he demanded. "Whatever's on your mind, ask it."

She picked at the edge of her blanket again before looking at him once again, her expression filled with compassion and regret.

"Did he do the tattoo to cover the scars on your face?"

Ilya stared at the top of the desk for a moment, hating the past and its memories. Thankfully, memories of his grandparents represented a short grace period of peace in his young life.

"He did," he finally answered her. "But the dragon would have been mine eventually. I'm the Dragon's grandson, and the Dragon heir. It's a tradition among my people."

But he should have been with the Dragon from birth and with their people, not trying to survive in hell.

"Is it tradition to place it on the face?" It was evident she liked his dragon there though. Of all the women he'd known, only Emma Jane had found pleasure in the ink.

"I'm the first to carry it on my face," he confirmed. "The son chooses where to carry his dragon, and though it's generally on the forearm, my father wore his on the left side of his neck. It has to be seen, be identifiable, or its protection is limited."

He could see her hunger for information, to know more than just his body, his here and now. And there was so much he needed to keep hidden from her.

"My father was Romanian, my . . . mother, for lack of a better term, from Russia. As the Dragon heir I'm head of our people when my grandfather steps down. Until then, the ink proclaims me the Dragon grandson and heir." He grinned in anticipation of how she would take the coming information. "When Grandfather steps down, I'll be head of all the dragon tribes and those loyal to them. You could say I'm a prince of a very large, far-flung nation of gypsies."

There were many in America now, Ilya thought, as he watched Emma Jane's eyes widen in surprise and anticipation. He'd stayed distant from his legacy, denied it whenever he had a chance, until now. If he had to take his place to protect her, then the sacrifice would be more than worth it.

No one could gather intel like gypsies, especially those of the dragon tribes. If he knew his grandparents, at this moment they were heading in from France, aunts, uncles, and cousins converging from other areas. Thieves, cut-throats, and assassins dropping good-paying jobs to come to the heir's aid.

He could feel them drawing near, he always had. It was his link to his people, his grandfather had always told him. Once they were there, he'd take his place as the Dragon officially, then no thief or assassin in the world could hide from him.

"Gypsies?" She sat up, breathing the word as though the thought of it were treasure. "Honestly? Ilya, what a man of mystery you are. I would have never guessed," she teased him.

His lips twitched at her mirth. "The tribes keep their secrets among themselves. They wouldn't survive other-wise."

Emma Jane watched him, a little awed now. She knew her dragon was so damned arrogant for a reason. And how could one boring receptionist hope to hold such a man? If she hadn't realized before how hopeless her love was for him, then she did now.

"When you have a son, will you do his tattoo?" she asked, aching at the thought that it wouldn't be her to give him that child.

"It's tradition." He nodded, his gaze somber, the dragon appeared despondent. "I've trained with the ink since Grandfather found me. He refuses to allow me to slip. Only the Dragon can ink those of his tribe with the dragon our name comes from, and each generation brings its own gifts in the work with the ink."

They would have made beautiful babies, she thought. Wild, intelligent, and bold as brass.

"Can you tattoo someone that isn't part of your group?" she asked, watching him intently, the question far more than it appeared, and he knew it.

"Only the Dragon or his heir can if it's a dragon image. So I can mark anyone I choose," he told her. "In any way I choose. But there are rules. You can ask for my ink, but you have to let me choose the design and where. The dragon image isn't one we take lightly."

There was nothing he wanted more than to mark her as his woman, to place his dragon on her wrist for all the world and his people to see. But the most dangerous of his enemies would only be more determined to destroy her.

Before she could say anything more, a knock at the closed doors leading to the entryway interrupted the request he knew she wanted to make.

"Enter," he called out, having already checked the entryway camera on his laptop

The door opened and Maxine stepped in, her blue eyes flicking from him to Emma Jane, then back again.

"Ivan's about two minutes out. He asks to meet with you privately when he arrives," she told him. "He sounded a little testy too. Journey must not be with him."

Fucking great.

Ilya stilled the rising irritation at the news. He'd asked Ivan to stay away from this. This wasn't a Resnova problem, it was his problem. And once he had proof, he'd take care of it.

Rising to his feet, he faced Emma Jane. "Do you want to wait on me here or I can help you to bed?"

"I'll just nap here." She shook her head, picking up the remote again. "I'm tired of bed."

He hated leaving her, hated seeing her pleasure in the small bits of information he had given her. Her eyes had lit up, filled with the same intensity other women showed toward diamonds.

Moving to her, he bent, took the kiss he'd been aching for, or at least a taste of it. As her lips softened beneath his, he pulled back.

"Rest," he ordered gently. "I'll be back soon."

He left Maxine with her and as he left he motioned Tobias to keep watch on the entryway as he opened the front door.

Ivan's car was easing to a stop in the driveway. Two agents stepped from the vehicle and flanked him to the house.

"Dammit, Ilya, stop siccing these fucking body-guards on me or I'm going to punch you in the face," Ivan cursed as he stepped into the house and closed the door before the other two men could follow him. "Ass-holes."

He glared at Ilya. "The day will come that I'll get you back for this."

Shaking his head, Ilya motioned him to follow him to the back of the house and the small office Emma Jane rarely used. Once Ivan stepped inside, Ilya closed the door, then strode to the bar and poured them both a drink.

"I checked on Nik before coming here," Ivan stated as Ilya handed him the vodka. "He's making the staff crazy, but other than causing Mikayla to roll her eyes at him and teaching his child how to intimidate doctors and nurses alike, he seems in good shape."

"I spoke to him earlier." Ilya nodded. "Had it not been for him, Emma Jane would be dead."

That knowledge weighed on him, Ilya admitted. Nik had created a debt that could never be erased, and for the first time in his life that thought didn't bother him.

"Journey and rug rat doing well?" he asked the other man when he remained silent.

The son Ivan's wife had given birth to had pulled together twelve shadow power families in Russia under Ivan's leadership, making him a force Russia's new president couldn't ignore.

"Journey and little Gregori are doing well," Ivan assured him. "Journey sends her love by the way."

"And mine to her," Ilya expressed, watching Ivan closely now. "Is this the reason you showed up tonight?"

A small grin touched Ivan's lips as his dark blue gaze remained thoughtful. "No, my friend, this is not the reason why."

Ivan was a pain the ass when he got in one of these moods. It was generally when someone within the family thought they could live a life without his sole permission.

"Are you going to explain it to me, or would you like to sleep on it first?" Ilya asked mockingly.

On a good day, he didn't have a problem with Ivan's little machinations, because he was usually in on them with him. They worked well together like that.

Ivan knew better than to use such delay tactics on him though. Still, the other man only grinned at the suggestion before finishing his drink.

Setting the glass on the table next to him, Ivan stared at it for a moment before lifting his gaze back to Ilya.

"Ms. Preston is doing well?" Ivan asked, then sipped at his drink. "Elizaveta said she's moving about easier now and, surprisingly enough, following doctor's orders."

"She's healing," Ilya confirmed the report as he sat down in the chair facing Ivan. "Nik took the brunt of the falling ceiling."

"Steele's a damned good man." Ivan nodded. "I brought that case of Dragon's Blood that you asked your assistant to send to you. You plan on drinking a lot, Ilya?"

Ivan was watching him closely now, as though wondering if he needed to worry about a problem.

"The Dragon's Blood is for Nik." He waved the suspicion away. "I hadn't known he'd been trying to find it to purchase for several years."

Ivan nodded at that, finished his drink, and looked around the office curiously. It was obvious the other man had something on his mind and hesitated to broach it. Which was highly unlike his friend.

"Goddammit, Ivan, say whatever the hell is on your mind!" Ilya snapped. "Don't play your games with me unless you want me to play mine against you."

Ivan glowered back at him then. "Fine, Ilya. Why the hell did I have to learn you had the mating ink done by going over your fucking records from the surgery when you took that bullet six months ago? Why didn't you tell me at least so we could have better protected her?" The look of disgust on Ivan's face was almost insulting.

Ivan stomped to the bar for another drink as Ilya stood still, watching the other man and saying nothing for long moments.

His medical records.

He'd taken that bullet six months ago, mere months after his grandfather had inked his chest. The bullet had slammed into the image, right next to the emerald the dragon's claws gripped so possessively.

The doctor would have seen it, but Ilya couldn't imagine him betraying either him or Ivan. The surgeon and his medical staff perhaps?

"She was targeted because of me," Ilya stated "Just as I thought. Which of the medical staff betrayed me?"

Ivan shook his head before quickly swallowing another drink. "The surgeon's office was ransacked, his files rifled. When he realized your file was missing, he contacted me. Unfortunately, that was this morning." Ivan pushed his hands into his pockets and shook his head. "I had your in-house records pulled and saw the image then. Then I checked out Ms. Preston. Are you aware she's the only female you've been around in the past years whose birthstone is an emerald?"

This was his fault. He had made it incredibly easy for his enemies to find her.

*The capriciousness of fate.*

*Go figure.*

"You inked your mate over your heart, but you didn't afford her the protection of the dragon's mark as well. Are you insane?" Ivan all but yelled at him now. "You could have at least told me, Ilya. We could have protected her."

Ilya glared back at him. "Don't start, Ivan, I'm not one of your damned lackeys you can insult and yell at," Ilya informed him with brutal emphasis.

The dragon's heart was inked with his woman's birthstone gripped in the shadow claws, but it was the dragon to be inked on his mate's left wrist.

It ensured that every criminal, assassin, or wannabe cutthroat knew the hell her dragon and his entire clan

would bring down on entire families should even one
dare harm her.

There wasn't a Mafia family, cartel, or gang that
wasn't aware and wary of the dragon's mark and of Ilya.

What criminals knew to steer well clear of someone
else was just waiting for, and she would delight in taking Emma Jane from him.

"Lorena," Ilya said, disgust heavy in his voice as he
let himself admit to someone other than himself who he
suspected was making the attempts on Emma Jane's
life. "Who would her or that fucker she married convince to challenge me in such a way?"

Ivan's expression of amazed disbelief was faintly insulting. "Anyone that's part of that family. Emma Jane
doesn't carry your mark, but if they know you carry
hers, they would be more wary. Whoever took this job is
spending more time jacking off than actually trying to
kill her. Third times a charm, dammit. Mark your mate
before they put a bullet in her head."

The words had that image slamming in his head, his
soul. It was his greatest fear, his nightmare, and he knew
the other man was right. If she was targeted by Ilya's
mother, and he was certain she was behind it, then the
only protection Emma Jane would have would be that
mark.

And with it, would come the truth of his past.

"God damn, Ivan, no one should have known about
her," Ivan snarled viciously. "If I ink her, she learns the
truth of what I am. She wouldn't understand . . ."

"Well, she'll be alive while she's thinking about it
then," Ivan sneered. "Now I brought your kit and your
inks. Damned if I knew which ones, so I just brought it
all. There's enough of us here to witness it. I'll have the

notices loaded to the dark web, then you can find your way with her without her death hanging over your head."

Ilya shook his head furiously. "Lorena will never honor that mark, Ivan. She'll find someone to strike against Emma Jane."

Ivan smiled. It was the smile of the shark he actually was.

"When we finish with her and her half-cocked bastard husband, she'll be lucky if she can hire anyone to acknowledge her. You're the Dragon heir and I head the Twelve Families of the motherland. There's no one stronger, Ilya. Even your brother."

But if the brother didn't remain neutral, then it would be a war.

"And the point is moot if Emma Jane doesn't carry the dragon where it can be seen," Ivan finished. "And she'll be too dead to give a fuck."

Plowing his fingers through his hair, he knew he had no other choice really. Lorena was but one, but if he didn't protect Emma Jane there would be no stopping the teams that came after her.

"I'll make the call," he sighed.

Ivan stared back at him, outraged. "What? You have to ask fucking dragon permission?"

Ilya glared back at him. "Only Grandfather can turn the reins of the Dragonovich families over to me. And only then can I ink her myself as the dragons mate. Otherwise, only his hand can do the job."

Ivan stared at him as though he were insane. "I've seen your work!" he snapped. "That's bullshit."

Ilya felt like punching the other man. Which was where many of their arguments led.

"There are rules, Ivan!" he snapped. "You should understand those. I can ink those that I consider warriors, or who are under my personal protection. But only the head of the tribes can ink a dragon or a dragon's mate. Get it?"

"Whatever." Disgust marked Ivan's face. "Make that goddamned call before it's too late. And get me another damned drink . . ."

# chapter seventeen

When the doors leading from the living room to the entry opened and Ivan and Ilya walked in, Emma Jane slowly sat up, instantly on guard to the tension whipping between the two of them.

What had transpired between two men during their meeting Emma Jane had no clue. One thing was for certain, Ilya was furious.

The anger made his icy green eyes like chips of frozen rage and the tattoos' iridescent scales seemed to shift eerily.

Sitting on the couch now, she watched them stride across the room, and something flashed in Ilya's expression that had her heart racing and panic edging at her mind.

He wasn't just angry. And it wasn't a hot blaze-and-expire anger. This was a rage long buried, tightly leashed for the moment but pushing at the bonds Ilya had on it. As though an old wound had been reopened, the bitterness of it leeching free and pulsing inside his soul.

She knew there were things inside him that were so dark, so hidden, they might never see the light of day or of love. A wild, dangerous cauldron of emotion brewed within him now and all those conflicting demons were hurting him.

The very fact that he had it contained was terrifying.

If all that murderous fury ever slipped his control, then whomever it was directed toward would never survive.

"Ms. Preston." Ivan's smile was pure charm as he moved to the chair to her left, unbuttoned his suit jacket, and practically plopped in the chair like a misbehaving teenager.

*Hell.*

"Mr. Resnova . . ." she began.

"Ivan." He gave a wave of his hand as a grimace crossed his face. "No formalities please."

"Very well," she said as Ilya sat right beside her, so close their thighs touched. "Elizaveta was showing me pictures of your son the other day. That's a future heart-breaker."

Pride suffused his dark face and blue eyes.

"Thank you." He grinned. "He'll be a handful I have no doubt."

Ivan already had a grown daughter, but Emma Jane realized he barely looked old enough. He was one of those men who would probably still be imposingly handsome at eighty.

He and Ilya both had those strong jaws, arrogant cheekbones, and chiseled features. And both their expressions reflected the tension rolling off them in waves.

Ilya sat back against the couch, still and silent as Ivan

made small talk. They talked about his son, his wife, her home, and the weather.

A half hour into the impromptu little visit, Emma Jane had enough. She was about to gag from the tension that seemed to thicken by the half minute. Ilya hadn't spoken half a dozen words, and only then because she shot him an irate look.

"Why don't I leave the two of you to discuss whatever has you strung so tight?" Why hadn't they just kept it in the office where it had begun?

As she moved to push herself from the couch, Ilya's hand settled on her leg in a silent demand to stay.

"Please, Emma Jane." Ivan smiled his most charming smile. "I must admit, I rather rushed in here to speak to you. If Ilya and I are left to our devices at the moment, I'm afraid we'll be using our fists on each other. That tends to get a little bloody."

Okay, she understood that, she thought, nodding.

"Mikayla's brothers are like that. She's hoping they grow out of it."

"He hasn't . . ." Ivan and Ilya spoke at the same time, with the same petulant hostility.

Oh wow, this was about to become precarious.

"So, why are you and Ilya disagreeing to the point of using your fists on each other?" No one spoke. "I mean"—she gave a little wave of her hand and continued with mocking cheerfulness—"Ilya and I were having a perfectly nice evening until you arrived. You want to mess up my evening, you can explain why."

Ivan's gaze flicked uncertainly to Ilya as though wondering how much he could actually get away with. Evidently, it was a question he wasn't certain how to answer.

Finally, he gave a heavy sigh, rose, and rebuttoned his jacket.

"Perhaps he'll tell you," her told her, though it was clear he didn't believe that was going to happen. "Either way, welcome to my family, Emma Jane. You have a lovely home, and once Ilya releases it for use I'm certain our clients will enjoy it."

Something resembling a growl left Ilya's throat as he tensed to rise, and Ivan visibly braced himself.

Emma Jane slapped her hand to Ilya's hard thigh and turned on him with a narrow-eyed warning glare.

"Not in my home, my yard, or my driveway. The two of you would no doubt break everything but yourselves!" she snapped, desperate to avoid the fight she could feel coming.

The tattoo at the side of his face flexed, rippled. The multi-hued scales seemed to come alive despite the emotionless gaze that met hers.

"Mr. Resnova." She gave the other man a disagreeable look. "Why do I suspect you've instigated a majority of those fights in the past?"

His smile was a somber acknowledgement of her accusation.

"That is unfortunately far too close to the truth," he sighed. "I'll bid you good night," he said with the utmost gentleness before turning to Ilya. "Anything you need, brother."

Ilya's jaw tensed to granite hardness, but he nodded to the man he called a friend and remained quiet as Ivan walked from the room and closed the doors behind him.

Slowly, Emma Jane lifted her hand from Ilya's hard thigh before turning on the couch to face him.

"What's happened?" Because she knew something had to have occurred. Something he didn't want to tell her, didn't want her to know.

"Nothing has happened." He pushed himself from the couch and moved for the small bar.

The liquor he pulled from the cabinet was one he'd stocked himself. She'd noticed the icy, almost faceted look of the vodka when she'd first seen it. Dragon's Blood, it was called.

Ronan's eyes had glazed over in liquor lust when she'd asked him about it.

"Ronan's threatening to steal your vodka if he finds it," she warned him, then watched in amazement as he tipped the bottle to his lips and drank from it as though it were water.

His fingers still gripping it, he paced across the room once more until he stood in front of her, where he extended the bottle to her. He watched her with the same icy interest he observed the world with but she had rarely seen out of him toward her.

Lifting her brow, she took the bottle and sniffed delicately. Beneath the strong liquor scent was an intriguing hint of something resonating with wild heat and glacier ice.

Still holding his gaze, she lifted the bottle and brought it to her lips.

She'd learned when she was young to show no fear when liquor was concerned and how to drink it. She took more than a sip but a hell of a lot less than a drink.

The instant wild heat stole her breath. A momentary reaction she had learned how to compensate for. A second later the ice hit her, a freeze that hissed through her senses. When it hit her belly, that wild initial burn multiplied before slowly dissipating and spreading through her senses. It left her face flushed and her toes tingling. Which was probably normal for her.

As he took possession of the bottle once again, his

lips kicked up in mocking acknowledgement that she had more than met his dare. Then he lifted it, drank deeply and when he lowered his arm turned away from her and paced across the room.

"My first memory of childhood is of Dragon's Blood," he said conversationally, but the tension in his body was building at a rapid rate. "I don't remember my age." He glanced back at her with a frown before moving to his desk, drinking as he walked. "I remember my thirst though. There was no water, but tucked beneath the cushion of an old couch was half a bottle of Dragon's Blood." He threw her a mirthless grin as she fought to contain her horror.

He drank again before leaning against the desk and watching her with a laser intensity that was frightening.

"I didn't die of thirst, obviously," he murmured, the words barely audible as he straightened and turned his back to her once again.

Emma Jane wanted to speak but didn't dare. Whatever had happened, whatever memories it had dredged up, had turned Ilya back into the icy, emotionless man she'd only seen in tabloids. And he was breaking her heart as he stood apart from her—the isolation that pulsed around him was killing her.

He stood so proud, so strong. There was no self-pity, and whatever he found so enraging he kept control of, though she had a feeling he didn't quite know what to do with it.

With his back to her, the straight line of his shoulders bunched again as he lifted the bottle to his lips, drank, then lowered it.

"Hunger, thirst, booze, isolation, does something to a child's mind, I believe," he mused. "I would sip from that bottle when the thirst was too much, and as it heated my gut, I would always imagine I could hear that dragon calling to me. At some point I remember Cook slipping into the hovel, taking the empty bottle, and leaving a small bowl of food and cold milk. By then, I preferred the vodka, I believe."

Shock held her immobile.

*Cook?*

*Someone had a cook, yet they'd starved him, isolated him, and let him go thirsty?*

"Legend says Dragon heirs will always be strong. They'll be fierce and like the Dragon they only grow stronger when touched by the fires of hell." He paused, then said rather ruefully, "Hell's fires were greedy when I was born."

Oh God, he was killing her. Her heart was breaking into shards.

"Ilya." She hurriedly covered her lips to hold back her sobs.

Ilya just watched her, his green eyes holding a faint glow as the rage he kept so contained rose to the surface.

The next drink he took was longer than the others. When he finally lowered the bottle he looked at it for a long moment before turning back to her.

"You weren't attacked because of Ivan," he stated, his voice harsh, his nostrils flaring as his teeth clenched. The dragon's scales shimmered, seemed to move and flex warningly. "You weren't attacked due to any fault of your own." Murder gleamed in his gaze and the red of the dragon's eyes were the color of fresh blood. "You were attacked because of me." He drank again. "Seems hell isn't finished with me yet."

He turned on his heel and stalked from the room.

A sob broke free, silent but powerful enough that her

whole body jerked from the force of it. Before the tears could fall, she jumped from the couch and rushed for the doors, throwing them open to follow him.

She rushed into the entryway to find Elizaveta sitting on the stairs, her face in her hands.

At the sound of the door opening, the other woman's head jerked up and Emma Jane could see the tears in the her eyes as their gazes met. Elizaveta shook her head before Emma Jane could say anything.

"Return to the living room." Elizaveta's voice was thick with unshed tears. "Leave him to himself. When he drinks Dragon's Blood, he prefers to be alone."

"Well, isn't that just too damned bad!" Emma Jane pushed past her. "As long as he sleeps in my bed, he doesn't have that option."

Finishing the vodka in one long drink, Ilya tossed the bottle to the small waste can, a mocking smile curling at his lips at the clatter and bang it created.

"Fuck," he muttered in disgust.

He should have brought the other bottle. What he had to do wasn't going to be easy. It would be the first step in destroying himself and any hope he'd harbored of holding on to Emma Jane—for a while longer at least. But then if he had thought his grandfather would catch him in a drunken sleep and place the dragon's heart mark upon his chest, then he wouldn't be in this mess. Because the fucking doctor had put a picture of it in his file, and when that file had made it into Lorena Vasilyev's hands, she'd had the proof she needed to strike out at Ilya in the worst way.

By taking the woman he loved.

Now, to protect Emma Jane, he'd take his place within the family he'd been born into, and he would do it alone. Because he simply couldn't imagine Emma Jane leaving her life to follow him into his.

Pulling the cell phone out, he made the call he knew he had no choice but to make now. He'd known from the moment he laid eyes on Emma Jane that this day would come though.

"Grandson." His grandfather knew he'd be calling of course. Ilya had never called him that he hadn't known beforehand. "I have been concerned for your grandmother, she has been worrying about you."

Or rather his grandmother was concerned and his grandfather was pacing the floors as he was wont to do.

He grimaced at the knowledge that his grandfather had always known when the past would return and paint Ilya's world in blood.

"Grandfather, when you chose the image for my mate's mark, did you draw it, or did Grandmother?"

Silence filled the line for long seconds and he could feel his grandfather's concern, his sorrow.

"When you were but a boy the image came to me," his grandfather said softly. "In the month that your dragon called for you to accept his power. In his song, he whispered his hope to my dragon, and I saw the image I was to one day draw."

Ilya sat down on the bed heavily. "Grandmother didn't draw it then." Had she drawn it he could doubt the truth of it.

"A dragon sings only to dragon blood," his grandfather reminded him. "I watched you after you took the ink and the dragon curled upon your face that night. You slept on the floor, close to the fire, unaccustomed to bed or blanket. My heart wept for you, and my dragon sang his sorrow and his rage with such strength that within hours the dragon warriors stood outside our door, demanding vengeance. We would have cut the head from that serpent bitch if possible."

Ilya closed his eyes wearily.

The murder by dragon guards of a dragon's immediate family was serious business. At the very least the tribes would have been forced to bar his grandparents from their presence forever. That would have killed them.

"Your dragon has whispered often to mine," the old man said. "He whispers in joy and hope of your woman. She is the light to the darkness, the strength of the sons that she will bear you."

"Sons?" Ilya stared into the shadows of the room, not even daring to hope.

"A dragon creates a dragon, but it is his mate that nurtures, that gives mercy and compassion to the babe's strong heart. I've told you this, Ilya. Rarely is a girl child born to a dragon, though your grandmother says one is coming soon."

*Mercy, compassion. Nurturing.*

"Then explain what fucked up with me?" he grunted. "Even you know the darkness that lives inside me, Grandfather."

His grandfather breathed out heavily.

"Fate will be cruel when a man denies it. Fate creates legacies, and those who will build upon it. Your father was strong. A warrior. A man of strong beliefs. He did not believe in what he could not see. The dragon called and he fought him, enraging the creature until he took the ink only to halt his fury." Heaviness filled his grandfather's voice and his heart, Ilya knew. "As I told him, the dragon can only guide you and only then if you open yourself to the song of his language."

*The song of his language.*

More and more often after meeting Emma Jane he awoke with such a song like a vibration around him, pulling at him. There were those times when he knew dragon blood kin were near, when he sensed the dragon guards just out of sight. There were those times when his grandfather sent them against his objections.

"Grandfather, I have my ink and would mark my *balaur pereche* should my dragon release to one of us the image of his mate," he made the formal request, the heir to the Dragon, who led the tribes.

"We are already on our way, though your dragon guards amass not far from you. The call they've heard has only grown more strident these last days."

Yeah, he could see that, he guessed. Son of a bitch, this dragon shit was hell on a man's nerves. He'd learned not to believe in fairy tales or legends, yet he felt as though he were living just that.

His grandfather chuckled as that thought went through Ilya's mind.

"All dragons must know the darkness and suffer in it before they will find their light. It is the light that guides their wisdom and the strength of the next generation. Your mate Ilya, she is your light. She is the only thing that can still that darkness within you."

And on that, Ilya cut the call.

Gustov Dragonovich laid the phone on the table in the RV traveling ever closer to the grandson who was more a son.

He sighed heavily once again and met the worried gaze of his still beautiful wife, Valaria. Age and all the lines of life's travels were etched into their faces, but all he saw was the woman who stole his heart when he saw her smile.

"He is in turmoil," he acknowledged. "What he

senses is in conflict with all he knows. And all he knows is stained in blood. Lorena will haunt him as long as she lives."

"Someone needs to kill that bitch and her demon husband," she said, her pretty brown eyes snapping with her anger.

"Perhaps," he murmured, holding his secrets for now, because sometimes in the telling of them, secrets are revealed. "Perhaps. But remember, love, dragons are sneaky creatures for a reason."

# chapter eighteen

Ilya jerked the door to the guest room open as Emma Jane was preparing to rap her fist against the wood. Who was more surprised, her or Ilya, she wasn't certain for a moment, then decided it was most likely her. All he did was lift a brow and stare at her fist before meeting her gaze. The dragon watched her with careful curiosity, waiting to see what she'd do next.

"What is going on? And what the hell do you mean, you're the reason I was attacked? No one could have known anything but for the fact that we had dinner with Nik and Mikayla," she argued, disbelief completely filling her as she faced him. "You are making me crazy, Ilya."

And that damned tattoo was more amused than outraged.

"Come on." Stepping from the room, he gripped her upper arm gently and led her down the hall to her bedroom.

Escorting her inside, he closed and locked the door, breathing out heavily and shaking his head.

"I should kill Ivan." He pushed the fingers of one hand through his hair. "That bastard has been the bane of my existence since I was five years old. Just one problem after another."

But it was said fondly, like one brother about another.

"Yeah, I can tell he's a real pain in the ass." She gave a roll of her hand. "Get to it and tell me what the hell is going on."

His eyes narrowed on her, the gleam of pale green glittering between thick black lashes. That was a sexual look, one of pure intent with no explanations forthcoming.

She moved several feet away from him.

"I want to know why you have this wild-assed idea someone is trying to kill me because of you. You can't just throw something like that out and walk away," she informed him with a hint of anger. "Especially when it doesn't make sense."

"I have enemies, Emma Jane. Russian enemies, as well as Romanian. We do not forget slights as Americans do. Vengeance, under certain circumstances, can follow from one generation to the next. Killing the offender is not considered the ultimate vengeance. Killing those they care for though is." He stared at her with an edge of torment in his gaze. "I have such an enemy, and somehow, they realized you are important to me."

Dragon's mate, he'd called her, Emma Jane realized, the light to his dark. And he had an enemy who knew it.

That was bad, Emma Jane thought, for her it was incredibly bad.

Clenching her hands together, she swallowed tightly, seeing the rage still burning in his eyes.

"What are we going to do?" she asked, her voice

trembling with the tears she wanted to shed for him. Tears he would never accept. "I can't stay locked in the house twenty-four-seven."

"I'll fix it, Emma Jane," he swore to her, striding to her quickly to take her into his arms and stare down at her with such a savage hunger she nearly lost her breath at the sight of it. "I'll fix it, baby."

Before she could she could ask how, before she could do more than part her lips, Ilya's head lowered, his lips covered hers, and instantly the raging hunger burning in him surrounded her. And she reveled in it.

Her arms twined around his neck, her fingers sinking in his hair as she went on her tiptoes to get closer to him. His hands stroked over her back, pushed beneath her top, and found sensitive bare skin.

The rasp of his callused palms stroking from shoulder to hip, his short nails scraping against her, his lips and tongue stroking hers, drawing her deeper into a hunger that pulsed with tormented need.

His hands moved from beneath her shirt, gripped the hem, and pulled it up. She barely had time to lift her arms and the tank top was gone. One hand pushed between their bodies, licked the metal tab of her cutoffs, and pushed them, along with her panties, to the floor. A second to get rid of her bra and he was lifting her, pushing her legs around his lean hips as he released his jeans and drew the heavy flesh beneath the material free.

"I can't wait," he groaned, his lips moving to her neck, exciting nerve endings that were way too sensitive. "God, Emma Jane, I can't wait."

Her back met the wall and, cupping the curves of her ass, he lifted her until she could grip his hips with her knees, and he guided the thick erection in position to take her. A shattered cry escaped her as his lips covered her nipple at the same time the broad crest of his cock began pushing past the slick folds between her thighs.

Any bruises she had were forgotten. Pleasure, sharp and intense, overcame her senses. With both hands cupping her rear, he lifted her, then let her lower on the throbbing flesh. The firm suction of his lips on her nipples, one after the other as he worked his cock deeper inside her, taking her with hard, quick thrusts, retreating slowly, then filling her again, intoxicated her senses.

The friction of the hard throb of his erection, the feeling of being stretched, being taken by her dragon, was addictive. She was greedy. She wanted more and more, no matter how many times he took her, all he had to do was touch her, look at her . . . God, all he had to do was breathe for her to want him

"Ilya," she gasped, her legs tightening around him as his hands separated the curves of her rear, his fingers stroking through the narrow crevice.

The rack of agonizing pleasure she felt poised on became thinner, sharper. As his fingers played and the thrusts inside her became harder, she could feel the sensations gathering inside her, the tension becoming sharper, drawing her tighter.

When one finger pieced the entrance to her rear and entered with a shocking surge of piercing pleasure, she came and cried out sharply. When he added another and pushed inside her again, the white-hot explosion of piercing sensation, a pleasure that rode that sharp divide into pain, shattered her. She felt her senses disintegrating, exploding, ecstasy rushing through her with a force that seemed never ending.

It was never ending, because he wasn't finished.

When the first hard waves of her orgasm came, his fingers eased free, and he turned, making the trip to the bed. He lifted her free of the still furiously hard shaft.

"On your knees." His voice was a hard growl, a dark rasp as she glimpsed the lust burning brighter than ever in his pale green eyes.

He didn't wait for her to find the position he wanted. Turning her, he pulled her hips up until her knees were balanced at the edge of the bed, then his fingers slid in her hair, the tug of the strands an erotic pain as she lifted herself on her hands.

"There, baby." His free hand ran over the side of her rear. "Just like that."

His palm stroked across both cheeks and a second later landed on one side, not forcefully, but destructive all the same.

Oh God, that was good. She was panting, on the verge of crying for more.

"You have the prettiest ass," he told her in that dark rasp his voice had become. "Let's see how I can make it blush."

The head of his cock pressed into her again. He thrust as his hand landed, pulled back, repeated. Controlled, deliberate, as he shook her to the foundations of her soul.

Her fingers fisted in the blankets beneath her, her head thrown back, his hard fingers holding her hair to keep her in the position he wanted her in.

"Feel good, *pereche*?" he groaned.

She shuddered, her vagina clenching on the flesh burrowing inside her, taking her with the maximum overload of sensation of his hand landing on her rear again. A heavy caress to each curve, his powerful body controlling hers, pushing her into that place where she was nothing but pleasure, one destructive white-hot flash of sensation at a time.

He didn't rush, he didn't hesitate at any time. The increased speed partnered with the increased heat on the curves of her butt, and his harsh male groans only pushed her higher.

"How beautiful you are." The words sounded torn from his lips as he delivered another heavy caress. "Made for my touch, for my hunger. There is no other pleasure such as this. Fucking you, taking you . . . ah God, Emma Jane, you are clenched so tight and hot around my dick."

He had to stop talking. She couldn't take so many sensations combined with the dark sound of his voice.

"Ahh, *pereche,* you grip me so well. That sweet pussy rippling over me . . ." His voice harder, the words more accented, his thrusts increasing.

His hand landed on her ass again. Once more.

As she felt herself tightening for the ecstasy building inside her, he gripped her hips with both hands and destroyed her senses. The hard, driving thrusts, the abrupt penetration and release, pushed her into a cataclysm of exploding ecstasy.

The blinding waves of release tore through her, sending shudders racing through her body, tightening her to the breaking point and leaving her shoulders collapsed to the bed as she lost the strength to hold herself up.

"Ah, sweetheart, we are not done yet." The silky promise in a dragon's voice had her womb clenching again, but she was certain she was definitely done.

Only to find out different.

He took her like a man desperate to hoard the memory of the pleasure, pushing her from one orgasm to another, from one peak of sensation into another.

Her cries turned to whimpers, her pleas to shattered gasps, when all she could do was lift her hips and hold on to his shoulders when another implosion overtook her.

He kissed her, her lips, her neck and breasts. Licked them, bit with just enough force, just enough of a flash of agonizing pleasure, to send her over the edge again.

And he followed, plowing deep, hands locked on her hips, the powerful, muscled lines of his body sheened with sweat, his pale, pale green eyes burning bright.

She collapsed against the bed, exhausted, replete, just trying to catch her breath.

Long moments later she forced her eyes open as she felt him sit on the bed, a warm, wet cloth sliding over her arms, her breasts, and lower.

He did that every time, she thought, dazed. He cleaned the perspiration from her body but, oddly enough, left the slick essence of their releases on the folds of her pussy.

"You don't wear condoms," she said somberly. "You're lucky I'm protected."

The cloth paused at her hips for one second before he resumed the path he'd set himself on.

"I have never taken a woman without latex, until you." The cloth slid over the top of her thigh. "I can't bear the thought of anything between us when I feel your pussy rippling around me, coming for me. Would you prefer I wear one?"

The gleam of his eyes was still fever bright.

"No, I wouldn't." She wanted every sensation, every lush pleasure he had to give her.

Her lashes drifted over her cheeks when he finally finished drying the perspiration from her, slid in the bed with her, and pulled her into his arms. Her hand fell to his chest, against the tattoo she thought was so unique, and she fell completely into sleep.

There were things she needed to discuss with him, answers she needed to questions drifting just out of reach. But she said nothing, she couldn't. Not when Ilya held her like this, when his hands caressed her without a need for anything more than her comfort, to ease her into sleep as he held her.

She loved him.

She loved him until when he walked away, she knew she'd grieve for him for the rest of her life. She'd go on, she'd force herself to find at least a measure of peace. But without Ilya in her life, she knew happiness would just be a glimmer of what-if.

What if she could have held her dragon? What if . . .

Ilya slid from the bed, careful not to disturb the woman sleeping so deeply beside him. Her palm slid from his chest to the pillow he placed against her before gently moving the long wave of hair from her flushed cheek.

Events were moving far too quickly to suit him now. Bitter acid roiled in his soul, mixing with the knowledge of what he would lose because of it.

Stepping back from the bed, he forced himself to dress, to tuck the weapon his at the back of his jeans. Pushing his feet into his boots, he left the bedroom, forcing himself not to look back at the woman who held every part of his being.

Avoiding the planks on the floor that announced any-one's passage, he moved downstairs, only to feel Eliza-veta's weapon at the back of his neck as he passed into the kitchen.

As quickly as she tagged him, she moved back.

"I'm going outside," he told her, his voice low. "Don't let anyone follow me."

She watched him through the darkness for a long moment.

"Especially her?" she asked with an arch of her brow.

"Especially her," he agreed, and went to the door and the security plate where he laid his palm, input his code, and when the light went green and the locks automatically slid free, stepped into the night.

Standing on the porch, he inhaled deeply, his head turning until his gaze centered on the tree line to the side of the house. As he stood there, five forms slowly emerged, stopping just short of completely revealing themselves. They were shadowed, a part of the night, waiting patiently for whatever he'd do next.

Ilya strode across the yard to meet them, his gaze meeting each of the team individually, reasserting his command though he knew it wasn't needed.

"Dragon son." Django, the commander of the group, stepped forward, his right arm extending, the dragon tattooed on his forearm staring out at the world in challenge.

Ilya had marked each of this team himself. He'd chosen them, aided in training them, then walked away from them to help Ivan fulfill his plans for the Resnova fortunes. Or so he'd told his grandfather.

The boy who had saved his life countless times. Ilya couldn't refuse to aid him. Then, once it was accomplished, Ilya had lingered despite the fact that he knew his life had to travel a different direction than Ivan's.

The world was one of technology. Science and facts. The old ways had been forgotten, bleached by men who were uncomfortable remembering that there was actually something to fear in the dark. So they lit it up with a thousand lights, kept it moving when it should sleep, and told themselves the old ways didn't matter because the old fears were just fears of the unknown.

Man was convincing himself evil didn't exist, even as their children, sisters, and wives disappeared, their sons lost their wild hearts, and their morals decayed by the day. Unfortunately, Ilya knew the evil that could touch an innocent life, just as he knew there was untapped good, as well as untapped evil, in each and every man or woman.

And the five he met at that moment had learned to fight both. The good and the evil, for each held their weaknesses.

Greeting each of the team in turn, he came to the last, the deceptively fragile cousin who had suffered herself as a child, lost to the dragon families and fighting just to survive. When they'd found her, she'd been like a demon, all instinct and fury. Now she was one of his dragon warriors, the only warriors he trusted at his back besides Ivan.

"We would have been here sooner, but others thought to delay us," Django stated as Ilya stepped into the shadows with them. "We had to kill them. We were unable to learn who sent them, but the tattoos they wore identified them as having spent much time in Vasilyev's prison."

Vladimir Vasilyev, the man his mother, Lorena Stefanova had married during the first months of her pregnancy with Ilya.

"I'd suspect Vasilyev anyway." He shrugged. "I talked to Grandfather earlier, he said he'd be here soon." A mirthless smile pulled at his lips. "He didn't give me an ETA."

"The Dragon rarely does." Django chuckled. "We

came as soon as we felt the need to do so. I'm thankful you called us to you."

He hadn't called them, but he let that go. It was yet another mystery that came with the life he'd walked away from.

Outlining the events to this point, he watched each of the team, gauging their strength, their readiness, and didn't find them lacking.

Django was a hell of a commander, and it was obvious he'd kept his team in peak condition.

He should have sent them to watch over Emma Jane the moment he woke at his grandparents' and saw the ink they'd marked his chest with. Never let it be said that his grandfather put off what could be done in that moment.

Ilya knew Gustov Dragonovich had despaired of Ilya's return. He'd feared the strength of the dragon the family had been given had died with his son's death and the hell his grandson had survived.

Like his father before him, Ilya fought his legacy, both the good and the bad, the instinctive as well as what had been taught to him. Again, like his father, he'd taken over the Dragon's Blood vodka enterprise, and within a few years had increased its demand until he could command an outrageous sum for it. But he'd fought the true gifts that came with his legacy.

The dragon at the side of his face had ensured wariness first among his enemies, then as his martial abilities were whispered of, the man with the dragon curving against his face was watched in fear.

There was but one person who didn't fear him, who lived for the danger that striking out against him could bring. Because she suspected the cost of killing her himself, or allowing his men to do so, wasn't something he'd been willing to risk. She had no clue that she only still lived because taking her life was a choice he feared would push him forever into the darkest part of the man he was. Now he knew, it wasn't her death that would do that, but the death of his Emma Jane.

When this was over, Emma Jane might force him to walk away, but at least she'd be alive, and the warriors who surrounded him now would ensure she stayed alive.

If she forced him to leave. Hell, what woman wouldn't force him to leave, especially one as sweetly gentle as his Emma Jane? When he had to walk away from her, at least he would know he had eliminated the only person insane enough to come after her because of him.

She wouldn't even let him kill her ex-husband, as fiery as she could be, there was no way she could survive his life and the legacy he brought with it.

"When your grandfather arrives, will you take his place as dragon?" Django asked when Ilya finished apprising them of the situation. "Or will he be directing the dragon soldiers that will amass with him?"

"When he arrives, and security will ensure the time needed, I'll take his place as dragon," Ilya affirmed. "Before I can do that, my mate's safety must be assured though. My enemy won't stop until she's dead, or Emma Jane is. And I won't risk my mate's life, and taking that path before I have the right to do so will only weaken the protection I can afford her."

Django nodded sharply. "Whatever your choice, our loyalty is with you," he assured Ilya. "You've only to tell us what you need done."

"Protect my woman," he ordered, his voice harder, colder. "Even above myself, protect Emma Jane. If she falls, then I'll follow quickly behind. There will be no dragon-heir, and no dragon-son, without her."

He loved that deeply, that completely. If Emma Jane were lost because of him, because of the evil that haunted him, then he wouldn't survive it. He couldn't survive it.

Without her, Ilya knew, he was lost.

Emma Jane knew the moment Ilya left her, just as she knew the care he took to ensure she didn't wake up. She was considering just lying there and slipping off to sleep again when her phone lit up with a green light, indicating one of the team with the palm print and code to get out had left the house. And she knew it had been Ilya.

Rising from the bed and pulling on her robe, she slipped to each of the two windows that looked out on the backyard. When she stepped to the side of the house, she watched the shadows shift at the tree line and five dark figures step just to the edge of trees.

Ilya walked to them, clasped arms with each, then when he reached the fifth, so obviously female, clasped arms with her, then drew her into a quick, hard embrace.

She jumped back, unwilling to see more, unwilling to let her world shatter just yet. Heart racing, hands shaking, she moved back to bed and wondered if he'd return, or if he had other things to do.

Funny, she should have been on guard for another woman, especially after Matt, and God knew Ilya was no virgin. He was so very experienced for a reason. And though her heart was screaming it wasn't possible, still the fear was like acid in her stomach for long seconds

Just for seconds.

Her Ilya wouldn't betray her, she told herself firmly. He wouldn't go to another while her scent still covered his body. There was a reason . . . an explanation.

But still, sleep didn't return, and neither did Ilya.

# chapter nineteen

Whoever, whatever, Lorena had sent to target Emma Jane because of him, was coming closer, Ilya acknowledged as he, Django, and Sylvanus moved silently through the trees the next afternoon, checking for any signs of anyone watching the house or attempting to access the device they'd left in the tree to analyze Emma Jane's security.

The group had surprised two men the night before, but before they could capture them, they'd managed to slip away. It was then that Django had made the decision to alert Ilya to their presence rather than staying back until needed.

Emma Jane's home was set on several acres of land, surrounded on three sides with a heavily wooded barrier between her and her neighbors. On one side was an old couple with hearing problems, on the other an older lady and her caretaker, with the two-lane road stretching in front of the house bordered by woods.

Neighbors at the scattered homes nearest to her had heard the gunfire the night of the attack but had excused it as kids goofing off. How the hell they did that Ilya still hadn't figured out.

"They've managed to hit her twice now," Ilya murmured as Django moved silently at his side, a black electronic detector in his hand while Sylvanus checked the area with a metal detector.

"Your suspicion that they're just sitting back and waiting seems sound," the other man murmured. "As you said, that would take deep pockets and a lot of patience."

Ilya paused, staring around the wooded area as Django fiddled with the display on the device he was using.

"Problem?" he asked, his voice low.

The soldier frowned, his dark brows lowering as he glared at the box. "It picks something up for a moment, then it's gone again."

Ilya turned his gaze up, scanning the overhead foliage curiously. "Another scanner like the one closer to the house?"

Django glanced up at him. "I'm taking that bitch down this evening and checking it out further." He fiddled with the controls to the detector again, only to quickly raise his head as Sylvanus motioned them over to where he stood with the ground-sweeping metal detector.

Both Django and Sylvanus had altered and modified various devices to suit far more important needs such as the ones they were using now.

Joining the other man, he and Django watched as Sylvanus knelt and began brushing back the leaves and wooded debris that covered the ground. Within seconds he uncovered a transmitter of some kind, the intermittent flash of the red light coinciding with the erratic signal Django had picked up.

"Bag it," Django ordered the other man. "Let's see if it has a buddy, then we'll take it back to the barn and dissect it." There was a hint of anticipation in the other man's voice.

"A buddy?" Ilya murmured. The other man only snickered.

"I'm going to bet someone has eyes on her house, day and night. Sabina found evidence of an old hunters blind on the other side of the road that had been used recently." He slid Ilya a narrow-eyed look. "Is it hunting season for something other than dragons' mates this month?"

"I'm pretty certain it's not," Ilya assured him.

"Well, she tagged it. Put a pretty little pressure detector under one of the steps. We'll see if anything puts it off." Django slid him a mocking look then. "What the hell you doing hanging out with us rather than your woman?"

Ilya crossed his arms over his chest and stared back at the commander coolly. "She was napping when I left."

She'd moved from the bedroom that morning, not long after he'd returned to the house to finish the briefs he'd been going over on his laptop. She'd gone to the kitchen, baked biscuits, and fried enough sausage and bacon that no one had gone hungry. Once she'd cleaned the kitchen, she silently went to the couch and turned the television on low. It hadn't taken her long to drift off to sleep.

"Bet she woke up soon as you left the house." Sylvanus proved he was eavesdropping at the comment. "If she's intuitive enough to know when her home's being invaded, then she'd know when her arrogant dragon left it." Amusement filled the other man's voice.

"Don't piss me off, Sylvanus," Ilya warned him. "I can still kick your ass."

"Wanna place bets on that?" Sylvanus chuckled. "I wouldn't mind sparring a little."

Ilya merely shook his head before he let his gaze go over the woods. No one was watching them now, but that wouldn't last, he knew.

"I'll have Drake come out and lay sensors before sunset," Django decided. "They're not foolproof, but it might give us a few seconds' warning anyway. And I know they're fully trained, but I want Maxine and Elizaveta pulled back from night watch."

Ilya restrained his smile. "See how far you get with that." Ilya shrugged. "You can give it your best shot."

Turning, they followed Sylvanus as Ilya kept his eyes on the surrounding woods, eyes narrowed for any anomalies. As he searched the woods, his mind was on Emma Jane though.

That woman was no dummy. Questions were coming soon and he knew it. The explanation he'd given her the night before was true enough but barely touched the surface of all the reasons his mother wanted him dead. Hell, he couldn't even bring himself to tell her who the enemy was. What man wanted to admit his mother had hated him even before birth because of the father who wanted his child but not her?

"You need to contact Alexi," Django sighed. "He'd tell you if she was acting strangely or was up to anything."

His half brother. Ilya refused to answer his calls, refused to contact him on his own.

"If he knew anything, he would have contacted Ivan,"

Ilya stated. "There's not much I do that he doesn't feel the need to know about." He was awful damned nosy for a younger brother.

They made their way from the forest, across the yard, and to the back door, where Django and Sylvanus broke off and headed to the barn where the team was staying.

Stepping into the house, he came to a stop when he saw Emma Jane sitting at the table using the laptop he'd rarely seen her pull out.

"How are you feeling?" he asked, closing the door and reactivating the security.

"Fine," she answered, turning to him to watch him suspiciously. "Who do you have hiding in my barn?"

His brow lifted as he restrained his smile and walked to the coffeepot. There wasn't much that got past her, he had to give it to her.

"They're part of the dragon tribes," he told her. "You find gypsies just about everywhere, it seems. They heard I was here and offered their services."

"And you trust them?" Evidently, he hadn't alleviated the suspicion.

"I trained them," he told her, watching the interest flare in her gaze. "All five of them, and inked the dragons they wear. Yes, I trust them."

Her lips tightened at the information. "And why haven't I met them? This is my property. I like knowing who's on it."

Pouring his coffee, he picked up his cup and moved to the chair to the side of the table. Pulling it free, he sat down, slouched back in it as he crossed an ankle over the opposite knee, and just watched her. And damn if he could intimidate her. She met his gaze and held it.

Not many men, let alone women, could do that.

Pulling back a grin, he sipped at his coffee.

"I thought we'd take care of that this evening," he informed her, glancing at the laptop. "Are you working or just playing?"

Lifting one hand, she very slowly turned the laptop until he could see the page she was reading.

The information site showed his picture, a black-and-white image of the dragon in exacting detail. And beneath it, information he'd hoped she wouldn't find. He should have known better. To be honest, there was so much conflicting information from site to site that he'd hoped she'd overlook the worst of it.

*Ilya Nicholas Dragonovich, called the Dragon heir, or dragon-son, grandson of the head of a gypsy tribe that only came into being in the past century. Rumored to be the older, illegitimate brother of Alexi Vasilyev, newly elected president of the Russian Federation.*

*No mother's or father's name listed but said to be the son of the late Nicholas Dragonovich and Lorena Stefanova.*

And there were pictures. Pictures of Lorena and her husband, Vladimir Vasilyev, pictures of Alexi and their teenage sister, Zorah.

He lifted his coffee cup and sipped at the hot brew again as she continued to stare at him, and wished to hell he kept vodka in the kitchen.

The article was incriminating enough for sure.

"What do you want me to say?" he asked her when she didn't speak. "Should I deny it?"

"Is it the truth?" she asked him quietly.

"Insomuch as the fact that I share their blood only." He placed the cup back on the table. "Lorena is no one's mother, she's a dam, nothing more. I wasn't raised with Alexi or Zorah, but should they be harmed I will exact vengeance. I rarely speak to either of them, and if Alexi and I do speak, we keep it carefully hidden lest Zorah be punished for it"

A few clicks and she turned the laptop back to him, her expression somber.

Oh yes, this article was much more incriminatory and a product of Lorena's viperous war against him.

The picture of her brother at perhaps twenty-five, laid out on the ground, blood staining his throat and chest.

*Lorena Vasilyev accuses the Dragonovich heir of murder at the tender age of fourteen. According to Ms. Vasilyev, who claims to be Dragonovich's mother, he murdered her brother in a psychotic rage, though there are those who state had Dragonovich killed him, he'd have had more than one good reason to do so . . .*

*Suspected enforcer of the former Resnova criminal organization in the Soviet Republic . . .*

*Rumored to be the sole owner of Dragon's Blood vodka, an exclusive, highly prized recipe . . .*

*Suspected in the disappearance of Russian crime tsar . . .*

*Suspected in the bloody murder and dismemberment of former Russian parliament member . . .*

There was a hell of a list there.

Checking the site, he realized it was a rather new one. Ilya had a fondness for crashing and deleting sites that included too much information about them. No one site needed to reveal too much, he thought.

Ilya didn't bother reading the rest of the article.

"Bastard never looked better," he murmured, realizing he was rubbing at the scars beneath the dragon with his index finger. "He died the same night Ilya's father did. Though I have to say Karloff Resnova died easier. Ivan was a bit more efficient at the time though he is older."

She turned the laptop back to her and snapped it closed.

"Is Vladimir or Alexi the enemy you believe targeted me?" she questioned him, and he could see the fear in her eyes.

Yeah, she'd been busy. But hell, he should have already explained all this to her anyway. She had a price on her head because of the little war Lorena had been waging on him since he was a child.

All because Nicholas Dragonovich had refused her.

It had never made sense to him. But then, he tended to be confused by psychopaths in general.

"Alexi makes a point to kill anyone who dares strike against me in horrible ways." There was no humor in the grin he gave her. "Sometimes, he and Ivan have screaming matches over who should have that pleasure while I take care of it myself." He leaned forward, holding her gaze and hating himself for the pain he glimpsed in her eyes. "I never claimed to be a saint, nor did I pretend my hands are free of blood, Emma Jane. I never claimed to be a good man, or even a man worthy of your touch. But I never lied to you and I never tried to hide the fact that you may have been targeted because of me."

Sitting back, he finished the coffee, then placed the cup on the table once more.

"And you didn't answer my question," she pointed out. "Which of them are behind that attempt to kill me, and why, Ilya?"

No, she wasn't going to be merciful and let this go.

"Not Vladimir." He shrugged and scratched at his cheek. "He's a bit lazy and rather stupid. I really believe Alexi does not belong to him. So by himself, he's not a threat." He paused, held her gaze, then continued. "When I was five, Lorena's bastard brother and Ivan's father held me to the ground and sliced my face open half a dozen times. Then they left me lying in the mud and the stink of my own blood and vomit while she stared down at me with a sneer. Lorena's behind this, I just have to catch the bastards she sent. As for why?" He grimaced, unable to come up with an answer that made sense. "I've been trying to figure that one out for as long as I can remember."

Rising to his feet, he moved to the sink, rinsed his cup, and placed it in the dish drainer before turning back to her.

"As there are five extra mouths to feed, I think I'll send one of the men to town for dinner. Any preference?" he changed the subject the only way he knew how.

Emma Jane could only shake her head. How could he talk about food? How could he be so distant, so cavalier, about the fact that his mother was pure evil?

"This doesn't make sense," she whispered.

She watched as a sigh parted his lips and his green eyes gleamed with icy mockery.

"Don't doubt the threat she is, Emma Jane. I was eighteen, and the lover I visited in Moscow I was rather fond of. Not in love with, but fond of." He glanced at the stone floor, somber regret creasing his face. "I returned to her apartment one night to find her laid out in our bed, the left side of her face shredded, a knife buried in her heart."

Oh God, she was going to throw up. Shock held her still, tearless.

This was the life he had lived? From five? He'd been a baby.

"Now, any preference for dinner?" he repeated the question as though they weren't discussing blood, death, and a woman so vile as to be demonic.

"No," she forced the word past her lips. "No preference."

She couldn't even consider food.

Never had she known such evil as what Ilya described to her. She knew it existed, knew some people just lacked any sense of morality or empathy. That didn't mean it made sense to her.

Ilya stepped to her, bent closer, one hand wrapping around the side of her neck to hold her in place as he stared back at her, the dragon at the side of his face seeming to flex restlessly.

"I don't want your pity. I don't need your compassion," he warned her, his lips pulling back from his teeth in a primal snarl. "And I won't tolerate it."

Releasing her, he stomped from the room, his head held high, pride and fury shimmering in the air around him until he turned into the entryway. Seconds later the front door slammed behind him.

Opening the laptop again, she stared at the pictures in the last article, especially those of Lorena Vasilyev. She had aged well anyway, Emma Jane thought, her chest aching for the boy Ilya had been.

She was pictured with Alexi Vasilyev, the newly elected president of the Russian Federation. Her husband stood behind her, thinning black hair, his features weak where hers were granite hard.

This was the woman who had allowed her brother and another man to so horribly mark her son's face that he'd had it tattooed over. The woman who had murdered his lover. And only God knew what that Emma Jane was unaware of. And she wasn't to hurt for him? She couldn't acknowledge the pain and horror he had suffered.

Closing the laptop once again, she buried her face in

her hands, determined not to cry. She wouldn't cry, at least not yet. Not while he might catch her.

"I'm surprised he told you." Elizaveta's voice was heavy with grief as she moved into the kitchen from the far entrance. "You okay?"

A firm hand gripped her shoulder for a moment before Elizaveta moved for the coffee pot and a cup.

She nodded at the question. How could she be anything but okay? Ilya would accept nothing less and she knew it.

Elizaveta moved to the table and sat down, silent for a moment as she sipped. Finally, she placed the cup on the table and frowned at Emma Jane.

"Do you love him, Emma Jane, or just love his touch?" Elizaveta braced her arms on the table as she asked the question. "Because if you love him, the road you travel with him will not be an easy one. But I think perhaps you are the only one I've met who would have a chance. If it is only his touch you love, then I beg of you, be kind and tell him now, before he destroys his soul for you."

Emma Jane pushed herself from the table, staring back at the other woman and forcing her lips not to tremble with emotion.

"I love him, Elizaveta, but I won't accept anything less from him," she warned the other woman. "And the point is moot, because Ilya hasn't mentioned love and he hasn't indicated in any way that he'll be here when this is over. Until he does, there's really nothing to talk about, is there?"

Picking up her laptop, Emma Jane walked gingerly across the kitchen to the door, where she paused and turned back to Elizaveta. "If he asks where I went, I'm going to bed. Having a ceiling fall on you, not to mention a Viking, takes a while to get over. Tell him to order whatever he wants for dinner."

She forced herself up the stairs, though her muscles protested and the bruises screamed at the abuse. Once she reached her room, after taking two aspirins and placing a heating pad beneath her side, she curled in the center of her bed and stared bleakly into the room.

She was exhausted, her body aching from one end to the other, and she wanted Ilya to hold her, to feel the warmth of him against her, his strength surrounding her. She wanted to touch him and remind herself he was really there, that the hell he'd lived through hadn't destroyed his ability to love.

Losing him would break her heart, though she was already preparing herself for it. Because the man who had just walked out of the house wasn't a man who wanted to love.

As she closed her eyes, a single teardrop fell.

# chapter twenty

Emma Jane made her way downstairs the next afternoon after a shower and change of clothes. The sleeveless blue-and-white print summer dress was one of her favorites. Barefoot, her hair left down to fall around her face in soft waves, she felt able to face whatever newcomers Ilya had brought in.

The fact that he knew them so well made it easier. He'd trained them, he said, and tattooed the dragons they obviously carried.

She'd spent some time trying to research the dragon tribes, as the articles online called the far-flung families. There seemed to be a running debate among several historians as to when the Dragonovich family might have begun, though it was readily agreed they'd originated in the mountains of Romania.

Either way, it was obvious she wasn't going to find the answers she needed without asking Ilya, and he seemed a bit testy when it came to the subject of his past or his family.

After she made it downstairs and stepped into the kitchen, she came a stop as she saw the young woman standing in front of the coffeemaker, hands on her hips. Long black hair was confined in a braid, and she was wearing black cargo pants and a black tank top with combat-type boots.

She swung around as Emma Jane came to a stop, and surveyed her with brown-gold eyes in a delicate, almost kittenish face. As she stood there, Emma Jane glimpsed the dragon on the inside of her right arm. The dragon Ilya said he'd inked.

"Can I help you?" Emma Jane asked, realizing this must be the woman Ilya had met outside with the small group of men.

"You must be Emma Jane." The girl looked back at her with a hint of a relieved smile. "I am Sabina Drag-onova, Ilya's cousin." She glanced back at the coffee-maker, then to Emma Jane once again. "May I make coffee?" She gestured to the pot. "I think I am going to go into withdrawal any moment."

Emma Jane stepped forward and moved to the cof-feemaker herself.

"There should be cinnamon rolls in the microwave if you want some to go with the coffee." Emma Jane ges-tured to the device before turning back to the coffeemaker.

"Perfect," a sound of bliss, and the woman stepped to the microwave and carefully removed the cinnamon rolls Emma Jane had baked that morning. "Ilya sent Sylvanus and Sawyer to town for food. I hope it is not pizza." She gave a shake of her head. "I am tired of pizza."

Emma Jane stepped back from the coffeemaker as the hot liquid began spilling into the pot.

"Where's Ilya now?" she asked as Sabina carried a cinnamon roll to the table, placing it carefully on a paper towel before turning to the coffeepot.

"He is at your barn talking to our commander, Django," she answered, causing Emma Jane to frown as Sabina sat down across the table from her.

"Ilya has a commander?" she asked.

Sabina frowned. "Django is our commander. We are the Dragon's personal security." She gave a little roll of her eyes. "Whenever he allows us to be. He does not enjoy playing with us, I think."

Emma Jane barely held back her smile.

"Sabina, Django needs to gag you." Ilya stepped into the kitchen from the hall, his gaze flicking between Emma Jane and Sabina. "I thought you were supposed to be unpacking the group's supplies."

Sabina sighed at the rebuke. "There was no coffee, Dragon," she complained. "I told you I must have coffee. I did unpack as I was asked, though, before seeking it out."

She lifted her cup with a charming grin as Ilya moved to the counter, leaned against it, and crossed his arms over his chest while leveling one of those icy looks on her.

"Uncle Gustov will be very upset with you if I have nightmares again, Dragon," she pouted. "Do not look at me like that."

"Sabina . . ." he began warningly.

"For God's sake, let her drink her coffee and eat her cinnamon roll," Emma Jane demanded, staring at him with a frown. "What's wrong with you, Ilya? I'm sure she's not on the verge of spilling any deep, dark dragon secrets."

Ilya slid that look to her.

Yeah, that was going to get him real far.

"You know, Ilya, that look would be more effective if that silly-assed tattoo of yours didn't seem to be winking at me." Emma Jane stared at the tattoo, hoping to catch it again.

From the corner of her eye, she saw the way Sabina froze in shock, the cinnamon roll barely an inch from her lips. She recovered quickly, though. Emma Jane could feel the other girl's tension.

"Emma Jane, tattoos do not wink," he explained to her, again. "It is ink, carefully applied by a master, I admit, but in no way alive."

"Yeah, well, tell that to the ink." She shrugged. "Now get some coffee and stop hovering over me or go be grouchy elsewhere. I have a headache and I'm not in the mood to deal with your attitude."

He moved to her instantly then, caught her chin between his fingers, and lifted her face to him. She frowned at the abrupt movement, then caught sight of the scarring against the tattoo again and wanted to cry out in rage.

"You should take the pills the doctor gave you," he chastised her. "You would not hurt."

"No, I'd be drugged out and unable to think. I'd never keep up with what the hell was going on around here then," she told him, pulling her head back from his hold. "Would you just sit down or something?"

He stepped away from her and moved back to the coffeemaker, where he poured himself his own cup before turning back to them.

"Sylvanus and Sawyer will be back with dinner soon. It seems Sawyer slapped down the idea of pizza." He ignored Sabina's muttered, "Thank God." "I believe Sylvanus texted something about enough ravioli and breadsticks to feed an army."

Emma Jane nodded, wishing she'd gotten her own coffee. As the thought went through her mind, Ilya set his cup in front of her and pushed it closer.

"Drink, Emma Jane," he said, his voice softening. "I don't like seeing you in pain."

She was all for being stubborn, but the damned headache was becoming irritating. She lifted the cup and sipped, thinking somehow that it tasted better for Ilya having drunk from it first. Which was ridiculous.

This was hopeless, she thought. She was going to cry if he left, and she really couldn't see him staying. Her home wasn't opulent, it wasn't anything like he was used to, but she loved it. Her blood, sweat, and tears stained the kitchen floor. She'd starved for the farmhouse sink for several months. She'd loved this house, fixed it up, repaired it, and given it all her love at a time when she didn't think anything or anyone could get past the hard knot of grief inside her.

"Sabina, take your coffee and return to the barn, I'm sure Django needs you by now," Ilya ordered as Emma Jane seemed more distracted by the moment.

"Yes, I have been away for a while." Sabina rose from her chair, refilled her cup, and with nothing further made her way from the house.

"You didn't have to run her off," Emma Jane told him as he took Sabina's chair.

"Django depends on her expertise with electronics," he told her. "She's new to the group and still trying to find her confidence. Thank you for taking time for her."

He hid a smile as she gave him a dark look. "I didn't take time for her. She was here and so was I. But she seems nice."

"She's a good soldier . . ."

"She's a woman. A young woman," Emma Jane burst out, her expression distressed now.

"She's also a soldier, Emma Jane, just as any young woman in the military is a soldier. She's highly trained in her area of expertise, and fully capable and proven in protecting herself as well as her team."

He was trying to be easy on Emma Jane's sensibilities. Son of a bitch, she was far too soft for the truth of the life Sabina had lived, let alone what Ilya had survived. She had no idea the monsters and the crazies who were in the world. And he didn't want her to know.

It was his job to protect her from it and hers to remain as innocent as possible, so he always remembered what he was fighting for.

"You mean she's been forced to kill," she whispered, her hands gripping the coffee cup desperately.

Yeah, she was too damned intelligent sometimes, he thought to himself, not for the first time.

"Emma Jane, the former Soviet Union is not often a kind place to grow up without a massive amount of power to back you. It is not America. The dragon tribes are stronger than many smaller groups, but still, we have our own problems and those who would harm us disappear from the face of this earth. If they did not, then young women such as Sabina would disappear instead."

It wasn't just Lorena who targeted the Dragonovich family. There were those who believed in the mythic tales of their tribe, suspected Ilya's bloodline, understood his legacy, and feared it. The former president of the Soviet Union had been one of those men. Because if it was what Ilya wished, he could step into that political arena and with little trouble gain the people's loyalty.

And it was the bloodline that would assure it, rather

than Ilya himself. He'd never felt challenged enough to even attempt it though. Being a ruler had never appealed to him. He much preferred working in the shadows.

"Children shouldn't be tortured," she whispered painfully. "A baby should be loved, cherished." The pain in her eyes and in her voice had him stilling, wondering at the emotion that resonated in her voice.

Her heart was too tender, and too much was happening to her at once. Learning she was in danger, that the reason for it stemmed from his inability to stay away from her. That would be enough to screw any woman's head up, let alone one as innocent as his Emma Jane.

"Yes, they should be, but even in America many are not," he reminded her. "Do not dwell on my past. I refuse to do it myself. I survived what I faced where others did not, and came to the other side stronger. Sometimes honor will only get a man killed. I do not believe I'd enjoy being dead."

Ilya allowed an edge of amusement to touch his voice, hoping to draw Emma Jane from whatever thoughts were tormenting her. She only shook her head, though, and turned to gaze out the window, looking out on the front drive just in time to see Ronan and the sheriff's cruiser pulling in.

"Eric's in sheriff mode," she said with a frown. "Something's wrong."

Rising to his feet, Ilya pulled his phone from his pocket and sent the team a "clear" alert to assure them that Ronan and Eric were considered safe.

They'd seen the men's pictures but hadn't yet met them. Until they did, who they thought they were wouldn't matter. They'd still put them in their kill sights until they knew for sure.

"Why do I have a feeling this isn't going to be good?"

Emma Jane sighed as Eric stepped from the sheriff's SUV, a file in hand, before striding to Ronan's truck.

Ronan stepped out of his vehicle and they seemed to disagree for moment as Emma Jane watched with a frown. Ronan and Eric hadn't seriously disagreed in years.

The two men started up the sidewalk to the house, with Eric leading the way. Ronan was still trying to convince him of something, though Eric didn't seem to be paying much attention.

"I'll let them in," he told her. "Drink your coffee." He pointed imperiously to the cup before turning away and heading for the front door.

Drink her coffee. She was going to have to do something about his propensity for orders. She didn't do orders well. Hell, she had enough problems with suggestions from most people.

Sipping at the coffee, she grimaced at the cooling liquid and placed it back on the table. She pushed the cup aside as Ronan and Eric came into the kitchen. Ronan's expression was concerned while Eric's was set in what she called his sheriff mode.

"What's wrong?" she asked as Ilya moved behind her, obviously taking a protective stance.

Eric removed his cap and shook his head before wiping his hands over his hair.

"I have to ask this and I hate it like hell." Eric grimaced, replaced the hat, and ignored Ronan's glare. "Has either of you seen Matt since the night he broke into the house?"

Well, that wasn't what she was expecting.

"Matt?" She shook her head in confusion. "He hasn't been back, Eric. I would have let you know if he had."

Eric lifted his gaze to Ilya. "You?"

"You'd have been the one helping me hide the body if he had," Ilya drawled. "What's this about?"

Eric and Ronan shared a speaking look before her brother turned back to her.

"Come with me, EJ, you don't want to be here for this," he sighed.

"Be here for what?" Emma Jane felt her chest tighten in premonition as she stared at Ronan's hand. "What has Matt done?"

She turned her gaze to Eric. "I know none of you believe it, but he's just trying to be a bully. You know how Eric is."

"EJ," Eric sighed.

"What did he do?" she demanded again, steeling herself for whatever Matt had managed to get himself into this time.

"We found Matt this morning," Eric told her, his voice low. "He's dead, EJ."

She stared at Eric, then Ronan. It was there in their expressions, in the concern that filled their eyes.

"He was murdered?" she asked, though she knew he would have been.

Eric nodded at the question. "We went to Mary's first, she's claiming Matt went to meet with you after her and Bart bailed him out. Said he was certain he had information about Ilya that would make you change your mind." He glanced at Ilya. "He was certain he could make you walk away from Ilya."

She was shaking her head even as Eric related the conversation. There was no way that would have happened, and she knew Ilya wouldn't have bothered killing Matt after he got out of the house.

"There's nothing he could have on me, Eric." Ilya's

hand brushed down her shoulders in a gesture of comfort.

"Yeah, I figured," Eric said, still watching Emma Jane closely. "Mary's inconsolable. She said Matt hadn't been the same since the divorce anyway."

Matt hadn't been the same in a lot of years, Emma Jane acknowledged to herself. After they'd married and he'd learned she had no intention of moving in with his parents and selling the house her parents had given her, their relationship had deteriorated rapidly. When his plans hadn't worked, he'd gone behind her back and mortgaged her property and the house for every penny it was worth before she'd realized what he'd done.

What he'd done with the money she'd never learned.

"He was like a child, always wanting more, always certain it was someone else's fault when he couldn't attain it," she sighed wearily, shaking her head.

"Mary asked if you'd come to the memorial," Eric relayed the message. "Her and Bart are leaving for her brother's place in Florida the next morning."

"That's not a good idea," Ilya stated behind her, his hands lying on her shoulders without pressure, but a reminder that he'd protect her.

Emma Jane shook her head. "I can't say no, Ilya," she disagreed, looking up at his expression for a moment. "Mary was always kind to me. I can't not go to the memorial."

She rubbed at her temples once again, the headache building as she tried to make sense of the abruptness of the information, the knowledge that someone she had known most of her life was gone.

She hadn't loved Matt as she should have; she'd accepted that a long time ago. For a while, she'd hated him for risking her home, for risking the only thing she had left that was hers. And finally, she'd just felt sorry for him.

He was a little boy in a man's body and he'd never wanted to try to mature, to learn how to live as an adult rather than as a little boy.

"I knew how you'd feel, EJ. I'll make sure Ronan and I are there," Eric promised. "And like I told Mary, she'll have to agree to your security as well or it isn't happening. She had no problem with it and Bart just wants to say goodbye."

Matt's parents had always been nice to her, as she said. They'd never understood why she couldn't remain married to him. Why she hadn't wanted to.

"Emma Jane . . ." She could hear the disapproval in Ilya's voice and the fight that was no doubt coming later.

It was all in that heavy rasp, the lower pitch of his voice, and what she thought of as the dragon roughness to his tone. She loved the sound of it, but she wouldn't allow it to sway her.

"I have to go, Ilya." Getting to her feet, she moved away from him before turning to stare into the heavy frown he leveled on her. "This isn't your choice, it's mine. Period."

He glared at her, then at Ronan and Eric.

Both men merely shrugged, clearly affected by whatever had happened to Matt.

"We're about to have a hell of a fight, Emma Jane," his voice roughened, his expression tightening arrogantly.

"Fine, we're going to fight over it." Placing her hands on her hips, she fought to keep from getting angry, from letting her own fears and the mistake she made marrying Matt to begin with burn into anger. "What will it change? It won't change my mind and it won't change the fact that I'll be walking out of this house tomorrow to attend the memorial. It wouldn't look right if I didn't and it would only level suspicion toward us."

"They will suspect me anyway," he snarled. "My reputation precedes me, remember?"

"As does mine," she told him, suddenly reminded of his comment that she was the light to his darkness. "Those who matter would know better than to believe I'd harbor a man who murdered my ex-husband simply because he could. But I really don't care what others think, and neither do you. I will be going."

# chapter twenty-one

There were times when a man just had to admit he was head over heels, stupid in love, Ilya thought later that evening as he pounded on the punching bag he and Django had hung in the barn. With a series of kicks, punches, and curses he beat on the bag, ignoring the sweat dripping in his eyes and the fact that he was beating the bag because he couldn't beat that fucking Matt Lauren to death.

*That dumb son of a bitch.*

He slammed his fists into the bag again, keeping the curses to himself, though he couldn't halt the rage that burned through his mind.

Yeah, he was crazy fucking in love with her and terrified for her. That woman was so damned trusting, so incredibly compassionate and merciful, that he couldn't imagine the horror she'd feel if she suspected half the things he'd done in his life.

Things he hadn't lost sleep over. He'd known before

he ever pulled the trigger, threw his fist, or used a knife who he was killing and whether or not they deserved it. They'd all deserved it in his estimation.

He was a fucking Dragonovich, whether he liked it or not, and there were times he'd honestly hated it. But he'd learned to accept it, learned to take the strength it brought him while ignoring the rest of it.

The rest of it—like the fact that he was a direct descendent to the Romanov line. That if he wished, he could take his brother's power, the people's loyalty, and make it his own.

If he wanted to.

There was nothing he would be more loath to do. Despite the current fascination and romantic view of the Romanov line, he'd never thought much of the family himself. There was a reason the people revolted against them. Why would he want to risk it happening again?

The Russian Federation needed a progressive leader such as Alexi for several generations before the wounds of the past could repair and the corruption within could be diluted. Alexi had the patience for such things. Ilya knew himself and he knew he'd end up shooting the bastards out of sheer frustration.

Pausing to catch his breath, his taped hands gripping the bag, he laid his forehead against it.

All he could do was curse himself because he was too stupid in love to do what he had to do to keep Emma Jane from going to that damned memorial the next day. He wanted to throw her over his shoulder and run away with her. He wanted to find a way to make her understand what it would do to him if he lost her.

He simply didn't have a good feeling about this, and he damned sure didn't have a good feeling about Matt's parents. Matt had been the way he was for a reason. His parents had raised him with that sense of entitlement and arrogance. They hadn't forced him to grow up, and by the time he'd married Emma Jane it had been too late. The boy was already set in the mold they'd created.

"You're going to put a hole in that bag," Django remarked as he walked slowly around Ilya until he could see his face. "I hear we're attending a memorial tomorrow."

The knowing amusement in the other man's expression wasn't helping his mood any, Ilya thought. It was fine to be amused if the situation was in the least funny. He didn't consider it funny.

"So she's trying to convince me!" Ilya snapped, his breathing still heavy.

"Or are you trying to convince her?" Django chuckled, his dark eyes flashing with amusement again.

"Don't piss me off, Django, or I'll use you for a punching bag," he warned the commander.

He hadn't sparred with the other man in a while, but he was sure he could take him. Hell, he was pissed off enough at the moment he wouldn't care if he had to spar with the whole damned team.

"It's interesting, seeing you with her," the other man commented as he stayed carefully out of reach. "Even Sabina likes her, which is unheard of. She's usually pretty critical of the women she sees you with in the tabloids."

No, Emma wasn't like the widows he'd fucked his way through. She would never be the type of woman a man could walk away from.

She was the kind of woman a man kept, cherished, and loved.

"I don't have a good feeling about this memorial." Stepping away from the punching bag, he grabbed a towel and dried the sweat from his face and shoulders. "Emma Jane won't relent. She's going."

And he couldn't come up with an argument he knew would sway her. He'd run through everything he could come up with. He'd stomped, he'd growled, and she'd just remained calm and stared at him with those haunted gray eyes.

"So, do what men around the world do and make her so damned tired she sleeps through it," Django suggested, wagging his brows suggestively like an overgrown feral savage.

Yeah, Ilya had thought of that.

"She can barely walk tonight from the bruising she took in that explosion." Not to mention the crazy, desperate hunger he'd taken her with the night before. "She's hurting. Physically and emotionally."

Matt's death and Mary's request had brought back memories he knew were painful for her. Things she never spoke of but he could sense she thought of often.

What she couldn't change she seemed to grow stronger from, but if she could change what she knew was wrong Emma Jane would fight tooth and nail.

Django nodded slowly. "From what I learned, he wasn't exactly a nice guy where she was concerned. Takes a hell of a woman to forgive that."

The other man crossed his arms over his chest, one hand rubbing at his rough jaw. "Some men just need to be killed, Dragon, and he was one of them."

Ilya shook his head. "I don't think it's so much forgiveness as pity. She's known him most of her life though, and she feels guilty. She knows he's dead because he was helping whoever attacked her and she's having a hell of a time telling the mother no."

He couldn't convince her that guilt was misplaced.

Oh, she'd agree with him, nod, and say she knew Ilya was right, but he'd looked into her eyes and seen the sorrow and the guilt as well as the pity.

"A woman that needs a dragon to protect her." Django flicked his fingers to the tattoo over his heart. "The mating mark you now carry is for her, isn't it?"

Ilya gave a short, tight nod. "When Grandfather arrives, I'll accept his position, then I'll ink her as well. I'm afraid it's the only way I can keep Lorena from hiring more and more assassins to come after Emma Jane. Then, I'll just have to deal with her."

The thought of killing Lorena without irrefutable proof that she'd killed Natalia all those years ago or that she had hired the would-be assassins coming after Emma Jane, didn't set well with him. If she struck out at Emma Jane in even the slightest way or if he learned for certain that she was behind this attempt, then he wouldn't be able to stop himself.

He was going to have to talk to his half brother, convince him to express to his mother that Ilya wouldn't have a problem killing her.

"Once you hold the position as Dragon, then it falls to us to protect those interests, even if it's against her," Django reminded him.

Ilya shook his head. "There's some things if a man can't do them himself, then he has no business having them done."

He had a feeling, much like him, Django would take his duties seriously though. Ilya would never know what the other man had planned and would probably never know he was behind it. It was that position he had taken in Ivan's life as they fought to be free of Russia and the Resnova crimes.

Survival was sometimes a dirty business. The blood

that had been shed wasn't innocent blood; Ilya had made certain of it. He'd ensured Ivan's hands remained as unstained as possible though. Ivan was the face of the Resnova name, and if he was going to make it respectable then he had to stay as above suspicion as possible.

"Your grandfather should be arriving soon, within the next twenty-four to forty-eight hours," the commander informed him. "Sabina received a text from them before I left the main house. When I tried to call, they weren't answering though."

That wasn't much of a surprise. His grandfather could be as conniving as hell, then laugh when he was caught up in it. It drove Ilya insane, amused his grandmother, and made everyone else wary.

"Let me know if you hear anything else," Ilya ordered him. "I'm going to go shower and see if that woman has given this insanity any more thought."

"Good luck there." Django laughed as he turned and loped the short distance to the back of the house.

Night had fallen since he'd left the house with a slam of the door and enough frustration to nearly grind the enamel off his back teeth. And Emma Jane had sat there watching him with those sad gray eyes, ensuring he felt like a complete heel. He wasn't looking forward to the fact that he knew he was going to take her to that damned memorial, and he knew he was going to regret it.

Unfortunately, he couldn't be certain that the reason he was going to regret it would be anything more than yet more grief heaped on Emma Jane's heart. He'd rather shoot a son of a bitch than see another tear on his woman's face.

Stepping into the house, he glanced around, searching for Emma Jane. She wasn't there, but Sabina was sitting at the table, a cup of coffee in front of her, an electronic pad in her hand.

"Emma Jane has gone up to rest," she told him, her head lifting from the tablet. "I've been scanning the social media on Lauren's death." Her lips twisted in distaste. "The world is a better place with such a man no longer in it."

The disgust in her expression as well as her voice was heavier than normal when it came to most men. Not that he could blame her. He should have just killed Matt to begin with. It would have been far easier.

"Anything that gives us a clue who he was working with?" he asked her. "There has to be someone new he was meeting with. The Vasilyevs wouldn't have contacts here."

He'd checked that first. He'd had every damned name of anyone who came in contact with Emma Jane run against any possibility of being associated with Lorena or Vladimir.

"Nothing. Sorry, Dragon. But if I find anything, I'll let you know immediately."

Not that he expected her to find anything. Hell, that would just be too easy, wouldn't it?

"I'm still looking though," Sabina promised him. "Most who knew Matt weren't the least bit fond of him, but his death has been a shock. It's making people come out and talk, and that's what we need."

*Social media.*

He shook his head. "Of the devil," he muttered.

The comment earned him a laugh from Sabina. "You are insane, Dragon. It's information. People talk here as though no one is reading. It's a free flow of fact, innuendo, and pure falsehoods, and sifting through it is rather fun."

Fun?

He'd have to ask his grandparents if Sabina was dropped on her head at some point as a baby.

"Well, you just keep having fun," he grunted. "I'm going to shower and head for bed."

She looked back at him then, her gaze concerned. "Emma Jane was very quiet after you left, Dragon. I think perhaps you hurt her feelings very much when you played the dumb man and stomped out."

That was Sabina. She never failed to call any of them on their "dumb man" moments.

"I know, Bina." And he hated it, more than she knew. "Let's see if I can fix it now."

Making his way upstairs, he went to the guest room to shower, not wanting to disturb Emma Jane if she was asleep. She was exhausted. The tension, the pain and fear, were beginning to wear on her. But hell, she'd made it far longer than she should have without breaking down.

If she decided to turn into a neurotic mess at this point, then no one could blame her, least of all him.

After stepping from the shower, he dried himself and, wrapping the towel around his hips, left the guest room and walked the short distance to her bedroom. Opening the door silently, he stepped into the room, a smile almost touching his lips.

Emma Jane wasn't sleeping. He could feel her awareness of him the moment he slipped into the room and locked the door behind him.

"You should be sleeping," he chastised her gently as he pulled the towel from his hips and dropped it to the floor.

Sliding beneath the blankets, he eased against her, pulling her into his embrace until he could wrap himself around her.

"I was afraid you wouldn't come up." Slender fingers gripped his wrist as his arm settled over her hip.

"Why wouldn't I?" He kissed the top of her head. "You have the more comfortable bed."

She didn't protest or give one of those soft laughs as he expected.

"Emma Jane." He tightened his arms around her as he felt the tension he'd been unaware of until now. "I may disagree with you and in my frustration stomp around like a stubborn man, but I'll never hurt you. You know this, don't you?"

He felt her nod against the arm beneath her head.

"I know." Her voice was low, sad. "You left the other night and didn't come back then or last night. I was afraid you wouldn't come back tonight."

"You woke up the other night?" He grimaced at the thought. "And I was afraid of waking you if I came back to bed. I didn't come up last night for the same reason. Django and I were late going over information we've had coming in and attempting to come up with some idea who the group is that's attacked you."

She gave a delicate shrug. "I woke when you left the house. I saw you meet with Sabina and the others. I knew where you've been. I guess I've gotten used to having you with me through the night."

He bent his head to kiss the curve of her shoulder.

"I knew the team was close, but until the other night I didn't know how close. I'll make certain I don't leave you again while you're sleeping," he promised. "You need your rest."

Tension still seemed to hum around her as though she was unable or unwilling to relax for some reason.

Rather than questioning her, he just held her, knowing when she was ready she'd talk.

"You know, Mom and Dad gave me this place when they built the new one," she said reflectively. "I'd just turned eighteen. I worked on it for years rather than getting a loan to make the repairs needed."

Ilya remained quiet, knowing from his investigation into her past what was coming.

"It was coming together. Dad, Eric, and Ronan helped with the heavier work, but I did as much as I could myself. I learned. Bled." A watery laugh whispered through the room. "When Matt and I married I still had a long way to go, but I thought it would be the perfect place to raise a family. To raise babies."

Ilya closed his eyes at the pain in her voice and the pain he knew she had experienced.

"You know he mortgaged it six months after we married. God only knows what he did with the money. The same day I learned of the mortgage, I learned I was pregnant."

He held her, he didn't know what else to do, because he knew what that babe had meant to her.

"I was so excited," she whispered. "By then, I knew I didn't love Matt, but I loved my baby." And the sorrow that filled her voice was shattering his heart.

He knew the details. At sixteen weeks into the pregnancy she'd been rushed to the hospital after a fall down the stairs. He listened as she talked him through it, knowing it was what she needed for whatever reason.

"I've never remembered what caused the fall," she whispered. "I remember Matt and I were arguing over the house. I had to leave for work. He was yelling. I just wanted to leave," she whispered brokenly. "I must have missed a step somehow . . ."

If Matt Lauren weren't already dead, he'd kill him,

Ilya thought, because he knew, beyond a shadow of a doubt, that son of a bitch had somehow caused that fall.

"I woke in the hospital." Her breathing hitched with tears, with the efforts to hold them back. "The baby hadn't survived the fall, but there were other complications as well. The doctor said I'd probably never conceive again, and I saw the thankfulness in Matt's face. The satisfaction . . ."

Turning her in his arms, Ilya held her to him and stroked her back, kissed her brow. He'd suspected when he read the report of the miscarriage that somehow her husband had orchestrated her fall, but he hadn't acted on it. He couldn't be certain if he attributed that crime to Matt Lauren because the bastard had truly set out to kill his child and possibly the babe's mother as well or if he was just that damned jealous of the son of a bitch.

"When Eric and Ronan threw him out of the house, he screamed that he was glad our baby had died. That he wished I had as well."

She cried then, her shoulders shaking, her silent tears breaking his heart.

"I don't want to go to his memorial because I care anything for Matt," she finally said, her voice rough from her tears. "I pitied him. I want to go for Mary, because she grieved with me. Because she wanted her grandchild as much as I wanted my child."

And she wouldn't turn her back on her ex-mother-in-law's grief. Ilya understood that. He hated it, but he understood.

"I don't want to lose you, Emma Jane," he told her, holding her like the treasure she was to him. "You don't know what it would do to me."

The silence stretched between them for long moments.

"I have to go." The pure conviction and stubbornness in her voice caused his jaw to clench in frustration. "I have to."

"I have to spank your ass at my next opportunity," he sighed.

"Okay." The lighter shade of her tone, the hint of arousal, caressed his senses and settled something in his soul.

It did nothing for his arousal, but he feared he'd taken her too hard the other day, and he was trying to give her a chance to heal more before he took her again. Because he was learning that the hunger he had for her went far too deep to control. And his fears for her were driving him crazy.

"Sleep, baby. We'll figure it out," he promised, praying he was right. "Somehow, we'll figure it out."

# chapter twenty-two

Ilya began his campaign to convince her to stay home the moment she opened her eyes.

"If we stay here today, we'll go on a picnic. I've never been on a picnic," he told her sincerely.

"We'll go on a picnic tomorrow." She dragged her butt out of the bed and headed to the shower.

The bruising along her body silenced him when she stepped into the shower. It looked horrible, she knew, and it didn't feel too damned good either. She was moving stiffly, aching from head to toe.

Ilya stood outside the shower cubicle just watching her, his expression still, though his pale green eyes seemed to glow with renewed fury.

"They'll heal," she assured him after she'd dried herself and moved back to the bedroom. "I'm just sore, Ilya. Another day or so and I'll be much better."

"Take your medicine," he growled, that irritable

sound sexier than she'd ever allow him to know. "Take it or we won't leave the house, goddammit."

She looked back at him warily. "Ilya, stop being autocratic."

"Emma Jane, stop making me wish I could take Valium." The words were pushed between clenched teeth. "Don't test me on this. Take your medicine."

She took the medicine, uncertain of this new mood and not really feeling good about testing it. He watched her swallow the pills, nodded, then went to the guest room to shower and change.

The black skirt and black silk camisole tank she chose she paired with simple black pumps. It was easy to wear, comfortable, and gave her a measure of ease of movement.

Sitting in front of the vanity mirror, she quickly applied her makeup, adding a pair of delicate pearl earrings and a matching necklace.

She tried to make sense of how she felt about Matt's death and the debacle their marriage had become. She knew her family had always suspected that he'd been the reason for her fall down the stairs. The doctor and surgeon who had taken care of her after she was rushed to the hospital had expressed their doubts that the extent of the damage could have been caused from the fall as well.

Ronan and Eric had both believed that after she'd fallen Matt had done something to ensure she lost the baby.

She touched her stomach, trying to remember, trying to pull free the truth from the blank slate that covered the event. There was nothing. There never had been. And she'd never forgiven him because she suspected him of it.

Quickly braiding her hair, she reminded herself that

none of this was Mary's or Bart's fault. And Matt's parents had grieved over the loss of their grandchild. Mary had collapsed into inconsolable sobs when she walked into Emma Jane's room. She'd held Emma Jane like a child, and they'd cried together.

Glancing at the clock, she realized if she put off leaving much longer then it would be too late to arrive before the majority of Matt's family did. She wanted to pay her respects to Mary and Bart, then leave.

Ilya would be more comfortable if he didn't have to deal with dozens of family and friends. She knew security would be a nightmare at the funeral home the Laurens had chosen. With more than one family milling around, it was never certain who was there to see who.

Leaving the bedroom, she walked down the stairs and could hear Sabina's and Ilya's voices in the kitchen. He still sounded disgusted, while Sabina seemed to be teasing him.

"Would you just tie the son of a bitch and stop lecturing me," Ilya growled as Emma Jane walked into the kitchen and came to a slow, surprised stop.

She'd seen Ilya dressed in silk suits and Italian loafers and jeans and boots, but she realized she'd never seen him wear a tie. On none of the society pages or at any of the events he'd attended had he ever bothered with one.

Sabina was carefully straightening the black tie and notching it firmly at his neck.

"Feels like a fucking noose," he growled.

"The better for Emma Jane to strangle you with," Sabina snorted. "Be nice to her, Ilya. She's the only woman I have seen you with that I like."

"And that's really important to me, little cousin," he mocked her. "You know it is."

"Of course it is." Sabina gave a little shrug of her shoulders, the dressy black blouse she wore emphasizing the delicacy of her build. "And it should be. I want only for you to be happy and to have a woman who will kick you in the ass often." She giggled at the last part, gave a final adjustment to the tie, and stepped back. "You are quite handsome, Dragon. She will be proud to be seen with you."

"Very proud," Emma Jane stated, causing the two to turn their heads in her direction.

When Sabina turned, Emma Jane saw that the blouse was actually a blazer. She wore black slacks, low pumps, and a navy shell. And though Emma Jane knew the other girl was armed, she could see no evidence of it.

Ilya was simply breathtakingly handsome though. The expensive cut of his clothes and shoes, the way the black jacket emphasized his shoulders and pale green eyes. Even the dragon looked proud of himself as he curled around the side of his face.

"You cannot wear that blazer," Sabina made the announcement, frowning back at her. "I have one for you."

Moving to the chair behind Ilya, she drew out a simple, tailored blazer that appeared a bit heavier than her own.

"Kevlar reinforced," Ilya stated, his expression tightening with command as he glared at her. "If we're going, I won't have you go in unprotected."

*His line in the sand,* she thought, hiding the amusement that wanted to break free.

"Very well." Shedding the jacket she wore, she let Sabina help her into the new one.

"Keep these two buttons secured," the girl directed, buttoning the two between her breasts. "The back and front are reinforced, not the sleeves. It's not as effective as a vest, but not as dangerous as going in naked."

Emma Jane's gaze lifted to Ilya's, and for a moment she could feel his concern as though it were her own. His fears of being unable to protect her adequately, of failing her. And she wanted to reassure him, wanted to promise him nothing was going to happen, but she'd learned better than that over the years.

"I'll be careful," she promised him instead, a momentary uncertainty pricking at her.

"We'll have you covered," he stated. "Ronan, Eric, Sabina, Tobias, and Sawyer will go in with us, the rest of the team will have the outside. They're at the funeral home now getting in place and watching the guests for anyone suspicious."

He would do anything he could to ensure her protection, she knew.

"It is time to leave, Dragon," Sabina stated. "Sheriff Quade and her brother have just pulled in. Ronan and I will ride with you and Emma Jane. Sheriff Quade will be behind us."

They had it all figured out, Emma Jane realized, watching how seamlessly she was escorted to the SUV they were riding in. She was surrounded, protected on all sides, which was faintly terrifying. She'd never recover from the guilt or the grief.

She was becoming fond of all of them. Tobias, Maxine, and Sawyer were laid back, appearing relaxed, but always watchful. The men with the dragon team, as she'd dubbed them, were like predators, ready to jump, to pounce, at any moment.

They didn't sit around and bullshit—they were always training, tracking, adjusting. Even Sabina when she worked her social media accounts would often clean her weapon as she scanned the news feeds and sipped at her coffee.

Both teams were confident and effective, just in different ways perhaps.

When they arrived at the funeral home, she almost winced at Ilya's muttered "fuck" and Ronan's concerned expression. The parking lot was packed, dozens of people milling around and spilling from the inside.

"This is a clusterfuck," Eric murmured, pulling into the parking lot, then stopping as another car pulled out of a handy spot.

The car in question was driven by Django, and he didn't look happy either.

"Report!" Ilya snapped into his comm link, then waited, his expression tight-lipped. "Stay on your fucking toes. We're heading inside."

For a moment, Emma Jane considered just having them go back to the house, but then she remembered Mary's voice when she'd talked to her the night before. How lost she'd sounded. How broken Emma Jane remembered feeling when she'd lost her baby.

It would be okay, she told herself as she went into the funeral home, Ilya's arm around her back, Eric, Ronan, and Sabina flanking them.

"Twenty minutes, Emma Jane," Ilya stated as they made their way into the crowded hall leading to the room the memorial was being held in. "You hear me?"

"I hear you." She glimpsed Mary and Bart standing outside the funeral director's closed office door, their expressions drawn, Bart's lined face damp with tears.

Barely six feet, portly, and balding, Bart was quiet and often buried in a book. Mary's salt-and-pepper dark brown hair was swept back from her face. She hadn't styled it as she normally did and wore no makeup. They'd aged terribly in the past years, and she blamed Matt for that too.

Nearing them, she had to fight her own tears as Mary saw her and looked away, her lips trembling.

"I'm so very sorry, Bart," she whispered as Matt's father hugged her firmly. "Mary."

Mary's hug was weaker, lethargic.

"I'm so glad you came," Mary sniffed, her eyes filling with tears. "We've missed you, Emma."

"I've missed the two of you." Emma Jane tried to smile, but the hurt in the other woman's face broke her heart.

"I have something for you," Mary sniffed. "I left it in the office. Some things that were yours that I found in his room." She touched Emma Jane's arm. "Please, Emma, can we go in without him?" she pleaded. "Please. I know you deserve a life but . . ."

Emma Jane glanced at Ilya and saw his "no way in hell" expression. Even the dragon at the side of his face appeared outraged.

"I can go in," Sabina whispered to Ilya. "Let's just get it done."

Emma Jane glanced at Sabina then. The girl was nervous, her gaze moving about the crowded hall, her hand resting at her hip, her weapon in easy reach.

Ilya's jaw clenched.

"I'll hurry." Emma Jane touched his arm. "Just a few minutes."

She followed Mary, turning to the door as the older woman opened it and stepping inside with her, Sabina moving behind her. The door clicked closed, and in that second Emma Jane realized her mistake.

She tried to scream, but before a sound could part her

lips a foul-scented rag went over her mouth. Eyes wide, screams echoing in her head, she watched Sabina take two shots to her chest before she could pull her weapon. At the same time, a neat little scarlet hole appeared in Mary's forehead and she crumpled to the floor.

The world faded in a flash of sorrow, grief, and guilt. There was no way she could bear the guilt.

Ilya stood at the door, adrenaline pulsing in his blood as he scanned the crowd, trying to detect whatever had the ultra-fine sense of danger rising inside him. The skin beneath the dragon ink was heating, warming, and his senses sharpening.

*God damn.*

He turned the doorknob, found it locked, and stepped back and kicked.

He could hear the commotion behind him—gasps and screams, muttered curses—as he stepped into hell.

Rushing for Sabina, he flipped her to her back, checked her pulse, and found a single breath as he felt it, steady and strong. The vest she wore beneath her blazer had stopped the bullets meant to punch into her body.

"They have Emma Jane. Sabina is down," he yelled into the comm link as he jumped to his feet, saw the windows opened on the other side of the room, and sprinted for them. "Emma Jane was taken from the office. Goddammit, find her."

Ilya could feel the ice begin to form beneath the ink covering his face and back. Each tattoo he carried flashed with frozen rage, and he knew every member of the team, save Sabina, would feel the same.

He jumped through the open window, clearing it without effort and landing in a crouch as he pulled his weapon free of his holster, his gaze sweeping around the crowded parking lot.

There were too many people milling around. Too many bodies.

"Report," he yelled into the comm link, his head beginning to buzz, blind fury racing through him. "Where is she?"

Pandemonium raged in the office behind him as well as in his ear. His gaze narrowed as he straightened, and he was preparing to run when he glimpsed the black Ferrari racing through the driving lane toward him.

*Fuck. Fuck.*

He stepped back and when the vehicle slammed to a stop he was ready. He was barely in the soft leather seat when the engine gunned and the vehicle tore out of the funeral home lot and into the traffic.

"All I saw was a tan Lincoln Town Car. Didn't get the plates." His half brother, the fucking president of a fucking goddamned nation, black sports glasses covering his eyes, leather driving gloves, and hard-set features, was loose on the American public.

God help them all.

Ilya snapped the description to the team, checked his weapon, then braced himself as the Ferrari increased speed.

"They're dead, Alexi," he stated calmly. "Lorena and Vladimir both. I'll fucking kill them."

"We have to find them first, Brother!" Rurik snapped as Ilya searched the traffic for the vehicle while digging a spare comm link from his jacket, activating it, and, rather than handing it to his reckless brother, simply reached over and shoved it in his ear.

"We have to find them first." The bitterness and fury

in Alexi's voice weren't new. "I just fucking arrived and haven't been able to find the jet yet."

"Django, do you have her location?" Ilya snapped into the link.

"Interference," Django reported coldly. "Last ping heading east."

"I have visual," an unknown voice patched through. "They just took the exit to the airport. Tan Lincoln, two males in front, heat signature reclined in the back."

"Identify." Ilya held on as Alexi turned on to the interstate in a scream of rubber and accelerating horses.

Dammit, the bastard was going to get them killed.

"Friends of Nik's," the voice came back. "There's a private jet taxiing to the runway. I'm good, but I don't think I can stop that jet."

"Well, let's see if I can." Alexi snapped his cell phone from the car cradle and quickly pulled up contacts. By the time he made the call while weaving in and out of traffic, Ilya was sweating.

"Delay takeoff or I'll turn you over to the dragon heir the second I find you. Do not alert my parents to my arrival and be prepared to explain yourself for not notifying me of your flight." He was silent for about three seconds. "I'm nearing the exit now, ETA in two to three minutes." He paused. "Well, unlock the cockpit door, you stupid bastard. If that plane moves I'll cut your dick off and parade you through Moscow as the moron you are."

Ilya sat silent, allowed the empathy, compassion, and what little honor he'd tried to salvage of his life evaporate. All that remained was the dragon. The killer. Avenger.

Death was coming, and it was hungry.

# chapter
# twenty-three

Emma Jane came to awareness as she felt every bruise on her body scream in protest. She was dumped on what appeared to be a couch of some sort.

Her lashes fluttered open, her gaze slowly clearing until she was staring into the cool, curious features of Lorena Vasilyev, the monster who haunted Ilya's life.

The monster who now had her.

Ilya was going to be so mad, was her first thought. Her second? She was so screwed.

"Awake now." The heavy Russian accent sounded coarse coming from the smiling lips of this woman.

Reaching out, she smacked Emma Jane's cheek, her pale eyes flashing with pleasure before she rose to her feet and ordered, "Have the pilot take off immediately."

*Pilot?* Despair rushed through her. Ilya would never find her until Lorena dumped her dead body some-where.

As she fought the lethargy and the roiling of her

stomach, her fingers curled against the leather beneath her face and she could feel the grief beginning to burn through her.

"Takeoff is delayed." The halting English was a bit garbled. "Pilot says tower will notify us when to taxi."

Ilya had to find her. She fought to control her panic and the need to sit up and tell this woman what a lowlife bitch she was.

"I hate America," Lorena spat out. "Lazy, crass bastards."

"My dear, you're showing base roots," another male drawled with faint amusement.

"I'd prefer we not be caught with this little tramp," the bitch sighed. "Ilya would be very put out with me." There was an almost girlish simper in her voice that was, frankly, sickening. "No doubt he's rather upset."

A male chuckle sounded at that observation. "I have no doubt, as he does seem rather protective of her."

A sound similar to that of ice rattled in a glass.

"She's not his mate or she'd carry his dragon mark by now," Lorena drawled as Emma Jane forced herself to sit up in the corner of the couch she'd been dumped on.

Pushing her hair back with shaky hands, she focused on Vladimir Vasilyev and his wife, their expressions curious, coldly calculating, as they watched her.

"You're crazy," Emma Jane whispered.

"Unfortunately for you, that is far too close to the truth," Vladimir breathed out heavily, and shook his head as though amused by his own words.

"Shut up, Vladimir," Lorena ordered as she sat back in a leather chair, the wine-red silk dress she wore sliding against the leather as she crossed her legs and continued to watch Emma Jane.

"Madam, I believe we have a problem." One of the men

guarding the closed exit looked through the window before turning back to Lorena, his expression alarmed. "President Vasilyev is outside along with the Dragon heir."

Emma Jane watched the long-suffering look that came over Lorena's face. "I must not have beaten Zorah enough the last time Alexi was so foolish as to interfere with my fun," she sighed.

Vladimir shot her a dark look. "You are testing my patience with your cruelty to my children, my dear."

Lorena smirked back at him.

"Madam," the pilot came over the intercom, his voice trembling. "Tower has grounded us until further notification from Homeland Security. They demand President Vasilyev be allowed to board."

Lorena turned to her husband. "You know, Vladimir, I know that boy is yours. He's so weak."

Vladimir's, "Hmm," was met by an expression of disgust.

"Well, open the door." Lorena flicked expertly manicured nails toward the exit. "Check the Dragon heir for weapons before he enters."

Emma Jane sat still, her eyes on the door as it slowly opened, steps extending automatically to the ground.

Alexi Vasilyev entered first, dressed in black silk slacks and an open-necked black shirt and leather gloves. He slid his glasses from his eyes, looked around the cockpit, and quietly clicked his tongue chastisingly as his gaze settled on Emma Jane.

"Really, Mother," he sighed, walking to her as the two men checked Ilya for weapons. "I was convinced you were actually smarter than this."

His expression appeared mildly disappointed, but if she wasn't mistaken she caught a gleam of cold, hard fury in his pale blue eyes.

"Your faith in me once again astounds me, my son." She gave him a hard, brittle smile before turning to where Ilya stood.

His expression was savage, the dragon at the side of his face staring back malevolently as Ilya stood, feet braced apart, his arms now crossed over his chest.

He'd lost the tie and the jacket and looked like a civilized savage.

Lorena's expression lost the bitterness and softened almost girlishly.

"Nicholas," she breathed almost reverently. "You are the image of your father."

She rose from her seat, staring at Ilya like a star-struck teen.

Ilya didn't move. He just stared at Lorena before his gaze flicked to the two guards watching him warily, then to Vladimir and Alexi.

"He's so very handsome, isn't he, Ms. Preston?" the older woman breathed out with something akin to lust. "So proud and indomitable."

Emma Jane gave Ilya a dubious look before her smartass side got the best of her.

"He's passable," she quipped. "That dragon on his face is cool though."

Before anyone could respond, a blow from Lorena's fist nearly shattered her face as it bounced her head against the back of the leather couch.

Alexi cursed viciously as Emma Jane fought not to puke.

"You fucking whore," Lorena sneered when Emma Jane make sense of the world again. "You have no idea who he is or the blood he carries. You're not fit to be in his presence."

"Lorena." The sound of Ilya's voice was terrifying now, and as Emma Jane focused on his face, she could see the piercing intensity in the color of his eyes, and the bloodred ink of the dragon. "I will kill you."

With a sound of disgust Alexi moved to the bar, fixed two drinks, and handed one to his obviously rattled father.

"You're a good son," his father muttered, taking a healthy drink.

"Really, Mother!" Rurik snapped furiously. "You're allowing your crazy to show. Rein it in if you don't mind. It's unbecoming."

Lorena flashed him a killing look before turning back to Emma Jane, her fists clenched, her once-pale face now a mottled red with rage.

"Do you even know who he is?" Ignoring her sons now, she focused entirely on Emma Jane. "He's royalty, Ms. Preston. A direct blood link to Nicholas the Second. His line should have ruled rather than that week-kneed boy that took the throne. Had they done so, Ilya would be the heir to a throne. He would be a prince."

Ilya arched a brow as she cast him a suspicious look.

"And here I forgot to bow and scrape," Emma Jane muttered.

Lorena's arm swung back for another blow.

"Lorena." Quiet but as sharp as a whip, Ilya's voice stopped her, had wariness flashing in her expression.

"She's trash," his mother accused him furiously then. "You could be fucking women of worth."

"Women like you?" he taunted her with a sneer. "Really, Lorena, I like to think I have some good taste and discrimination."

Lorena's face flushed in humiliation.

The scene would have been farcical if it weren't for the potential of death. If the woman standing only feet from Emma Jane weren't a psychopath.

"You could have taken control of the Soviet states." She pointed an accusatory finger at Ilya. "I made certain you understood strength and survival. No mercy. Power. You were born to fulfill the Romanov legacy."

Ilya merely stood watching her. His eyes eerie as hell were so pale now. "You're fucking crazy," he enunciated with the utmost clarity.

"My God, look at those eyes," Lorena whispered. "The power in them, like a mystical warrior."

Sickening distaste filled Emma Jane at the unabashed lust in the woman's voice and expression.

"Let Emma Jane go, Lorena, you don't need her here." The rough, enraged rasp of Ilya's voice was almost mesmerizing.

"But we do need her." Lorena faced him almost pleadingly. "I have to make you understand what you were born for. I can't do that if she lives."

Ilya smiled. There was no amusement in the curve.

"If she is harmed further, I will peel your flesh from your bones as you watch. That is a vow," he told her, and even Emma Jane believed it.

Lorena looked from Ilya to Emma Jane again, calculation flashing in her gaze.

"Lorena," Vladimir drawled. "Alexi can fly home with us. Let Ilya and his little pet go. The odds are against us, my dear."

Emma Jane knew that wasn't going to happen.

"This is over, Mother." Alexi's voice hardened as he turned to the two guards watching all of them warily. "You have one chance to walk away from this if you leave now."

The two men glanced at each other.

"Oh for God's sake!" Lorena exclaimed in disgust, turning to the guards as she drew a weapon from the pocket of her dress and fired twice.

Emma Jane watched in shock as they fell to the floor, her heart nearly exploding in her chest, disbelief and terror exploding inside her.

At the same time, Ilya moved in a blur of speed, picked her up from the couch, and all but threw her into the chair behind him, covering her body with his own.

"Dragon," Lorena breathed, then turned and leveled her weapon on Rurik before glancing at Ilya from the corner of her eye. "Your whore or your brother, Ilya. Choose now."

Sorrow creased Alexi's face then. "Mother . . ." he whispered despairingly.

"You're weak!" Lorena snapped. "Such a disappointment, Alexi." Her finger tightened on the trigger. "Perhaps I should choose for him."

The harsh, explosive retort of a single shot caused them all to flinch. Emma wanted to scream, wanted to hide, then watched as Lorena went backward as though in slow motion. Blood rapidly stained the silk of her dress over her chest as she slid to the floor, shock reflecting in her expression.

Emma Jane's gaze went slowly to Vladimir. He sat in his chair, the gun held confidently in one hand, the drink his son had made him in the other.

"Well, I did warn her," he injected mildly. "A man has to protect his son." He nodded to Alexi. "Shall we return home now? I believe it's poker night and General Grosky should be there. He owes me quite a bit . . ."

Emma Jane stared at the blood and death that filled the small plane, the scent of it hitting her. She gagged, one hand going to her mouth as she fought desperately to hold back the bile desperate to escape.

"Take your woman and go, Brother," Alexi sighed heavily. "Go. This mess is mine."

With his arm supporting her, Ilya rushed her from the plane, and as they passed the final step, in front of a dragon team, brother, friends, and family, she lost control and began retching, sobbing.

The nightmare was over, for her, perhaps for Ilya.

But for Alexi it may have just begun.

It was hours later before Homeland Security finished with them. By then, Ivan had flown in along with several political backers of Ivan and Ilya's work in the shadow criminal world they still had connections into. His grandparents were escorted from the airport parking lot to where Ilya, his men, and the security members of Brute Force, along with Eric and Ronan, waited.

Alexi's jet was pulled into an empty hangar along with a limo a very powerful senator showed up in. Emma sat in the limo, a blanket wrapped around her, the door opened to allow Ilya direct access to her in case she was sick again. His grandmother sat on the other side of her, speaking to her softly.

Vladimir was convinced to leave the plane and wait in the Ferrari, though he wasn't questioned. The man was almost childlike as he spoke with Alexi, smiling and patting the Russian president's face as he had when he was a boy and Lorena had managed to punish him, Ilya thought.

For whatever reason, likely Lorena, Vladimir had slipped into his version of reality years before and only visited theirs when he had no other choice.

Finally, Alexi rose from his crouch next to the car,

wiped his face, and turned to meet Ilya's gaze before sliding the dark glasses over his face and sauntering over.

Alexi wore those glasses because he was well aware that were times he couldn't hide the emotion in his eyes. He hadn't been burned by the fire enough, Ilya thought, almost thankful that his half brother had escaped a measure of the cruelties Lorena could have heaped on him.

"She's well now?" Alexi asked as he stood next to Ilya at the limo.

"I don't think she's going to throw up again." Ilya glanced at Emma Jane's bent-down head and wished he could just take her home. "It will take her a while, but she'll make it."

"I tried to keep Lorena reined in—" Alexi broke off, his jaw tightening, his hands shoving into the pockets of his slacks. "She became worse by the year. She couldn't accept your hatred, couldn't accept she'd lost Nicholas, even though she killed him."

The other man turned and stared off into the distance. "She couldn't handle reality."

"I should have had her killed when I found Natalia," Ilya growled.

He wouldn't have regretted it, wouldn't have lost sleep over it, if it hadn't been for his little half sister.

"No one would have blamed you, least of all me," Rurik sighed. "Until I had Zorah safe, I couldn't let you do it, Ilya."

Lorena had held Zorah's safety over Alexi's head like a double-edged sword.

"She's safe?" Ilya asked.

Rurik nodded sharply. "I left her in Hagerstown with Nik and Mikayla. They promised to look after her until I could have her flown home to Moscow."

Moscow was the one place Zorah didn't need to be.

"Let her go with Grandfather when he leaves," Ilya suggested. "They need someone young around now that they're retiring. Grandfather has his security, they can easily guard her as well."

Alexi rubbed at his neck before dropping his hand and staring around the organized chaos of the hangar. "Perhaps," he finally said. "Fixing the hell I've walked into isn't going to be easy."

Being president of the Russian Federation and fixing the mess his predecessor left would be more than hell.

"Get out, Alexi." Ilya turned to him, feeling the certainty of what he was about to say. "You won't survive there. The people aren't ready yet. Not yet."

His brother's face creased with momentary grief before he shook his head. "I can't believe that. I have to believe they're ready. I have to believe it can be done."

Yeah, the difference between him and Alexi was the fact that Ilya accepted the world for the fucked-up place it could actually be sometimes.

"I have a dozen men ready for a challenge," he said then. "I've worked with them myself over the years and they're damned good. You need a security team that can't be bought if you're going to do this."

"A dragon team?" Alexi said with interest, using the title Emma Jane had used when Django had brought her water and she'd asked if the dragon team was all there.

Ilya nodded. "They're fully blooded and inked." Trained in war, men who knew the value of life but all the ways of death and inked with dragon blood.

"I'll take the offer." Rurik nodded. "And I'll let Zorah go with the grandparents. She'd enjoy that."

"Go do what you have to do, Alexi. My team will arrive in a few days. When they do, pay attention to the commander, he knows what the hell he's doing."

Alexi nodded, extending his right arm. As they clasped arms, Ilya felt the presence of the dragon ink his brother wore even through the shirt sleeve covering it. He had been one of the first Ilya had inked.

"Visit soon," Ilya ordered. "Visit secretly."

Alexi grinned at that, tipped his fingers to his forehead, then turned and strolled to the Ferrari. Ilya stepped to the limo, lifted his woman from the back seat, and headed for the SUVs outside the hangars.

His grandparents, dragon team, and security force followed, ignoring the Homeland Security agents who started to protest. Started to because men they knew not to fuck with called them back.

It was time to take his dragon mate home. The grandparents were there, his ink was there, and his dragon was ready to mark her.

# chapter twenty-four

### One week later

The dragon song woke him. It wasn't often he heard it, the haunting, mystical notes drifting through his senses, there but not.

He'd never been able to make sense of the reality of dragon song. It wasn't music notes, wasn't really a song. The sound would have been deep and filled with bass if he could tune it in fully in his head, he always thought. But there was no tuning it in, there was just the knowledge of it calling him, pulling at him.

His first memory of the dragon song had been when he was three. Hungry, hurting from Lorena's cruel blows, and wanting only to close his eyes and disappear. That song had held him.

Opening his eyes, he stared up at the ceiling, the sensation of the skin his dragon was part of ultra-sensitive, uncomfortable.

And that song . . .

Beside him, Emma Jane shifted, the hand that lay against his chest caressing the mating mark he carried there, stroking it lovingly. She seemed to enjoy that quite a bit. He knew he damned sure did.

Yeah, he was crazy, stupid in love. He hadn't had a restful night's sleep in a week due to the need to just watch her, to be certain she was actually lying there beside him, He'd refused to allow the guest room in the house to be used, because people wandered at night and when they wandered it woke Emma Jane.

The bruises from the explosion in the office, and the horrific one Lorena had given her, were finally fading away. Had Vladimir not killed that bitch, Ilya would have done it himself for that act alone.

And the fact that Vladimir had done it still had the power to shock Ilya and Rurik as well. His half brother admitted there were days he was afraid it was a dream.

Thankfully, it was no dream.

"Sounds pretty," Emma Jane muttered, shifting against him, mumbling again before running her hand over the tattoo on his chest once again.

Tilting his head, he couldn't help but grin. His Emma Jane did have a habit of talking in her sleep, he'd learned.

Easing her gently to her back, Ilya rested on his side, just staring at her. The way her hair framed her pretty face, the delicate arch of her brow, the fragile line of her jaw.

Lifting his hand, he couldn't help but brush his thumb over her lips, loving the feel of them. There was nothing about his Emma Jane that he didn't love.

"Are you waking me up?" Her lashes lifted, her gaze drowsy and languorous. "I was having a wonderful dream."

"Were you then?" He grinned. "About me, of course."

She lifted her arms over her head, gave a little stretch, then looped them over his neck with a smile.

"Did you know dragons can sing in my dreams? Like the haunting, deep-throated sound filled with mystery," she sighed, her smile filled with remembered joy. "It was beautiful."

Oh yeah, he knew dragons sang.

"As beautiful as you?" His lips lowered, brushed over hers as he pushed the blankets past her naked, sleep-warmed body

"Hmm, I'm not nearly that beautiful." The fingers of one hand trailed over his shoulder, his chest, and began to make their way down to the thick crest of his cock.

He was iron hard, his balls drawn tight. Her thumb stroked over the damp head, then, as she stared up at him, her eyes heavy lidded, she lifted her tongue and licked the taste of him from her thumb.

*Fuck.*

"Oh, baby." He smiled slowly. "That is very bad."

"Does that mean you're going to spank me?" She lifted, her thighs parting at the touch of his hand, giving him free access to the sweetest pussy in the world.

"Oh, I'd say you're definitely getting spanked."

Emma Jane breathed in against the rush of pleasure as Ilya's lips slanted over hers, his kiss becoming carnal, greedy. A branding of her senses all its own.

His lips plundered her kiss before nipping at her lips, the line of her jaw, and continuing along the column of her neck. She loved his lips, the dominant kisses and sharp, heated little love bites.

"Ilya," she moaned, the heated rush of need building quickly.

He bit her shoulder, licked the little wound.

"The things I want to do to you, Emma Jane," he groaned, his lips moving lower, his kisses becoming hungrier. "Love your nipples." His tongue stroked over one. "Let me have those pretty nipples, baby."

He sucked one into his mouth, licked at it, and sucked her firmly as her fingers threaded through his hair, her nails raking at his scalp. Like a man desperate to memorize the taste of a woman, he moved from one breast to the other, devouring her nipples and enslaving her senses.

He nipped at the tender buds, licked the little hurt, then did it again before sucking the hard tip. Hard flashes of sensation raced from her nipples to her womb, where they sent spasms of greedy pleasure rushing to her clit.

"Oh God, Ilya, it's so good," she gasped. "I love your mouth on my nipples."

He jerked back, ignoring her cry as he pulled her hands from his hair and brought them to her breasts.

"Let me see you play with them," he demanded, his expression wicked. "You make your nipples feel good and I'll see what else I can make feel good for you."

Tentatively, her expression dazed and filled with excitement, she cupped her breasts, her fingers finding her nipples, gripping them, rubbing over them.

Hell, he wasn't going to make it long, he thought. But when did he ever make it long with her?

Moving over her, he pressed her thighs apart, lips lowering to her abdomen, his tongue stroking lower. Her hips arched to him, her gasps driving him crazy with the sound of her need.

He nudged her legs apart, bending her knees, opening her fully.

"Sweet baby," he whispered. "So damned good."

His tongue licked through the flushed, moisture-glazed folds, the taste of her filling his senses with sweetness, driving him mad for more.

Emma Jane lifted to him, crying out as she felt his fingers easing into the heavier layer of slickness, stroking it, easing it lower to the sensitive, much smaller entrance of her rear.

There his fingers rubbed, pressed, had her craving more.

The deep male groan that vibrated against her clit had her crying out, jerking against his mouth. Her head tossed on the pillow, her hips arched, and a shattered cry tore from her as she felt the first finger penetrate the tender entrance he was caressing.

"Just a minute, baby." He lifted, reaching for something, but before she could make sense of the move he was back, his lips on her pussy, his fingers teasing her tender rear entrance again.

His lips were at her clit, licking, flickering over it, driving her insane as she fought to increase the pressure. At the same time, slick and cool, two fingers pressed against her, parted the ultra-tight flesh, and began pushing inside.

"Oh God, Ilya," she gasped.

His fingers slid free, returned slicker, parting her, pressing in.

"Fuck, baby. Your sweet ass is so tight. Just let me inside, baby, let me have you."

He pushed inside her again, retreated, returned, spreading a heavy lubricant with each slow thrust of his fingers inside the tender entrance.

And still, his lips, his tongue, tormented her clit, keeping her on edge, desperate for more. The bite of heat at each inward push of his fingers, each thrust inside her rear, had her senses humming in anticipation, the slight pleasure-pain of his fingers making her crave more.

"Oh, Emma Jane, sweet baby," he breathed against her clit, easing his fingers free of her again. "Turn over here, baby. Let me see that pretty ass."

He held her as she rolled to her stomach before he positioned her on her knees, her rear lifted to him.

His fingers returned, lubricating her further, making her slick and so very hot. They slid inside her, the bite of sharp sensation flashing through her senses and only making her crave more.

She was burning inside, outside. Desperate for every sensation now, every flash of agonizing pleasure.

When his fingers returned again, he eased three fingers inside her ass, ignoring the thrusts of her hips, her shattered cries. Each shallow thrust and retreat worked his fingers deeper inside her, until he was gripping her hip with one hand and, stroking inside her ass with his fingers, making her mindless. That was what did, he made her mindless.

"Ah, Emma Jane, almost, baby," he crooned, his fingers sliding free of her again only to return again, lubricating her further. "That's it, sweetheart," he groaned behind her. "Fuck, you're so tight you're going to kill me."

With each retreat, his fingers returned, slicker, worked inside her, pulled back, and repeated until she was bucking against him, poised on the edge of a hunger that was becoming unbearable.

"Here we go, baby." He moved behind her, one hand gripping her hip firmly, the other guiding his cock until the engorged crest pressed against the flexing opening. "Breathe in, honey. Slow and deep."

She breathed. His cock pressed against the nerve-laden entrance, parting her, stretching her, burning her.

She fought to breathe, to process sensations she'd never known before, had no idea could be so destructive.

"Now, baby, breathe for me." He paused, the pressure at her rear a blistering tease she had no idea how to ease. "Now, Emma Jane. Breathe, baby."

She inhaled.

Flash fire rocked her, streaked up her spine, then back down. She could feel the once-untouched tissue, flexing, rippling around the intrusion.

"Fuck," he groaned behind her. "That's it, baby, milk my dick. So damned sweet."

"Ilya," she gasped, panting, racked by sensations she fought to make sense of. "Ilya, help me."

A heavy caress along a rounded curve had her jerking, driving into the heated slap of his hand.

"We're almost there, baby," he groaned. "Come on now, breathe in for me."

She inhaled, then exhaled on a scream of pure sensation as she felt the engorged head of his cock stretch a tighter band of muscles as his hand landed on her rear again. Behind her, his harder groan, one of agonized male pleasure, came as he began working his cock inside her with short, shallow strokes.

Sensation raced through her. The feel of his cock buried up her ass, the desperate ache in her clit, her pussy. She was wanton, out of control with need.

Emma Jane pushed her hand down her body, between her thighs, as Ilya gripped her hips and buried full length inside her.

Years of fantasy, of need, of hungers she'd never understood, and now she let them free. She sent two fingers burrowing inside her pussy, the heel of her palm rasping her clit.

"Oh fuck, yeah," he groaned. "Ride your fingers, Emma Jane. And I'll fuck this sweet, pretty ass."

Her fingers buried deep as he began moving, thrusting inside her hard and deep, thrusting every thick, iron-hard inch of his cock inside her before drawing free and thrusting back. And Emma Jane loved it. The pleasure and pain, the feel of his cock throbbing inside her, the brutal flash of sensation, the whirling chaos of ecstasy that began whipping inside her.

When he came over her, his hips shuttling faster, his cock shafting inside her, his teeth bit into her shoulder and she shattered. The muscles gripping his cock, her fingers, tightened, rippled, and she felt herself disintegrating from the inside out, buried in such pleasure.

A pleasure that only increased as Ilya pushed in deeper, harder, the buried full length. She could feel his release, each violent pulse of semen jetting inside her, extending the pleasure tearing through her. She could feel his release pumping inside her, filling her rear, marking her in a way she knew she might never completely understand.

The white-hot flash fire left her wasted, collapsed beneath him, her breathing harsh as she fought to get her bearings, to recover from the heavy shudders still trembling through her.

Behind her, Ilya's breathing was hard, rough, as her inner tissue continued to ripple and stroke the hard flesh penetrating her.

"*Balaur pereche*," he whispered at her ear, the lyrical sound so beautiful, his voice that deep dragon rasp she so loved. "*Te iubese*. I love you, my Emma Jane. My dragon mate."

# chapter twenty-five

He loved her.

Emma Jane was keeping her dragon.

The next day, she watched as his grandfather re-touched the tattoo on his face, telling her softly how Ilya would now become the head of the Dragonovich family. It sounded rather formal, but she'd learned since Ilya had come into her life that Romanians had a romance and a mysticism all their own.

When the ink was finished, the skin still a bit red-dened, the ink appeared a bit more silvery black, the dragon's eyes no longer red, but a pale green to match Ilya's, and he was still flirty all the same.

When his grandfather finished, he handed something to Ilya, then everyone left, leaving her and Ilya in the kitchen alone.

Her lips parted in wonder as he went to one knee, asked her to marry him in the deep rasp he got that indicated stronger emotion, and at her teary "yes" slid the obviously old, exquisite diamond on her finger.

"My dragon mate," he whispered, turning her hand to stare at her inner wrist before turning it again to run his thumb over her lower arm. "Will you let me ink you?"

He looked up at her, his pale green eyes brighter, filled with love. With love, for her.

"I would love to have you ink me," she whispered.

"Here?" His thumb stroked over her wrist. "With my dragon?"

She smiled. "Yes, Ilya, with your dragon."

Minutes later, his dragon team, his grandparents, Ivan and his wife and her brother were once again in the kitchen, watching silently as the lights were turned off and the candles were lit.

There, in the chair he had sat in himself while his grandfather had refreshed his dragon, Emma Jane sat, her arm resting on the table, staring at Ilya as he began. He didn't need to sketch the image on her skin, he explained. His dragon was as familiar to him as his own face.

"We light candles for new ink," he explained, though he used the electric needle. "Where skin shifts with less effort, and the muscle is more dense, is far easier to sense with candlelight. And because the bond between a man and his woman deepens with the intimacy of candles."

Emma Jane watched, curious, amazed that she felt no pain as the ink was placed beneath her skin.

"Each artist mixes the ink himself. What marks your skin I had prepared myself. Ivan brought it when he first arrived.

The needle moved over her skin, then his fingers, testing the muscle, the feel of her flesh before he resumed.

"There are those that say the dragons live and breathe upon the flesh of dragon blood," he stated, his gaze lifting a moment to meet hers. "Some say they flirt or glare in rage. The gift of the ink and the one trained to lay the color in just the right manner, in just right position, can give the appearance of life, or knowledge. And all dragon-sons, heirs or artists chosen to lay the ink, have an instinct for that placement. It is not done quickly, nor is it done without reason. The image comes to the artist, no pattern is needed."

As he talked, his words washed over her, holding her. The legend of the dragon tribes, the sons and heirs and where it all began was told. Those who watched ebbed and flowed through the room. Coffee and food were consumed by everyone but Ilya and Emma Jane. Morning became noon, then flowed into evening. Candles burned away, others were lit to replace them. And in that moment between night and morning, Ilya leaned back in his chair, realizing, only as he finished, how stiff his body had become.

But his dragon marked her now. It twined around her left wrist and rested against her forearm. A promise of his protection, a warning to anyone who would harm her. As he looked up at her, a grin tugged at his lips. Her head rested on her other arm as she dozed, her breathing deep and even.

Only the dragon guards still held vigil, and as they realized he had finished, they gathered around her in a semi-circle, and with Ilya, whispered the words of the Dragon Song.

When they finished, Ilya picked up his drowsy mate and carried her to their bedroom.

There, tucked against his heart, held within his arms, his woman slept, her protection assured. His woman.

For the first time in Ilya's life, he slept, knowing he belonged.

He belonged to his Emma Jane.

## The Dragon Song

We remember when you walked the land, regal and
    wise, benevolent and proud.

We remember your rage when they came.

When your mates were stripped of their hides, your
    babes spilling their blood to the land.

We remember your sorrow when we found you, once a
    clan so large, to become so few.

We fed you from our stock.

We brought you black stone to replace your fire.

We led you to that place that the ancients call that
    place not known.

We returned to our homes.

We returned to our farms.

And the invaders had destroyed all we owned.

Lead them to the beasts, they demanded. The one of
    legend, strength, and wisdom. We told them you
    were not known.

They searched the mountains high.

They searched the mountains low.

They burned our homes, they raped our wives, they
    killed our stock and stole the black rock, leaving us
    cold.

And still we cried, you we did not know.

We would not go to you.

We would not sing the mournful call.

We did not betray the legends, we refused to reveal
    what we did not know.

And so the day came that we like you, once so many,
    became so few.

Weak and hungry we huddled in the caves, lost and
    alone.

Then came you.

Your fire warmed us.

You fed us of your stock.

You strengthened us with your care.

Then to you, you drew but a few.

With your claw you drew, upon the arms of the few, an
    image of you.

Into the few you gifted the essence of you, and whisper
    you did, of warriors renewed.

Part of us, part of you, merged and melded to create a
    legacy true.

The legacy of the Dragon-Sons.